The Raskin Family

Cherry
Orchard
Books

The Raskin Family

Dmitry Stonov

Translated by
Konstantin Gurevich
and Helen Anderson

Library of Congress Cataloging-in-Publication Data

Names: Stonov, Dmitriĭ, 1898-1962, author. | Gurevich, Konstantin,
  translator. | Anderson, Helen, 1956- translator.
Title: The Raskin family / Dmitry Stonov; translated by Konstantin Gurevich
  and Helen Anderson.
Other titles: Sem'i͡a Raskinykh. English
Description: Boston : Cherry Orchard Books, an imprint of Academic Studies
  Press, 2019. | The Raskin Family was first published in Russian in 1929,
  in Moscow. | Translated from the Russian.
Identifiers: LCCN 2019023028 (print) | LCCN 2019023029 (ebook) | ISBN
  9781644690574 (hardback) | ISBN 9781644690581 (paperback) | ISBN
  9781644690598 (pdf)
Classification: LCC PG3476.S786 S413 2019 (print) | LCC PG3476.S786
  (ebook) | DDC 891.73/42--dc23
LC record available at https://lccn.loc.gov/2019023028
LC ebook record available at https://lccn.loc.gov/2019023029

ISBN 9781644690574 (hardcover)
ISBN 9781644690598 (ebook)
ISBN 9781644690581 (paperback)
©Academic Studies Press, 2019

Book design by Lapiz Digital Services

On the cover: *Exodus*, by Leonid Osseny, 2014, Oil on linen

(a fragment)

Published by Cherry Orchard Books, imprint of Academic Studies Press.
1577 Beacon Street
Brookline MA, 02446, USA
press@academicstudiespress.com * www.academicstudiespress.com

To Yuri Slezkin

The author's family is deeply indebted to Aaron Hoffman, Elaine Koffman, and Ludmila Epshtein for their generous help, enthusiasm, and moral support in preparing this novel for publication.

CONTENTS

About the Author   ix

Part One   1

Part Two   61

Part Three   133

In Place of an Epilogue   197

Photographs   202

ABOUT THE AUTHOR

Dmitry Stonov (Motl/Mitia Vlodavsky, Motya Raskin in the novel) was born January 8, 1898 in the village of Bezdezh (Kobryn District, Grodno Province), in the backwaters of Belarus. His father Meyer Vlodavsky (Meyer Raskin in the novel) was a Jewish merchant of the first (the highest) guild who leased and ran an agricultural estate. Stonov was not only a witness to, but an active participant in, many of the dramatic events that shaped the history of Russia in the twentieth century. His life, rich in transitions, quests, tragedies, and ordeals, was quite typical of intellectuals under the Soviet regime.

The Raskin Family covers the author's youth, ending with his departure to a railroad construction site in the hills of Valdai. There, he lived through the revolution of 1917 and the civil war that followed. Aged eighteen to nineteen, Mitia Vlodavsky enthusiastically responded to calls for liberty and equality and to slogans like "Power to the people!" or "Land to the peasants!" In the civil war, he was on the Bolsheviks' side and even joined their party. He later became a member of the Workers' Opposition, headed by Alexander Shliapnikov, a prominent communist. This group argued for a greater role for the workers in running the state.

At the same time, he developed an interest in literary work. He wrote articles on battlefield-related topics and worked for newspapers in Vladimir and Kremenchuk. His native language was Yiddish, so writing in Russian was both a great challenge and an impressive achievement for him.

When Mitia Vlodavsky was twenty, he wrote two sketches based on his own life, and rashly mailed them to Vladimir Korolenko, the famous writer and humanitarian, known among other things for his strong stand against the notoriously antisemitic Beilis trial of 1913. In his essay on Korolenko written forty-two years later, Dmitry Stonov described the torturous feelings of fear, shame, and remorse that overwhelmed him the moment he dropped the letter in the mailbox. Within a week, however, Mitya received a warm reply from Korolenko, with helpful suggestions and advice for the future.

This was not the end of his dealings with Korolenko. A few years later, Vlodavsky started the magazine *Raduga* [Rainbow] in Poltava, Ukraine, where Korolenko and his family were living at the time. Since Korolenko had openly rejected Soviet rule, he could no longer publish anything, and his family was in very dire straits, literally starving. When Mitia Vlodavsky learned about it, he persistently invited Korolenko to write for his magazine and even tried to obtain material help for his family through the local Communist Party committee. Sadly, nothing came out of it: Korolenko responded that he had nothing against Vlodavsky personally, but that he would not accept any help from "the bloody hands of the Communists." When Dmitry Stonov was arrested in 1949, the original letter was confiscated. If it still exists, it will be in the KGB archives.

Also in Poltava, Mitya Vlodavsky met two literary authors: Yuri Slezkin and Mikhail Bulgakov. By then, Yuri Slezkin (1885–1947) was already a prominent, established novelist, who was very helpful to Vlodavsky in mastering the Russian language. He became Mitya's literary mentor and a dear friend for life. *The Raskin Family* is dedicated to him.

During the early 1920s, Vlodavsky traveled across northern Russia and saw endless trains of boxcars packed with convicts and exiles. This is when he fully understood the nature of the Soviet regime and rejected it. The persecution of all groups opposed to the regime had already begun, and Shliapnikov's Workers' Opposition was no exception.

In 1923, Vlodavsky tore up his Communist Party membership card and changed his name to the pseudonym Dmitry Stonov, from the Russian for *moan*. Pseudonyms reflecting the suffering of the working people were popular at the time (see Maxim Gorky—meaning *bitter*). He then moved from Poltava to Moscow, where the only people who knew him were Yuri Slezkin and Mikhail Bulgakov, so there was no one to report on him.

As an author, Stonov flourished in Moscow. He wrote for the newspapers *Izvestiia*, *Gudok*, and *Trud*, as well as the magazine *Nashi dostizheniia*, and also taught at the Literary Institute. His first collection of stories, entitled *The Fever*, was published in 1925 by Zemlia i Fabrika, the publisher responsible for opening the way to many future classics of Soviet literature. Within the next twenty-plus years, Dmitry Stonov established his literary reputation with more than ten published books, including *The Raskin Family*.

In 1942, during the war with Nazi Germany, Stonov went into military service and wrote for several army newspapers. Two years later he suffered serious shell shock, was discharged, and returned to Moscow, where he worked for the Soviet Information Bureau and in radio, while continuing to teach at the Literary Institute. He was active in the Jewish Anti-Fascist Committee (JAC), writing for its Yiddish-language newspaper, *Einigkeit*, and maintaining close friendships with many members of the JAC board, most of whom were arrested in 1948 and 1949.

By that time, Soviet intellectuals were being arrested en masse. Fear in anticipation of arrest was a common aspect of Soviet life, especially for Jews, since by that time, Stalin was already openly pursuing his anti-Semitic policies.

In the early morning of March 13, 1949, state security agents burst into Stonov's apartment, arrested him, and took him to the secret prison at their headquarters, the Lubianka. In September 1949, he was sentenced to ten years of hard labor "for anti-Soviet agitation and propaganda."

The questioner who interrogated Stonov mistreated him and demanded not only that he confess his anti-Soviet activities but also that he implicate other writers—his friends such as David Bergelson, Vasily Grossman, Ilya Ehrenburg, Yuri Olesha, and many others. After a series of fruitless interrogations that took place each night, Stonov was transferred to another prison "for persistent lack of cooperation." For a whole week he was held in a special punishment cell, a damp stone-walled closet where it was physically impossible to lie down and difficult to even sit. Stonov gave a vivid description of this experience in his short story "Seven Slashes."[1]

Stonov's fortitude saved his life, for had the interrogator found out that he had been part of the Workers' Opposition, most likely he would have been executed.

Stalin died in March of 1953, and the wind of freedom could be felt in the air.

Owing to the relentless, truly heroic efforts of Stonov's wife Anna, his case was reviewed long before those of many other innocent victims of the Gulag. At Anna's urging, some prominent authors like Konstantin Fedin, Leonid Leonov, Konstantin Paustovsky, and Semyon Kirsanov also worked on his behalf.

---

1   *In The Past Night* (Lubbock, TX: Texas Tech University Press, 1995), 172–190).

In early 1954, Stonov's conviction was overturned. He was freed and fully exonerated "in the absence of *corpus delicti.*"

After his release, Dmitry annually visited the areas where he spent his childhood and youth, collecting material for his new books. Within a few years, he published several short stories and two novellas.

Dmitry Stonov died in hospital on December 29, 1962, on the eve of his sixty-fifth birthday, a full twenty-three days after he had had a heart attack. The ugly aspects of Soviet life caught up with him: incompetent doctors, negligent personnel, and horrendous hospital conditions all contributed to his death.

Stonov summarized the lessons of his own life in the Soviet Union with an epigraph to his Siberian stories:

All his life, he fought against the Revolution—and the Revolution destroyed him.

All his life, he was neutral—and the Revolution destroyed him.

All his life, he fought for the Revolution—and the Revolution destroyed him.

Leonid Stonov

PART ONE

PART ONE

1

Meyer Raskin was fifty-four years old when the lease expired on Telyatichi, the large country estate that had been his family's home. Before closing his business, the old man, who had only a vague idea of his worth, finally sat down to count his money. Not including his sons' assets, Meyer himself turned out to have seventy-five thousand rubles.

At his usual brisk and somewhat agitated gait, Meyer went to find his old wife Chava, who had never been happy living among the Belarusian peasants. Her father had been a cantor and kosher butcher in the Antopol shtetl. When he was young, he once managed to put together two hundred rubles and publish his work on religious philosophy. It was a long time ago, the publication was a failure, and his hope of becoming a rabbi came to naught. He was poor, always in need, but he kept his head high, guarding his pride and independence. He married his only daughter to a poor country Jew named Raskin. The young man, who was seventeen at the time, arrived in the shtetl with his father in a simple farm cart. The two purchased paper shirtfronts and stiff collars to look good, and went to see the butcher. Three days later, after weeping on the withered chest of her gloomy philosopher father, the girl left her home and went to live in the country with people she hardly knew.

At first, she was afraid of the vigorous young Meyer, then she grew accustomed to him, then she fell in love with him. They were poor too, living in a shabby peasant hut. Its thatched roof leaked in the springtime, and in winter the half-rotten log walls creaked loudly. Chava did not sleep much at night.

Meyer's father ran a tavern. From morning until evening and from evening until late at night, the poorly lit tavern was filled with peasants who sang, drank, cursed, brawled, and collapsed on the floor. Drunk, they would now and then break a window, then sober up and pay for the damages. It appeared that Meyer's destiny was to open a tavern too, and live the way his father did. But even as a young man, Meyer possessed energy that his ancestors lacked. He was incapable of sitting in one place doing nothing—some force always pushed him out of the house. For a while he bought up flax seed, another time he signed up to supply firewood to the village administration, yet another time he found a business partner, hired some peasants, and began digging for lime. . . . He kept starting new projects, rushing around, going on trips, and doing business with what seemed like incredible ease.

Within a few years, the hut where old Raskin sold vodka was replaced by a large house with a tile roof. Meyer opened a small store. His children were growing up. Young Chava quietly walked through the rooms, sat pensively by the window and, resting her arms forlornly at her sides, dreamed of her past life in the shtetl. When Meyer built the house and opened the store, she hoped against hope that her husband would settle down, stop traveling all the time, and perhaps just quietly live with her in the village. She was sick and tired of grim winter nights spent listening through closed shutters to the distant barking of dogs and the howling blizzards. Alone with the children, she had trouble getting to sleep in the large house that never felt cozy. The sound of dry floorboards cracking and the popping of wallpaper separating from the walls drove her insane.

But Meyer had no intention of relaxing or settling down. Sporting a suit jacket, a beard, and a rosy complexion, he was robust and resembled young Leo Tolstoy of the 1860s. He was brimming with energy. Whenever he stayed home for a few days, he would move the furniture around, change the dining room into the bedroom, the bedroom into the children's room, or tidy up the barn. During such work-free days at home, he would walk through the village dressed in his fine bowler hat, with his nimble hands clasped behind his back, humming Sabbath tunes, and making the peasants vaguely envious.

"How about that Jew?" they would say, clicking their tongues. They weren't quite sure how to treat him, and always began with his lineage.

"You're Yossel's son, aren't you?"

"Yes, Yossel's!"

Scratching the back of his head, one of them would say,

"And I thought you were a landowner or something. . . . Some Jew you are!"

Involuntary idleness made Meyer suffer, so in order to kill time, he would offer,

"Want me to show you a trick?"

"What trick?"

"Here's what I'll do: I'll put a stick through your arms and legs, and you won't be able to stand up."

"Really?"

A skeptical smile would appear under the peasant's thick mustache. In his own secret way, Meyer would push the stick through, leaving the man trussed like a sheep and begging,

"For God's sake, let me out!"

But the Jew would walk away, chuckling and humming.

For weeks on end during all seasons of the year, Meyer rode around in his cart. You could find him in the most remote estates, villages, and shtetls of the district. Meyer had become indispensable; even some landowners turned to him for advice. Watching his children do their homework, he learned in passing how to read and write in Russian. He observed the landowners and picked up their refined manners: he said "thank you very much" to his wife after dinner in Polish, and once even kissed her hand, making her blush in embarrassment. The young woman grew more confident, and one night, after her embraces had put Meyer into a peaceful sleep, Chava gently shook him awake.

"Meyer," she said, her voice trembling with self-pity. "Meyer, I'd like to ask you something . . ."

"What? Who's here?" Meyer asked, alarmed and still half asleep.

"Nobody's here. . . . It's just me. . . . Meyer, enough of this wandering all over the world! You have a family, and you aren't that young anymore. . . . Listen, let's just stay home together. You don't need to travel all the time . . . or . . ."

Her heart started beating faster.

"Or . . . I know you have money. Please, let's move to Antopol, and start living like all Jews do. Here, I even forgot how to talk, I don't speak to anyone for weeks on end. And in winter time . . . alone with the children . . . I'm terrified . . ."

She burst into tears.

At first he frowned, but then he patted her gently on the shoulder.

"Ah, you're such a silly woman! And I thought . . . , Well, stop that. I know what I'm doing. Just wait a bit longer—we'll live so well! We'll ride around in a two-horse carriage."

But Chava didn't need a two-horse carriage. All she needed was the simple shtetl life, with old women, a synagogue, Friday night candles, and warm comforting tears at Rosh Hashanah and Yom Kippur. She sighed and wept softly for a while, then waited for the dawn with her eyes open, listening to her husband's robust, healthy snoring.

The years were rolling along, and the first three children were growing up: sons Ilya and Isaac and daughter Sarah. When the children had been younger and other Jews lived in the village, the families had hired an old melamed for a small fee to instruct the children in biblical wisdom. The melamed would dispassionately tell the children how Jacob fell in love with Rachel, how he was forced—against his will—to marry Leah, how Leah's children found the apples of mandragora, and how Rachel wanted to obtain those apples.

"Fine," Leah said, "But first let Jacob sleep with me."

So when Jacob came to his tent, Rachel met him and said to him,

"Tonight, you are sleeping with Leah."

So he slept with Leah, and they had children . . .

Sometimes the melamed grew angry and spanked the children on their bare bottoms. When he had to punish the girls, he shut his eyes and whipped their rosy behinds, asking the boys,

"Children, am I hitting the right place . . . ?"

As an observant Jew, he was not allowed to look at a girl's naked body.

But as other Jewish families left the village, the Raskin children started going to the village school with peasant children. The Raskins kept to themselves. On their way home from school, the peasant children would scream at them:

"Dirty Jew, dirty Jew,

Devil's hiding behind you!"

Looking at her children, Chava would shake her head and wipe away tears. If her father were to rise from his grave and see how his grandchildren were growing up, one would think he would die all over again! And these are the grandchildren of a cantor, almost a rabbi! No synagogue, no proper prayers—they will forget everything among these Christians!

It didn't trouble Meyer at all. It was as if he didn't notice his wife's concerns, he was too busy. The children? Let them grow, they will be good for something! He did love them enough, though. At first he brought them toys and candy from Pinsk and Kobryn, later he brought books.

After a break of ten years, Chava became pregnant again. At three-year intervals, she gave birth to Hersh, Motya, and Sheva. The older children were growing up and finishing their studies. They were healthy, but more and more Chava thought about what would become of them.

"It's no joke! Ilya, the oldest one, is fifteen. The boy is fifteen, and how does he spend his time? He wheedled fifty kopeks out of his father and gave the coin to a peasant who made a fiddle for him. Now he spends entire days scratching out sad Jewish tunes on that piece of wood. Oh, if only the cantor, their wise grandfather, were still alive!"

Chava, however, without noticing it herself, began to hum along with her son's playing. She wiped her reddened nose often and swayed her head in tune. "What does Meyer think of the children? Does he think of them at all?"

Meyer did think about the children, of course, but he never talked much with his wife anyway, and he especially did not like to share his plans with her. He observed his children, but not through their mother's sad eyes. He observed and noticed what he needed to know. He loved his children with a caring, practical love.

Ilya was an industrious young man. From his early days, one could sense a hard worker in him. When Meyer gave him a ruble, he created a ledger to keep track of his funds, binding several sheets together and separating the income and expense columns. He was meticulous, and even his handwriting was neat—straight and round. He respected his elders, counted every kopek, and played violin in his spare time. What more could you want from a fifteen-year-old?

But when Ilya turned sixteen, his father asked him,

"Ilya, if I gave you a project, do you think you'd be able to see it through?"

Ilya put down his violin and paused. He bit his fingernails for a while and answered the question with a question,

"Why shouldn't I?"

"Excellent," Meyer said. "I've just purchased a forest parcel in Adryzyn. Of course, there will be a man there to oversee things, but you will need to keep an eye on the operation, too. A hired hand is one thing and an owner is something else."

"Yes," Ilya replied readily. "Why not? Of course!"

So, Meyer took Ilya to Adryzyn. The parcel was located fifty miles from their village. They made Ilya a sheepskin jacket and two pairs of good boots, one from leather and one from felt. Ilya enjoyed being treated like an adult, and he tried to emulate the merchants he knew in every possible way. He worked hard. During the day, he crisscrossed the forest on foot. In the evening, he recorded income and expenses in the ledgers in his neat handwriting. He respected his elders, he was humble and curious. He tweaked his upper lip; he liked to listen and even tried to tell stories of his own. His father was a master storyteller, but Ilya wasn't nearly as good at it. Even though he added "in short . . ." to every sentence, his stories weren't nearly as lively and engaging as his father's.

Meyer continued with his travels. He gained weight. He wore stiff collars instead of just wrapping a scarf around his neck like most Jews did. People in the shtetls started calling him "Reb Meyer," and some tried to invest money with him.

"A smart Jew," other Jews said of him. "He's on fire! He comes from a simple family, but he's not your average man!"

2

At home, the older children—Isaac and Sarah—continued to mature, and the younger three were growing out of their diapers. Isaac also played the violin, but not the sad Jewish tunes favored by Ilya. He composed his own music, and at times even he couldn't tell exactly what he was playing. However, Isaac was more concerned with his looks. He was handsome. He loved to stand in front of the mirror for hours when no one was watching. Once, when his father was at home, a landowner came to visit, bringing his son with him. The son's hair was slicked down. After that, Isaac began to wear his hair the same way, and the result looked quite striking on him.

Sarah was a reader. She was a quiet girl, somewhat secretive. People often thought that she was unhappy about something or thinking sad thoughts. She made no friends, not even with the rabbi's children or those of the woman who worked at the liquor store. Only after Sarah had finished the few books that they had at home, did she start visiting the saleslady at the liquor store and borrowing books from her, because the woman had subscribed to *Niva* since time immemorial. The illustrated magazine came with literary supplements. The supplements didn't last Sarah very long, though. The saleslady was a stylish woman, always following the world's fashions through magazines. She once told Sarah that wearing a red ribbon in her braid was ugly and in poor taste. Sarah blushed and burst into tears. She stopped visiting the liquor store and even avoided leaving home if she could help it.

When summer came, Meyer took Isaac and Sarah to the city of Pinsk. That journey had a lasting effect on the way the children chose to lead their lives.

They stayed in Pinsk with Daniel Yaglom, a distant relative. Oh, this was a very different household! On the way there, however, Meyer had spoken of Yaglom with scorn.

"What is wrong with these people? One day they have money and live like magnates, the next they have no money and are dying of hunger. Hah! They think they are nobles! Oh yes! And at times, other people's money somehow sticks to their fingers. Nobles, huh!"

But no matter what their father said, Isaac and Sarah were absolutely enchanted by their relatives. The Yagloms had curtains covering their windows, their maids wore starched aprons with shoulder straps, their two daughters studied at the gymnasium,[2] and everyone in the house—even the parents—spoke Russian rather than Yiddish. Students from technical schools came to call on the daughters, who were fifteen and sixteen years old. The older daughter played the mandolin and sang romantic ballads like a grown-up.

Sarah was all ears and tried to catch every word that the young people said. Now these were real people! Isaac quickly realized that he couldn't possibly compete with the students—they spoke unaccented Russian, they were far more knowledgeable than he was, and they knew how to court young ladies. So he set out to distinguish himself in a different way. The students wore black uniform jackets with gold buttons, and simple shoes. Isaac convinced his father to buy him a real grown-up suit, complete with collar, cuffs, and tie. The barber did his hair in the latest style. Isaac's plan paid off handsomely. Rachel, Yaglom's older daughter, couldn't take her eyes off him. She started complaining that she was bored, that the students were stupid and dull. She said all this openly and without hesitation, as no one in the Yaglom household was afraid of candor. But the Raskins—even Meyer—were taken aback when Daniel bluntly asked Rachel, "Do you like Isaac?," and she replied without even lowering her eyes, "Very much so!"

"Listen, you village capitalist," Daniel Yaglom said, moving his glasses to his forehead and putting on a pair of silver pince-nez. "Here is what I have to say. Leave your children in Pinsk, and I will make them into real people! For Isaac, we will hire a tutor. The technical school director doesn't ask too much: five hundred rubles will make Isaac a student. We'll enroll Sarah in the gymnasium. I won't charge you much for room and board either."

In his head, Meyer quickly added up what all this would cost him. "Oh, no," he thought to himself, "I haven't lost my mind yet! Nothing good ever

---

2   A fairly privileged secondary school in old Russia, with emphasis on humanities. Technical schools were nearly equivalent to gymnasiums but emphasized sciences. All notes are by the translators.

comes from getting involved with these penniless aristocrats!" Still, he was pleased that Yaglom had called him a capitalist.

"Well, I'm no capitalist, are you joking? No, Reb Daniel, I cannot afford to send my children to schools like that, I just can't."

Sarah flushed. Oh, God! If only she could continue her studies, live in the city, meet educated people. Read books! She even tried to bring it up when she was left alone with her father.

"Dad," she said, "would it still be possible, by any chance? Times have changed, but we continue to live like wolves in the forest. What will become of us?"

Isaac wasn't too interested in school. Put his fine attire aside and study day and night? Thanks, but no thanks. But stay here as a guest for a month or so—that's another matter. That he wouldn't mind.

"It won't cost you anything," Daniel said to Meyer wryly. "So why don't you leave the young man with us for a while?"

And Meyer agreed, "Just for a month. One month only! I want him to start working with me." With that, Meyer and Sarah set out for home.

Oh, how excruciating it was for Sarah to be back in the countryside! Goodness, other people study, they become doctors, engineers, or mid-wives, and she is doomed to sit here in the country and wait for some boor to propose to her! Her eyelids became swollen from crying, and Chava could not fathom what was happening to her daughter. Did someone put the evil eye on her in the city? Why did Meyer have to take her there? He's always coming up with something!

A week passed, and Sarah was still beside herself. She wasn't doing any chores, she wasn't taking care of the children. She read books on all kinds of subjects with no rhyme or reason, so that they all became mixed up in her head. At night she quietly wept, burying her face in her pillow so that no one would hear. One day, she'd immerse herself in Pushkin, learning dozens of his poems by heart; the next day, she'd study Russian accentuation in Kirpichnikov's grammar because she had difficulty pronouncing Russian words and made them sound Jewish. She kept pestering her father until he bought her Pavlenkov's single-volume encyclopedic dictionary, then she began to memorize words. Oh my God! So many words out there—and she doesn't know any of them! She knows nothing!

And Isaac? Look at him! A new man returned from Pinsk. Even his own father, who had seen all sorts of things in life, opened his mouth in astonishment—but then immediately furrowed his brow. What did it all cost, how much money did Isaac borrow from Yaglom? He had hairbrushes and combs, and a razor, and another suit, and a small photographic camera, and a pair of stylish shoes. He must have spent at least thirty-five rubles, more like fifty! But Meyer wasn't the kind to mention this to his son directly. He just furrowed his brow even more so that everyone could see that he was displeased.

"Fine" he thought, "what's done is done. Now it's time to get down to work. When Ilya was Isaac's age, he was already at Adryzyn . . .

But Meyer was even more displeased when Isaac began receiving letters from Rachel Yaglom. Those penniless aristocrats! As soon as they smell cash, they start putting a "spell" on the boy! But Meyer did not mention this to his son either; he just complained to his wife at night. That's the kind of man he was.

A few weeks later, he took Isaac to Ilya at Adryzyn. Their forest at Adryzyn was large, since Meyer kept buying more and more parcels.

Ilya had made himself into a true owner in the full sense of the word. All evening long the old Jew who oversaw the work was shaking his head, sighing, and expressing admiration.

"This young man will go far," he told Meyer, nodding in Ilya's direction. "You ask why? Well, when he got here, he was pretty much blind, blind as a puppy. And look at him now! Look how he understands everything! He's got a golden pen and a golden eye. And his head! It's really something! You should hear him bargain with the drovers—you really should!"

And indeed, Ilya had done really well here. That same evening, after Meyer and Isaac had tea and something to eat, Ilya took them to his room and showed them the ledgers. Speaking in a whisper, so that the overseer—who wasn't part of the family—couldn't hear, he used an abacus to add up the profits. The operation was really lucrative, and Ilya knew how to keep expenses to a minimum.

"Well done," Meyer said. "Here, I brought you a helper. If you work well together, everything will be fine!"

Ilya glanced at his dandy brother and didn't say much. Ilya was a kind and warm man, all he said was:

"You'll ruin this suit here, better save it. And actually, you need felt boots here, not these shoes . . ."

Isaac stroked his closely shaven cheeks and suddenly pulled a flashlight from his pocket. Ilya examined it, pressed the button, and shook his head. He was captivated, like a true country boy . . .

3

Well, how about that Meyer Raskin!

The story was rehashed in all the shtetls of Kobryn District. And not just the district—the entire province! The Telyatichi estate is nothing to sneeze at!

This is an interesting story, so we'll take our time to tell it.

Let's start with the old Polish magnate who once lived at Telyatichi—His Lordship Boleslaw Żuk. This Żuk had his own personal "Yankel"—Ephraim Livshitz. Żuk didn't care for Jews and wouldn't allow them anywhere near Telyatichi. Every once in a while, he would catch a careless "Chaim," force him to climb up a tree, and make him sing *Ma-Yofis*, a Sabbath song.

But his feelings toward Livshitz were totally different. "This is an honorable Jew," Boleslaw Żuk used to say of him. Whatever Żuk did, he did it through Ephraim. And, of course, Ephraim prospered. He built himself a two-story house in Antopol and bought Polushen, a small estate nearby. Ephraim had ten sons and one daughter. He married all of them off. All of the sons helped their father in his business, and the entire family was well off.

In time, Boleslaw Żuk died. He had no children. The heirs came from St. Petersburg—an engineer nephew and his wife. Of course, Ephraim and his sons immediately set out to ingratiate themselves with the new owner.

But the new owner did not want to manage the estate himself. He was a landowner of a new type: he spent his winters in St. Petersburg and only visited Telyatichi in the summer—unless he went abroad.

So the younger Żuk decided to lease out Telyatichi for a period of ten years. It was as though God himself wanted Livshitz to be the tenant. After all, he was tied to Telyatichi in more ways than one: he kept his oxen in the Telyatichi barn, he purchased Telyatichi's entire output of Swiss cheese year after year, he provided the malt for the distillery and bought up the rye crop from Żuk.

Then suddenly, this country Jew named Meyer Raskin, a freshly minted money bags, if one may say so, appears on the scene. On his lucky day, he arrives at Telyatichi together with some enterprising broker.

"Is your Lordship offering Telyatichi for lease?"

"Yes, I am."

"How much?" asked Raskin.

But the new landowner was not much of a businessman, so he directed Raskin to his wife, a woman not to be trifled with. Twelve thousand rubles per year in rent, plus the tenant must purchase a forest parcel for another twenty-five thousand.

Now, let's hear Meyer tell the whole story himself.

"Of course," Meyer says, "the first thing to do was to inspect the forest. Twenty-five thousand is nothing to sneeze at! But then the broker appears and tells me confidentially, 'Reb Meyer, you should know that the Livshitzes are on their way! I swear, strike me dead—they will be here in five minutes!' It made my head spin. All my money is in business, I only have three thousand in my pocket. It's enough for the deposit, of course, but then what? But there is no time to think, the clock is ticking. So I go back to the lady, take the deposit money out of my pocket and put it on the table—done!"

Legends tend to grow around all major events, and some grew around this episode, too. One of the stories was that the Livshitzes had been pre-warned, that they were supposed to arrive at Telyatichi before Raskin. But on the way over, one of the sons lost his silver cigarette case. They stopped their carriages and went searching for it. While they were at it, the lease on Telyatichi was signed.

Whether it's true or not, one thing is clear: when the Livshitzes arrived at Telyatichi, Żuk's office door was locked. Through the keyhole, they could see Meyer Raskin inside. The Livshitzes knocked on the door and heard the lady reply from inside the locked room:

"We did not call for anyone. You can't come in!"

Thus began a tale of slander and intrigue—in short, the war between the Livshitzes and the Raskins. This war had a completely unexpected outcome—the marriage of Ilya Raskin to Rachel Novogrudski, Livshitz's granddaughter. . . . We'll get to it later; for now, back to our main story.

Time flies. At first glance, its passage may seem monotonous. If a person is bored and feels suffocated, he might feel as though time has stopped. Each morning, the Raskins open their store. Here are two brands of cheap tobacco in four ounce and two ounce packages. Here is sulphur—to treat scalp disease. Matches. Here, for the local intelligentsia especially—the clerks from the administration office, the doctor's assistant, the priest's sons, and the saleswoman—Butterfly cigarettes, twenty-five for seven kopeks. A drum of kerosene, a barrel of tar, salt, glass shades for oil lamps, homemade yeast. The latter must be concealed, or else, God forbid, the tax inspector might appear and write up a citation, which would spell big trouble. . . . Also, sugar. That's about it.

Business is slow during the day. A peasant might walk in, look around for a while, sigh, and finally ask,

"How much for a ten pound bag of sugar?"

Chava starts calculating, then responds,

"Sugar is expensive. Two rubles twenty kopeks, can't go any lower."

The peasant would bargain at length, taking his warm hat off and putting it back on, swearing, and spitting. He searches deep in his pocket and pulls out a small bag of copper coins, counts them slowly, then finally gives up and makes a decision,

"Give me a quarter pound for four kopeks. That's all I have, I swear to God . . ." Or he might shout,

"Just give me some time, I'll pay you when I have the money!"

In the evening, all hell would break loose. The big room would fill with peasants, who come here night after night. They sit on the floor, the benches, the stools. They banter about the goings-on in the village, spit on the floor, and endlessly smoke disgusting cheap tobacco. The house turns blue with smoke, and there is no air left to breathe. This doubles Sarah's suffering: she develops a migraine, chokes, and sobs quietly and bitterly over her wasted life. Then the village idiot arrives, his bare feet covered only with torn galoshes, despite the winter frost. All he wears is a hemp shirt and a pair of homespun pants. He has a thick beard, black and curly, and his hairy chest is bare. His eyes and teeth sparkle unpleasantly in the dim light. He can stand motionlessly for hours, leaning against the wall. The peasants, for lack of anything else to do, tease him and pick on him, driving him into a rage. He runs around the store like a wild animal, cursing and swearing, his white teeth sparkling from within the thicket of his black beard.

Ominous clouds—taxes, fire, disease, failed crops—frequently hang over the village. Then the peasants' faces change, and all of the filthy curses and all the anger that has been growing and festering for centuries is poured onto the Raskins' heads. The Belarusian peasants, normally tranquil and unflappable, suddenly recall that Jews crucified Jesus, that they don't want to do real work, that Meyer, for instance, opened the store where his wife robs ordinary people blind, while Meyer himself, that greedy bastard, makes more dirty money on the side. If these drunk and angry men run into chubby three-year-old Sheva, one of them might spit on her head; another, as if by accident, might step on her little foot with his ice-laden bast shoe: "Take that, you Yid spawn!" The child cries, Chava wrings her hands and begs for mercy, while Sarah and the boys hide in the cold larder. Someone boldly breaks the lamp with a stick, the store goes dark, and the peasants continue to scream in the darkness . . .

On those winter days, when the bright cold sun makes the snow sparkle with blue, gold, and purple diamonds, rose-colored smoke rises from the chimneys toward the clear skies. The village suddenly feels joyful and light, like a play set. On such days, Sarah dresses her brothers warmly and takes them for a walk. Before long, the boys are treated to her remarkable view of the world, in the form of a didactic sermon:

"Some people lead happy lives: no vicious peasants, no miserable, dirt-poor villages. These happy people live in big cities. They read good books and go to theaters and lectures in the evening. They do intellectual work and enjoy their work tremendously. Children, your future depends upon you! We three older children are doomed, we have failed to escape this pit. But you have to make something of yourselves. Study, children! Study! I should be able to convince father to send you to school; you will graduate from the gymnasium, and not just graduate—you will earn gold medals! Jewish boys must graduate from the gymnasium with a gold medal in order to be admitted to university. Imagine, Hersh and Motya going to university. My God! Hersh and Motya as university students, in uniforms with gold buttons and blue peaked caps! You, Hersh, will become a doctor, I know it in my heart. You will be a doctor. And you, Motya? What would you like to be?"

Motya wipes snot from under his nose with his sleeve, pulls his wrap-around hood to one side to free his mouth, takes a deep breath, like a fish out of water, and says,

"I want to be a tax inspector."

"No, that won't do, Jews cannot be tax inspectors. Not to mention that it's boring. You will be a big lawyer."

"Fine," the boy agrees, sniffling, "I'll be a big lawyer."

The children love fairy tales that feature themselves. Sarah paints a vivid picture as she instills her own sweet dreams in the younger children. "Study, children! Here's a book, *Good Seeds*. It has a wonderful true story about a village boy who traveled to Moscow in a winter just like this one and went on to become the great Russian scientist and author—Lomonosov. Let this be a model for you, children. Never, never forget it!"

Sarah cannot help shedding a tear onto the page, which has been crumpled by the children's little hands.

"It's nothing, boys; it's just that my eyes hurt from reading, that's all. Hersh, why don't you read aloud, and I'll listen. Watch your accentuation carefully."

And so it goes, day after day, week after week, month after month. Winter is followed by spring, summer, autumn, and then winter again. Every once in a while, father comes home, almost always unexpectedly. The gloomy house returns to life; the floors squeak gaily under Meyer's excited, energetic footsteps.

And look, all the sourpusses here are ready to cry!

"What do you want?" Meyer asks Chava. He cannot bear her sobbing or her face, red from trying to hold back tears. "What do you want?"

Chava rubs her eyes with the sleeve of her cotton blouse and says nothing. During long, sleepless nights after dealing with drunken and rowdy peasants, she thinks a lot about what she is going to say to her husband and how she will say it. She prepares long speeches in her mind, arguments that Meyer will not be able to counter. "He is a good man, Meyer, he will surely see that my life in the country is silent torture for me, no matter how well we eat. This cannot go on forever! I'd rather live on stale rye bread, but in the city, among our own people."

But now, in her husband's presence, Chava feels that all her carefully rehearsed words will vanish like smoke into the sky. What exactly can she say to him?

Angry with herself, Chava begins to talk about the children. Their Jewish daughter is growing up in a Belarusian village—does Meyer ever think about that? At Sarah's age, she, Chava, was already a woman. What will become of Sarah? What kind of people can she meet here? Who can be a role model for her? She reads Russian books all day long and must have already forgotten all her Jewish prayers. And the younger children? At least the older ones studied with the melamed, but the younger ones are growing up like gentiles. What will become of them?

Meyer furrows his brow. He doesn't like his wife's whining. "We'll see what will become of them! Right, Hersh?" "That's right," Hersh replies with his childish lisp. "Me, I'm going to be a doctor!" "See," Meyer laughs, "he'll be a doctor!" "And I'll be a tax inspector!" Motya chimes in, forgetting about his future in the legal field. "Very good! Excellent!"

Meyer absentmindedly flips through the pages of the children's notebooks and furrows his brow, as is his habit. "Drawings, drawings," he mumbles. "Hersh, why do you draw so much and write so little?" Sarah, who had been silent until now, cannot hold it any longer. Flushing, she says: "The boy has a natural talent for drawing. He will make a first-class artist, you'll see. No one has shown him how to do it, no one has taught him, but look at his drawings of people and horses! Like it or not, these children ought to go to a technical school or a gymnasium. They need to be properly educated . . ." The girl's eyes are sparkling. Meyer sees right through her; he understands. "Yes, maybe she herself should have been educated properly, maybe she should have gone to a gymnasium. Maybe Yaglom was right. But, as God is my witness, I couldn't have possibly done it back then, and now it's too late. Soon we'll have to start thinking about something else, something completely different! Sarah is already sixteen . . ." He gives the girl a hug. Chava cannot understand anything. Doesn't Meyer love his children? Why does he work so hard if it's not for their sake?

4

The Telyatichi episode took place in late spring.

The preceding winter had been long and tedious; drunken peasants harassed the women and children with growing regularity. Meyer did not return home until the first days of Passover. He seemed distracted, preoccupied with something important. Then the springtime floods and the gentle sun marked the arrival of Russian Orthodox Easter. Something roiled the Belarusians again, and again they recalled the grave crime once committed by the Jewish nation . . .

The snow melted quickly on the hill where the village sat, and young blades of green grass sprouted in search of sunlight. The wide street was littered with the painted shells of Easter eggs. Loud drunks were not uncommon. Sarah took the children to the fields, where space was more open, dreaming was easier, and life seemed less ugly and hopeless. Then they heard bells tinkling in the distance. The only two people who drove with tinkling bells were the bailiff and the tax inspector. The bailiff was to be offered tea with jam and bagels; his bawdy stories and crude innuendoes had to be borne with patience. The tax man would rummage through the store and endlessly nitpick.

"Why are the tax stamps on this tobacco peeling off? There's something fishy here. Are you trying to pull a *schacher-macher*?"

The tax inspector was very fond of this Jewish word for shady dealings.

The dark spot on the horizon grew in size, and it was neither the bailiff nor the tax inspector. Their horses were not nearly as fast, their carriages were not as lavish. It must be some landowner on his way to the train station.

Was Sarah dreaming? She could not believe her eyes when she saw that it was her father, Meyer, riding in this magnificent carriage.

Yes, it was Meyer Raskin. He was very excited. He placed his heavy hand on the coachman's shoulder, and the black stallions stopped in their tracks, their mouths foaming, their bits jangling. For some reason, Sarah noticed just then that her father looked much older, with gray showing in his beard.

The following hours and days were like a dream. When Chava caught sight of the carriage and the stallions stamping their hooves, she began to weep mournfully. She just knew that something was wrong!

"Wrong?!" Meyer furrowed his brow and paced the room nervously. "Something's wrong? Even on a day like this, you can't set your foolish premonitions aside!"

And then he told her the whole story about Telyatichi. A customer was knocking persistently on the door of the shop, urgently needing tar. Meyer opened a window and called out cheerfully, "We are closed today! Actually, we are closed for good."

Sarah was sitting on the side, her face flushing. The question of the children's future has now been resolved. She senses that their life here is coming to an end. As for herself. . . . Is it too late for her to make up for lost time, too late to go to a proper school?

Chava listened to Meyer quietly. There was not a word, not a sound from her while he was talking, and no delight showed on her face, as he had hoped.

"So we'll be leaving here?" she finally asked softly.

"Of course we will! In the next three days, I'll try to sell all this junk," Meyer said, pointing with his hand, "and off we go! From now on, I'll be at home with you. Enough is enough! Chava, this is your dream come true!"

Chava sat silently for a while, then asked,

"And what about the store?"

"What store?" At first, Meyer didn't even grasp what she was talking about.

"Our store! What will happen to it? Who will run it if we're gone?"

Meyer burst out laughing: "What a woman you are! You've been dying to get out of here your whole life, and now you're worried about the store! We'll sell it, what else? We'll sell everything: the tables, the benches, the wooden couch. To hell with it! We are moving to a seven-room house furnished for the gentry. The moment we get there, we'll bring a tailor from town so that you and the children can get proper attire. Let no one think that we are some kind of ragamuffins. We'll have two servants, like landowners have—one to cook and one to clean. Didn't I tell you that one day we would ride around in a two-horse carriage?"

The woman didn't say a word.

That night, Meyer awoke as if someone had nudged him. Chava was sitting on the edge of the bed, a white figure in the dark room. She must have stayed up all night, just sitting there thinking.

"Why aren't you sleeping?"

"Well, I can't go to sleep somehow," she answered sadly. "I just keep thinking . . . , Maybe we should stay? We've lived through so much here! I had all my children here . . ."

"I don't understand," Meyer said, and it was clear from his tone that he genuinely did not understand her. "You've complained all along that you are bored here, that we should move elsewhere, and now you're saying that maybe we should stay here? You're nothing but a silly woman."

"You don't understand. . . . Every corner of this house has been washed with my tears. I have memories of every single log in these walls. . . . Oh, God!"

In the end, the local peasants were also sorry to see the Raskins go. They stood there shuffling their feet, not knowing what to say. Only Semyon Chukuyski found the words to express what everyone was feeling.

"We had one good Jew here," he said, "and now he is leaving. You could come to the store, sit around and chat. If you had no money but you really needed something—no problem, they trusted you to pay later. You were good Jews!" he said to Raskin. "Why do you have to leave?"

"Come to Telyatichi in the summer," Meyer replied, "to mow the grass. It's as tall as anything there. Everywhere you get a quarter for yourself, but I'll give you a third, fine."

The word spread quickly through the nearby villages that Raskin was moving away and selling his house, his store, and everything in the house for next to nothing. Peasants had been crowding into the store since early morning. They examined every trinket and listened carefully as they knocked on the walls to make sure the wood wasn't rotting. They asked the price for every useless trifle, climbed onto the roof, inspected the chimneys. An old man with a long thick beard wanted to buy Raskin's cow. The cow was for sale, too—there were two hundred cows at Telyatichi.

"Give me a good, honest price," the old man said, lifting the cow's tail and looking under it. "My son will be coming back from the Japanese war. He's fighting in Manchuria now, yes . . ."

The connection between the son and the purchase of the cow was left open.

Clearly, the peasants enjoyed haggling tremendously. They would whisper their offers into Meyer's ear, watch his face closely, and swear to God, hiding their hands under their brown jackets.

This went on all day and would have gone on for a few more days had it not been for Shmuel, an old blacksmith from Zastave, who arrived when it was already getting dark. Shmuel came with his son. They both looked old, and it was hard to tell which was the father and which was the son. Both had watery eyes, probably because of the work they did, and both had raspy voices.

They sat down for tea and opened with complaining about the price of iron going up every day, while the peasants become more and more frugal. In the winter, hardly anyone gets all four of their horse's hooves shoed, they just do the front ones, and shoeing in the summer—forget about that. They rambled on and on, finished up two samovars of tea, and rose to leave. But as they said their goodbyes, they paused at the door, and the old man asked offhandedly: "I hear you're leaving?"

Meyer caught on to their game, but he had no desire to take part in it. He responded bluntly:

"Yes, I am leaving, and everything is for sale—the house, the store, the merchandise, the furniture, and the cow. Three thousand for everything. And you, Reb Shmuel, will buy it all in the end, because you have a married son. You need customers, and for now, there is no other blacksmith in this village. I am asking next to nothing, but if you want to convince me otherwise, Chava can refill the samovar again."

Anxious tears welled up in the blacksmith's eyes. He started with two thousand rubles, promptly raised it to two thousand five hundred, and then kept on adding a hundred every half hour, wiping his face and neck with a red handkerchief. Shmuel's son quietly watched his father doing the talking. He was not his own man, this son, not at all.

All through the peasants' haggling and the blacksmith's bargaining, Chava sat by the window, her arms resting heavily on her knees. She stared through the window motionlessly, without blinking, and it was impossible to tell whether she was listening or thinking her own thoughts. And only when the blacksmith pushed his glass away and firmly declared, "My price is twenty-nine hundred rubles!," she briskly got up and said,

"One minute, please. You can have everything except this wooden couch. It's no good anyway, it really isn't. I'll take it with me."

"What do you need it for?" Meyer asked, surprised.

"Well, I just do. . . . I'm not selling it, we'll take it with us."

She said it so resolutely that Meyer did not dare to argue.

"Fine," said the blacksmith. "Twenty-nine hundred rubles without the couch."

"Twenty-nine hundred," his son echoed.

"*Mazel tov* on the purchase, you got it for nothing," Meyer said and stood up.

"Take good care of it. . . . It's a very nice house," Chava said sadly.

5

So began the Raskins' new life.

Neither Sarah nor Chava—especially Chava—were able to imagine that their father and husband could possibly "play such an important role." As an entrepreneur, Meyer was developing away from home, out of their sight, but now the family suddenly saw a completely changed man. It's not that he was trying to show off, not at all. He was too smart for that and didn't engage in foolish pettiness. He did, however, make it clear from the start that he was the one in charge.

When the manager of Telyatichi, Mr. Plavski, an elegant-looking man with good manners and a long mustache, came by to greet "Mr. Meyer" and his family on the day of their arrival, Chava felt sheepish. They were in the dining room, and she herself went to the living room and brought a comfortable chair for Mr. Plavski. Meyer winced, but said nothing. However, when the assistant manager, who everyone called by his first name, David, showed up with similar greetings half an hour later, and Chava, after pouring him a glass of tea, wanted to offer him that same comfortable chair, Meyer said in rapid Yiddish,

"Take that glass away and never, ever do that again!"

Oh yes, Meyer knew how to present himself!

A tailor was summoned to the house the same week, and Chava and the children all got suitable new clothing. Chava found it hard to part with her simple cotton blouses. She felt ill at ease at Telyatichi. Who in the world needs two servants? What will be left for Chava to do? What will keep Sarah busy? Oh my, people just don't know what they want: very often they leave a bad situation behind—only to find themselves in an even worse one! Chava sometimes recalled her life in the village. There, at least she had the peasant women to talk to, and here she can't even do that. One day, a woman came by with eggs to sell. Chava invited her into the dining room for a cup of tea and spent several hours talking to her, finally unburdening herself. But then Meyer showed up, and he was not at all pleased.

"You think this is the right company for you?" he grumbled.

New people started appearing in their house, and even when old acquaintances came by, they didn't act the way they used to. Take the tax inspector, for instance, who had been visiting the Raskins in the village for the past few years. He used to be utterly unpleasant. He found fault with everything, he wrote up citations, he pounded his fist on the table and screamed at them. That same taxman started coming to the Telyatichi distillery. My God, he was a completely changed man now! On one occasion, Meyer invited him for supper. The taxman accepted eagerly, came in, and— imagine that—kissed Chava's hand! He kissed Chava's hand and asked her in the sweetest of voices,

"How are you doing, Madam?"

Oh yes, Meyer knew how to present himself! Maybe he still had some difficult moments from time to time, but he knew how to smooth them over. If Chava were to find out that money was tight at times, she would have immediately suggested to let go the household help. But that was not Meyer's way. He had the carriage prepared for him and went to the shtetl of Drahicyn, as if on business. He was dressed up like a magnate. Peacock feathers swayed on his coachman's small round hat.

And what do you know? In less than five minutes, a crowd of Jews was all around him.

"Would the Telyatichi leaseholder be interested in borrowing some money at a good rate? We don't know what to do with our money, honestly, and here's such a good investment opportunity!"

Meyer furrowed his brow and replied,

"Money? Everyone wants to loan me money, you know, I don't know what to do, I really don't. But on the other hand, why not help out your neighbors? Your new neighbors, who also happen to be Jews? All right, fine, I'll take some—at seven percent!"

And money came pouring in from all sides.

It was amazing how quickly Meyer got the gist of it, how he threw himself at operations that were new to him. Take the distillery, for example. Did he know anything about distilling just a month earlier? But within a few weeks, Levkovich, the old distiller and a friend of Livshitz, was only shrugging his shoulders and cursing Raskin under his breath:

"Damn it! You can't fool this Jew, you just can't!"

Meyer was now trying to divest himself of all his prior business commitments and give his full attention to Telyatichi. The Adryzyn forest venture had been wrapped up, and Meyer welcomed two new helpers, Ilya and Isaac, who were returning from there. The brothers had lived together in the forest under one roof for several years, and it appeared that they didn't see many people while there. One would think that they would have grown very much alike and developed similar habits. Think again. Two grown men arrived at Telyatichi, and one look at them was enough to tell that they were very much changed.

Ilya, the older of the two, became a true forester, with a yellow folding ruler sticking out of his pocket, with a whiff of tree resin and an air of hard work about him. He was short and wore tall boots that had not seen a brush in months. He had largely abandoned his violin. The only thing he had in common with his father was his willingness to work hard, but even in this respect the two men weren't equals. Frankly, he lacked vision. He was able to handle any assignment, but "inventing gunpowder," coming up with something new, negotiating with landowners, thinking strategically—this was not for him.

From his very first day at Telyatichi, Ilya quietly began working. He put on his tall boots and walked the estate. Here's the distillery, the ox barn, the cowshed, the cheese factory, the storage barn, the kitchen for seasonal laborers. Ilya observed everything, learned how things worked, and made notes in his notebook.

When Mr. Plavski told him that today was the first day to sow wheat, Ilya drove out to the fields with him. Ilya walked purposefully across the already plowed, lustrous black earth, cheerfully answering the workers' greetings. "God help you in your work!" he said to them. "May God help you, too," they replied and pressed their oxen forward. Ilya followed them with his eyes. He was about to mop his brow with a handkerchief, then suddenly stopped and ran after the laborers instead. Red-faced, his upper lip trembling, he yelled out to them:

"What are you doing? Who taught you to drive oxen like this? You'll break their skin, you'll injure them! This is not good! Pull those nails out of your sticks right now!"

The farmhands removed the nails from the sticks that they used to drive the oxen.

"If I ever see this again," Ilya said, "I will dock your wages. Understood?"

"Understood," the farmhands replied.

Meanwhile, Mr. Plavski walked through the field, looked into the distance with his blue Polish eyes, and said,

"Aw, God damn it! These sons of bitches, they won't get the job done today. They're dragging it out on purpose so that they'll have to come back tomorrow and get paid for another day."

Ilya thought for a moment, looked at his watch, and then paced the length and width of the field, measuring it with his short steps.

"Listen, boys," he said as he called the young workers to gather around him. "We have to get this job done today no matter what."

The workers blew their noses, glanced at the sun, scratched their heads, and said nothing. Only one of them, a bald, good-natured man with a bad leg that had been mangled by a falling wagon, stepped forward. Fixing Ilya with a penetrating look, he gestured with his stick toward the crimson summer sun and said,

"It can't be done, Master. It's like we told Mr. Plavski, it's just not possible."

"Nonsense!" Ilya retorted. "Together, we'll get it all done. Three quarts of vodka on me!"

"Now, that's another story!" the man said, beaming and winking at the others. "Hear that, boys? Vodka's on the Master!"

"Thank you very much indeed!"

And with that, they got down to work.

At twilight, after the cows came home and the bell rang to summon the milkmaids, Ilya went to the cowshed. He enjoyed the pleasant smells of the animals, of damp hay, of manure and fresh milk. Strong streams of milk rang out against the metal pails. Girls and women sat on low benches with their heads buried in the cows' warm bellies and did the milking. Here, Ilya learned everything he needed to know, and within an hour, he had given his first order—to wash the cows' udders with warm water before milking.

"That's what they do in Zakoziel, their German manager told them to," the cheesemaker said.

"And that's what we will be doing here as well; we can match the German," Ilya replied.

In the evening, while sitting in the dining room and noisily sucking weak tea from a saucer in his hand, Ilya said,

"We definitely need to buy five more horses for the summer. They will pay for themselves, and we can sell them in the fall. There's a fair in Kobryn in five days, we'll have to go."

"Why horses?" Isaac said, shrugging his shoulders. It was not clear whether it was a question or just an idle comment.

Meyer quietly hummed under his breath as he listened and furrowed his brow.

"Do you think we really need them?" Meyer asked.

"No question about it . . ." Ilya replied, pulling a notebook from his pocket and proceeding to prove beyond any doubt that more horses were indeed a necessity.

Then Ilya said to his father,

"Livshitz has two railcars worth of oxen waiting in our ox barn. The distillery will stop operating in a week. . . . Do you happen to know when he plans to send the oxen to Warsaw?"

Meyer drummed his fingers on the damp tablecloth.

"His man came down last week and said that they will move the oxen in a few days. There is one problem, though: Ephraim Livshitz owes me three thousand rubles!"

"He won't pay you back" Ilya said. "He's mad at us for beating him to Telyatichi." "Then he won't get his oxen."

Ilya was speechless, but Isaac said grudgingly,

"That's all we need! Do you want to cause a provincewide scandal?"

"What scandal?" Meyer retorted. "He'll pay the three thousand and we'll release his oxen right away. I don't have extra money lying around, you know."

Isaac was perpetually displeased with everything, and even his face always showed discontent and aggravation. It was as if he was telling the world, "Do as you please, but I already know that it won't work." Yet he never suggested exactly what should be done and how.

He made everyone around him feel uncomfortable somehow. When he was particularly angry and moody, he sensed acutely what would hurt the others, and he knew how to express it in the most painful way.

He enjoyed dressing stylishly, wearing stiff collars, cuffs, and yellow shoes. For some reason, he started turning gray at the age of twenty, even though he did not drink alcohol and, apparently, did not chase after women. He played his violin in the evening, and people could not understand how such a callous man could produce such mournful melodies. He also bought a flute, and when he played it in the evening, Chava would wrap her shawl tightly around her shoulders and mutter quietly,

"God, please make him stop. . . . I can't bear it anymore!"

But to him, she never said a word.

Everyone was wary of Isaac and avoided arguing with him. And he was always unhappy about everything no matter what it was. He did not start pulling his weight on the estate right away. Instead, he watched his father and Ilya for a few days, and even though he didn't say a word, one could clearly see that he was already prepared to be unhappy in advance. Just in case, one might say, which always allowed him to claim, "See, I never agreed, I knew it wouldn't work . . ."

Meyer kept quiet for the time being. Forthright with everyone else, he was very solicitous and gentle with his children. Had it been Ilya, he would have casually told him that it was time to get down to work, that there was more than enough for everyone to do. But he would never say that to Isaac. So Isaac took advantage and kept dragging his feet.

After a week, Isaac said to his father,

"We need to decide who does what around here."

"What for?" Meyer asked, bemused.

"For the usual reasons. We all need to have certain responsibilities. I, for example, can do all the paperwork. It's plenty. We're taking over the distillery in the fall, which will mean even more work: the distilling journal, the cellaring journal, all kinds of reports."

On the surface, it sounded completely innocuous, but his tone made both Meyer and Ilya cringe. It was as if Isaac was saying,

"I'm doing you a big favor. . . . You would have made a mess of it, since you don't really understand anything, but I felt sorry for you and came to your rescue. But remember: if the whole thing fails—it will be your fault. After all, you didn't ask for my opinion when you decided to lease the estate . . ."

Meyer promptly agreed, if only to end the unpleasantness.

"Fine," he said, "please do take over the paperwork."

But Isaac wasn't finished yet. Looking stiff and annoyed, he took a few steps across the room.

"Well. . . . Look, we aren't little kids anymore." He smiled wryly. "We need. . . . We should have an ownership interest in the business. Or else we're just like hired help . . ."

Ilya found this so unpleasant that he turned away.

"Oh, God . . . ," Meyer said, throwing his hands up. "Everything here is yours!" He smiled, hoping to put an end to it. "Everything here is for you!"

"Well, that's all well and good, but it would be better for the business if each of us knew exactly what's his. If you give us fifteen percent each, I think everyone would be happy."

Ilya was about to jump in and refuse his share, but Meyer got in ahead of him again.

"Fine with me," Meyer said. "You will each get fifteen percent. As long as we have good luck. . . . Would I really . . ."

He didn't finish his thought. Isaac's expression clearly stated, "Well, no one knows whether we shall have good luck or not. After all, nobody asked for my opinion. If anything goes wrong, you should blame yourselves; I had nothing to do with it . . ."

However, it would be unfair to think that Isaac was a greedy man. Not at all. It's just that he was a skeptical and unhappy man. Unhappy about everything without exception.

6

Life weaves its own intricate patterns and keeps people on their toes.

Just as the keen interest in the Raskin family was beginning to subside in the towns and shtetls, just as curious Jews in synagogues and market squares had reached an agreement on burning questions such as how much money the leaseholder of Telyatichi had, how good his next harvest would be, or how much Meyer would make during the ten-year period—and, accordingly, how much Livshitz would lose—a striking new development resonated throughout the area. Now everyone could see what kind of people the Livshitzes were and how low they could sink.

It is true that the Livshitzes had been wronged by Meyer Raskin, and rather cruelly at that. Would an honest Jew do what Raskin had done? Is it acceptable to grab something that doesn't rightfully belong to you from under someone else's nose?

And so the Livshitzes took action.

About ten days later, the district police chief from Kobryn visited Telyatichi. Meyer welcomed him as he would a dear and eagerly awaited friend. A sumptuous dinner was prepared, and fine wine was ordered from Drahicyn. "Would His Excellency be interested in seeing the estate in the meantime?"

Of course, His Excellency was interested in seeing the Telyatichi operation in the meantime. He was a fat and clumsy man. He breathed noisily and heavily, which made his red neck and face even redder. He had a habit of sounding unpleasantly surprised, and his expressions of surprise invariably ran toward the same end.

"Look at all of these cows!" he exclaimed upon entering the cowshed, and his breathing grew even heavier. "I had only one little cow, and now even she is dead. Honest!"

"Your misfortune can surely be remedied," Meyer observed. "Might I humbly offer to sell you a cow?"

The police chief huffed and puffed and said nothing. In the ten years that he had been serving in the Pale of Settlement, he had learned to read these Jews very well.

"Looks like you have some lovely hay here," he said with surprise a little later.

"Indeed, we do," Meyer replied. "Your cow is used to this lovely hay."

Again the officer said nothing. Then they entered the cheese factory.

"Your Swiss cheese is excellent!" the policeman exclaimed.

"I'd be happy to sell you some," Meyer said.

A young maid in a white apron ran out from the house, with her hands on her breasts to keep them from swaying. She coughed into her fist and said,

"Dinner is ready, Master."

"Look at her!" the police chief said, immediately brightening up. "Dinner is ready!"

They returned to the house slowly, the police chief walking heavily and panting with exhaustion.

"I just have one favor to ask you, Meyer Yosselevich. It is my official duty, if you will, so I must, you see. . . . Please, don't spoil your local police captain too much! For your own sake! I know, you will shower him with gifts right away—and he is not entitled to anything. He already has a wealthy wife. I know all my captains, I know them very well! So I am asking you, Meyer Yosselevich. . . . And the police sergeant—don't even let him set foot in your house. Just throw him out, no ifs, ands, or buts!"

The dinner was splendid—a true Russian feast. The police chief could not have been happier. He said,

"Between you and me, I am against all restrictions on Jews. I am against the Jewish Pale of Settlement. Jews are people just like everyone else, I assure you. But," he said, downing another glass of wine, "what can you do, my friend? I'm just doing my job, and that's that."

He unbuttoned his tight collar and continued, lowering his voice:

"And besides, Meyer Yosselevich, all that snitching, all that ratting, my friend. . . . What can you do? I'm a fair man, but I have to say that you Jews love to snitch, you love to rat each other out, and all that . . ."

He illustrated his last words with a characteristic gesture and leaned back on the couch. Then he opened his briefcase, dug through it, snuffled just enough, praised the wine belatedly while Meyer kept quiet, and finally said:

"Look, I have folded it here to conceal the signature. Of course, as an officer, I am not supposed to show you the complaint itself either, but, my dear friend. . . . I'll tell you in strict confidence: it was your fellow Jew who sent this document to the provincial Governor. And I was asked to investigate."

Meyer started reading. Ilya also approached and cautiously glanced at the document. It was a denunciation. Someone was informing the Governor that "a Jew named Raskin has leased the Telyatichi estate, even though, as a Jew, he had absolutely no right to do so. Not only that, "the said Jew, along with his family, resides at Telyatichi," again with no right to do so.

"I see Mr. Livshitz has sprung into action," Meyer said, putting the paper on the table. "Well, Your Excellency, you've known me for a long time . . ." He paused, probably deciding to approach it from a different angle. "Whether or not I am a leaseholder—that still needs to be proved. As for my staying at Telyatichi—I had thought about it before Mr. Livshitz did. Here are all the papers: I am the manager of the distillery and I have the residency permit. As for my family, they do not live with me. Isn't that right, Your Excellency?"

Ilya bit his fingernails and moved aside. Isaac shrugged his shoulders, but said nothing.

"I see," the chief of police said. "All right, we'll record all your testimony, so to speak, and after that—it's out of my hands. Personally, as you know, I am against the Pale of Settlement."

The complaint was set aside. Meyer had a chat with a man who had nothing to do with any of this, who in turn conveyed to Livshitz—also in strict confidence—Meyer's advice that he cease the unpalatable practice of writing denunciations. "Because," Meyer said, "if I take this route as well, Reb Livshitz would get into serious trouble. After all, I do have a little something on him too!"

This "little something" was, of course, Ephraim's "tiny bit of land" in Polushen.[3]

The complaints ceased, but the Livshitzes still wouldn't let it go. Ephraim requested that a rabbi make a ruling on his conflict with Raskin. And here again, Meyer demonstrated what an unusual and cunning man he was. He brought the rabbi's wife a few chickens and a calf. Let no one think, God forbid, that he was trying to influence the outcome of the case

---

3   The right of Jews to own agricultural land was severely restricted by law.

somehow. No, not at all. As for the rabbi, Meyer had a good heart-to-heart with him before the case came up for review. Once again, let no one think that Meyer was trying to get ahead and influence the outcome in any way.

The rabbi groaned over the yellowed pages of the old folios for so long that he ended up developing indigestion. He repeatedly proposed that the two Jews reconcile, but "the contesters' souls were as unfeeling as iron." Finally, the rabbi had no other choice but to rule that according to our laws, Reb Meyer was in the right—you see, he may not have known that Reb Livshitz had wanted to lease Telyatichi himself.

"But what about my right of priority?" exclaimed the incensed Livshitz. "The fact that I've known old Żuk for forty years?"

To that, the rabbi said nothing; he was rushing to the lavatory. May God save him from having to handle such a case ever again! He'd rather reconcile twenty husbands with their wives than sort out a conflict like this.

It was exactly at this point that Meyer requested, in the presence of other Jews, that Livshitz pay him the three thousand rubles, as detailed in the promissory note.

"Reb Ephraim," he said respectfully, as if nothing had happened between them. "Reb Ephraim, you've informed me that you will be taking your oxen soon. Please remember to send me my three thousand with the man who will be coming for the oxen."

This took place at the home of Antopol's rabbi on Tuesday, and on Friday, when twilight fell and Chava lit Sabbath candles, a cart drove up to the porch. In it was Kratz, a broker and freight forwarder quite well known in the area. Kratz was his nickname; his real name was actually Meyshe.

Why did Kratz arrive at such a late hour? This is how he explained it:

"I was in Zakoziel on business, and then I stopped in Ludvinovo to see the landowner Kantorov. I was hoping to be in Drahicyn before sunset to spend the Sabbath there, but, as you can see, I didn't make it, and the Sabbath caught me in Telyatichi."

Who on earth needs all these explanations?

"God has sent you here," kind Chava said. "Please be our Sabbath guest."

Kratz did not need another invitation. Maybe because Kratz had been trading in oxen for so long, in the end he himself started to look like a bull who had spent a good six months in the ox barn. He put on his Sabbath jacket, combed his beard with his chubby fingers, and suddenly started screaming as if he himself was being slaughtered: "Glory to our Lord!"

On Saturday, Kratz, still wearing the same Sabbath jacket, walked around the estate, visiting the shed, the barn, the distillery, which was about to wrap up within a few days, and the stables. Casually, he took a peek into the ox barn. Mr. Livshitz's fat oxen were awaiting their sad fate—to be shipped to Warsaw for slaughter. Kratz walked back and forth, silently counted the animals—the number was right—and smirked into his beard.

Now we can finally reveal the real purpose of Kratz's visit. As some of you may have guessed already, he was dispatched to Telyatichi by Livshitz with a particular goal in mind. The plan was for Livshitz's men to come to Telyatichi from Polushen in the middle of the night and "liberate" the oxen. Kratz was to accompany them to the train station and then on to Warsaw.

Kratz, however, decided not to limit himself to Livshitz's errand. Why not have a chat with Reb Meyer? Why not get to know this newly rich man? Why shouldn't a broker and a Jew get a little something out of Raskin? And Kratz got right down to business.

"I haven't seen such an excellent operation in a long time," he told Meyer, not yet knowing where he was going with it. "And you have really good helpers—your sons," he continued. And that's when he had a bright idea: why not earn some money from matchmaking? Wouldn't Ilya Raskin make a good bridegroom?

And so he shared his idea with Meyer. Oh, those brokers! Can you guess who he suggested as the bride for Ilya? None other than Rachel Novogrudski, Ephraim Livshitz's granddaughter! True, her stingy grandfather would not offer much money for her dowry, but don't forget that she can expect an inheritance.

"I don't think it would work," Meyer replied quickly. "You know that Reb Livshitz is angry with me."

"What do you mean—angry?" Kratz exclaimed. "You are both Jews!"

That is what Kratz proposed to Meyer, even though Livshitz had sent him there for a totally different purpose.

Now we have to set the matchmaking story aside and relate what exactly happened early Sunday morning.

That night, Livshitz's farm hands arrived from Polushen as planned. When everyone was asleep, Kratz quietly got up, put his clothes on, grabbed his small suitcase, and jumped out the window. The men were waiting for him near the ox barn.

The oxen would have been taken away, no doubt, had it not been for pure chance.

This time, Ilya, who usually slept like a log after working hard, woke up for some reason. Chava can claim all she wants that it was God's doing; you can believe it or not. What's important is that Ilya did wake up. It was quiet; the night watchman was beating his wooden clapper, as usual. Ilya glanced at the clock—it was three in the morning. He had another four or five hours to sleep. He tried, but no matter what he did, he could not fall asleep. Then he dressed himself and went outside.

"Is it quiet?" he asked the watchman.

"Yes, Master" said the watchman. "They're done with the oxen; they'll be driving them off now."

Ilya had no further questions. He rushed to Mr. Plavski's and urgently awakened him. Mr. Plavski put a revolver in his pocket, and a minute later, he, Ilya and the farm hands that they had awakened headed for the ox barn. The Polushen boys, even though they were armed with stakes, fled in disgrace. It turned out that Mr. Plavski had a heavy hand, as Kratz had a chance to find out.

Despite his treachery, the battered Kratz nevertheless decided to justify himself to Meyer.

"Reb Meyer," he said, holding his chin and moving one eye, as the other was swollen from the beating, "Reb Meyer, you do understand that I had nothing to do with it! I'm a hired hand. I was told to go, so I went. . . . I hope you're not angry with me . . ."

"Oh, my God! Nobody is angry with you; just hold something cold to your face," Chava groaned. "Does it hurt badly?"

By the end of the day, the Livshitzes had sent the three thousand rubles, and the oxen were released. That same Kratz, even though he was hurting all over, took "the goods" to Warsaw.

A naïve person might think that after this skirmish, the Livshitzes and the Raskins became enemies for life. By no means. Kratz needed something to live on. This is what he himself said about the incident,

"Business is business, and the cause of humanity is the cause of humanity."

That Kratz was quite a philosopher! During the next ten years, Kratz received more than just a few hundred rubles from the Raskins. And the first fee he earned was for matchmaking . . .

7

Ephraim Livshitz had ten sons and one daughter. To sons, God gives legs to follow in their father's footsteps, and to daughters He gives wings—to fly away from home.

And so it was with Ephraim's family. The sons helped their father, boosting his fortune and expanding the large Livshitz family. People used to say that on holidays, when all the sons, daughters-in-law, and grandchildren got together, fifty-five people sat around the table.

So why didn't Ephraim's only daughter and her husband stay with the old man? The old gossips at the synagogue would have much to say about that, but let's leave them alone. Some claimed that Ephraim didn't love his daughter and was happy to be rid of her; others said quite the opposite—that he adored his daughter, but couldn't stomach his son-in-law, Novogrudski. Who knows? This is of no interest to us. Livshitz's daughter died long ago, leaving her husband with two sons and daughter Rachel—Ephraim's grandchildren.

What can we say about Akiva Novogrudski? He smoked very strong cigars, shaved his beard, could down twenty-five glasses of tea in one sitting, and read and wrote in nine languages. He was also known in Kobryn as a big *apikoyres*—that is, a nonbeliever.

After his wife died, Novogrudski remarried and sent the children from his first marriage to live with old Livshitz in Antopol. Ephraim took a dislike to these grandchildren, his late daughter's kids. They had not been in Antopol for long before he hired a melamed to look after them and sent them all to Polushen.

The girl stayed put in Polushen, while the boys finished a four-year primary school and were send to Warsaw to live with a distant relative. There, they studied to become dental technicians.

When they were already young men, the grandsons came to Antopol for a visit. They did not stay with their grandfather or any other of the

Livshitzes. Instead, they took rooms at Isaac Rubinstein's boarding house and didn't call on Ephraim until the next day. No one knows for sure what kind of conversation the grandsons had with their grandfather. But afterwards a maid, who was frightened out of her wits, went from house to house telling everyone in strict confidence that the young Novogrudskis had banged their fists on the table and demanded money. One of them allegedly grabbed Ephraim by the throat and choked him to the point that the old man fell to his chair, losing the yarmulke from his head. The culprit was the younger of the two, who "let his temper get the better of him" on account of his youthful stupidity. The older one stated that if Grandpa did not come to an agreement with them peacefully, the Committee would become involved. That's exactly what the frightened maid was telling everyone in strict confidence. What Committee? What about this Committee? She had no answers.

Of course, the way old Livshitz was, he could well have reported the matter to the police, and the police could have easily dispatched the perpetrators of such a brazen act to the middle of nowhere. But what would the Jews say? How would they feel about it? This isn't Meyer Raskin, after all—a stranger who is fair game for reporting to the authorities. Remember, these boys are his own flesh and blood!

So old Ephraim made peace with them. He gave the two "loafers" five hundred rubles each, on the condition that he would never see them again. The loafers accepted the money, but three months later they were back, this time in the company of some young men in black tunics. The men were armed—at least according to the maid, although no one could confirm it. The men disappeared as quickly as they had appeared, leaving Ephraim a letter from the "Committee." Rumor has it that the letter contained a skull and crossbones, and a single Russian word in capital letters—"Death!"

We are unable to vouch for the veracity of this information, so we are just reporting what we know of the story that has been rehashed for years across Kobryn District and beyond.

The grandsons of Ephraim Livshitz continued to visit Antopol every now and then. Sometimes it was just the two of them, other times they brought their associates "from the Committee," only to vanish like evil spirits.

Rachel Novogrudski, on the other hand, stayed at Polushen and only rarely visited Antopol. The shtetl made her uncomfortable. Rachel was a fairly attractive, plump brunette; her numerous cousins considered her "rather odd." "Imagine," they would say, "she likes the primitive life at Polushen. She doesn't find it boring at all—can you believe it?" And indeed, Rachel was not bored there at all. She had quickly become accustomed to country life and happily embraced it. She did not go to school for long and never engaged in serious study. A brood of fuzzy yellow chicks interested her more than the young men of Antopol, more than the most exciting novels and short stories. "She is not stupid," some people said of her. "No," others countered, " in fact, she is quite stupid. To have such a rich grandfather and yet choose to live in the middle of nowhere—now that is stupid!"

So it was this girl, Rachel Novogrudski, who, "with God's help," was to marry Ilya Raskin. That was the idea that took shape in the determined brain of broker Kratz. Some hotheads might very well ask, "You mean, despite the episode with the oxen that the entire province talked about, despite the denunciations, despite taking the case to the rabbi?" Such hotheads would, of course, fall on their faces. Even before the episode with the oxen, Kratz had said to Meyer, "What do you mean—angry? You are both Jews!" Kratz never retracted his words even after the episode. As soon as he came back from Warsaw, and his swollen face started returning to normal, he got down to business. A practical man, he smelled success, and with it more than a few hundred rubles for himself.

Without going into too much detail, let us say a few words about the lineage of the two families involved. Keep in mind that Ephraim Livshitz's grandfather was already a member of the merchant class, and not just any merchant—he traded in timber, floating it downriver to Danzig. He was a pious, honest, and learned Jew; when he had a free evening, you could find him in a synagogue studying the Talmud. Likewise, one can only say good things about Ephraim's father. As for Ephraim himself, everything about him is in the open. Is there another Jew in Antopol who is as distinguished and as rich as he is?

And Raskin—well, what can we say? We can disclose in strict confidence that Meyer's grandfather probably didn't even know any prayers. He spent his whole life in the country, working the land like a simple peasant. Imagine: a Jew working the land! It was only Meyer's father who opened a tavern and left the plow behind. And what could be lower than keeping a tavern? Not much.

As for Meyer—you already know his story. Nothing special either. A Jew who got lucky once, that's all. And who knows which way God may turn the wheel tomorrow? No one yet knows how much profit Telyatichi will actually bring.

So, the Livshitz and Raskin clans have been following very different paths. Their paths would never have crossed had it not been for Kratz.

Kratz reasoned: "True, the Raskins do not have distinguished roots. On the other hand, who is Rachel Novogrudski? A country girl, an orphan, nothing more."

And so Kratz got down to work.

There is no need to dwell on the obstacles that Kratz had to overcome. Anyone with a head on their shoulders can easily see that. To reconcile the two enemies, and not just reconcile, but to make them into one family. . . . That was no laughing matter! Meyer's father had brought his son to Antopol in a farm cart. Twenty-five years later, Meyer brought his son Ilya to Antopol. But what a difference! How things had changed during these years!

The entire shtetl came out to witness the Telyatichi leaseholder's famed arrival in town. People had not seen horses and carriages like this in many years; not even the landowners had anything like it. Both Raskins, father and son, were impeccably attired, as befitted the occasion. As the carriage pulled up in front of Ephraim's large house, the curious onlookers would have paid dearly to see firsthand the two enemies reconcile. Would Ephraim's servants really be capable of properly relaying the scene afterwards?

Oh, those long shtetl tongues! It was reported that Ephraim's other granddaughters had dismissed Ilya Raskin from the start. Because, the long tongues maintained, who is this Ilya Raskin after all? He may be an earnest young man, a hard worker—but that's it! In contrast, Ephraim's granddaughters had gone to gymnasiums; they could discuss literature and philosophy. Out of pride and refinement, they occasionally conversed in French. What would they talk about with this working stiff?

But as luck would have it, Rachel Novogrudski actually took to him. As it happened, the two of them did have common interests. They talked about how this year's good snow cover and low-hanging mists promised an excellent harvest for the coming season. They also discussed how it is best to feed the chickens with finely minced boiled eggs, and noted that yearling calves should never be put in the same field with the rest of the herd, because a bull could injure them, God forbid. How do you like this kind of talk between bride and groom? How is that for "common interests"?

Seeing the lavish style in which Meyer Raskin arrived at his home, Ephraim Livshitz suffered a momentary weakness and offered two thousand rubles in cash as a dowry for his granddaughter. He later came to his senses and never actually delivered the money, but that is beside the point. What mattered was that Meyer did make quite an impression on him.

Ephraim also took a liking to Ilya, the groom. "A capable man, very solid, very much so," he kept repeating. "It's a pity he's not a very observant Jew. But," he concluded, "what can you do? Times have changed. What can you do?"

The old men, Ephraim and Meyer, sat in one room, while the youngsters, Ilya and Rachel, sat in another.

"I hope," said Ephraim, "that Ilya will get something from you as well."

"But of course," Meyer replied. "He already has a fifteen percent interest in all of my affairs. Actually, "in all of my affairs" was a bit of an embellishment, but we shall forgive Meyer for that.

"And on top of that," Meyer continued, "he will remain with me. I have no intention of parting with him!"

The two future relatives agreed on everything. Meyer Raskin, however, was not a man to make important decisions for his son without his knowledge. "How do you like Rachel Novogrudski?" he asked Ilya. "I think she will run the house very well," Ilya replied.

Only Ilya and no one else could possibly give this answer.

"May the two of you be happy together," Meyer said to his son. "I will be the same father to her that I am to you."

The next day the formal engagement took place, complete with plate smashing for good luck. Three months later, Ilya and Rachel were married.

8

The wedding was held in Polushen.

Admittedly, it was more of a contest than a wedding. Meyer, after all, was marrying off his first son, and he was determined to make a real splash. First, he was becoming one family with the Livshitzes, second. . . . Well, what is there to talk about? What is the point of making a list? Every man has his own motives, every man knows why he is doing what he is doing, so it's better not to pry and fish for the reasons why and what for.

Tailors and seamstresses worked for three whole weeks to outfit the groom and his family. A full week was spent boiling, baking, and frying.

"What would Chava say, our sad soul, our lovely lady in charge?" Meyer wondered.

"Well, well, well . . . ," he thought to himself. "When something important happens in your life, you can't help but pause and look back. You can't help but start philosophizing—yes, that's the way it is, my dearest Chava! Has it really been that long since you were my bride, and I brought you to the village in a simple cart? Remember that? And all the way home, my silly girl was crying. You are often sad, Chava, but your heart is warm, this I can say. Please don't cry. Please, for me . . ."

"Well, well, well. . . . How time flies! It feels like it was just yesterday, Chava, it certainly does. And yet—look in the mirror! You hair has gone gray. Why are you crying, my silly girl? You shouldn't be crying, you should be rejoicing! Thank you, God—that's all I can say. Thank you, God! Well, well, well . . ."

Meyer smiles wistfully and looks in the mirror. He can see more than one gray hair in his beard, more than ten, even more than a hundred. . . . This is so foolish. God, it's so foolish!

"Well now, Sarah, let's see you in your new dress. My goodness, you are so beautiful! You'd make a beautiful bride yourself! Really!"

Sarah looks away. She is not interested, this is not what she would like to have heard. They have already been at Telyatichi for nearly a year, yet her life has barely changed. True, she can now buy as many novels as she wants, but that's not enough, not at all! Whenever she sees a young man in a gold-buttoned student uniform or a gymnasium girl in a brown dress with a black pinafore, her heart starts beating faster, her eyes fill with tears, and she bites her lips so hard that they start bleeding.

Maybe, instead of whining and daydreaming in silence, instead of tormenting herself, instead of burning inside, she should scream at the top of her lungs to be heard? Why won't God give her the strength to do that? Why does nobody—nobody!—understand what she is going through?

And what of our groom, Ilya? What is Ilya saying? What is he thinking?

When the family was preparing to go to Polushen, filling more than a few carts with relatives, servants, and luggage, he let his displeasure be known.

"How could they schedule the wedding for the spring, when there is so much work to do, when every hour counts? How incredibly thoughtless!"

As he pulls on his black frock coat, he continues to grumble. That's the kind of man Ilya is!

Isaac just turned away and shrugged his shoulders. That was how Isaac usually reacted—by shrugging his shoulders. No one really knew what he meant by it. No one liked this gesture of his, not at all. But everyone kept quiet.

Many people gathered at Polushen to watch the two camps face one another at Ephraim's estate in the greatest of contests. If Ephraim's hired band started playing Hungarian dances, then the band that came with the Raskins—not to be outdone—responded with German, French, Jewish, or all kinds of other tunes. If a Livshitz relative gave the young couple a gift of ten rubles, then some show-off from the opposing side immediately pledged twenty-five. Let the world know! Let everyone see!

There was, however, one eccentric guest who couldn't care less which side prevailed. This was Akiva Novogrudski, Rachel's father. He showed up with his second wife and gave the impression that his daughter's wedding had nothing to do with him. He puffed on his cigar incessantly, wearing a sneering expression on his face. Even during prayers, he didn't bother to put his hat on.

Rachel's two brothers were also in attendance. "See, they are family after all," the women whispered among themselves. "Even though they are at odds with Reb Ephraim, their grandfather, they still came to the wedding!"

Sarah blushed the moment she caught sight of the siblings of her would-be sister-in-law. Blood rushed to her head. These young men live in Warsaw! They went to school there, they associate with wise and culti-vated people. They will surely laugh at a simple country girl like her. They will talk about some new novel that she has never even heard of. Her dress will probably look provincial to them, hopelessly old-fashioned. Her own brothers, Ilya and Isaac, are sporting black suits with gleaming, carefully pressed cuffs, but these two cosmopolitans, one might say, are wearing plain black satin tunics with simple sashes. This must be the latest fashion!

The heart of this tormented young girl was beating anxiously. She sat hiding in the corner, as if she came here to be humiliated rather than to attend her brother's wedding.

But nothing terrible or humiliating actually happened.

The old Jewish women, endowed by the grace of God with sharp eyes and infinite curiosity, even launched into whispering. "See how easy it is these days? Take a look! Sarah and the Novogrudski brothers didn't even know each other before. The Raskin girl was just sitting in the corner, blushing. And look at her now! It's as if they are glued together. They can't let go of each other, they can't stop talking. Wouldn't it be interesting to hear what they are talking about, ha ha! Maybe Meyer Raskin, the Telyatichi leaseholder, needs to start preparing for yet another wedding?"

The wedding gossips kept whispering and moving from chair to chair, edging ever closer to the corner where Akiva's older son, Moses, was sitting with Sarah.

Apparently, Sarah and Moses were so engrossed in their conversation that they didn't even notice the old women encircling them. Sarah was no longer blushing. Her eyes were shining, her cheeks were rosy from a cer-tain lightness that she was feeling inside. And it was only then that the old women realized that Meyer's daughter was not plain-looking at all. She is even pretty, if you will. Love is in the air! The women would have bet any-thing that Sarah Raskin had fallen in love with Moses Novogrudski! Another wedding awaits, yet another wedding!

Before long, however, the old women's faces had turned sour. First, the young couple were conversing in Russian. Second—and this is something the women caught on to in no time—it had nothing to do with love. But then why was the girl beaming like this?

This time, the wedding gossips were dead wrong; missed it by a mile, so to speak. The couple had been discussing matters of a totally different nature . . .

Oh, how cruel life can be, how awfully cruel! And yet it weaves such intricate patterns at times. It takes just a few hours of a heart-to-heart talk for one's eyes to start seeing things that had been totally hidden before. The conversation was not about stylish dresses, or schooling, or even the latest novels. It turned out that Moses Novogrudski and his younger brother read even fewer novels than Sarah. So what do they read, what do they care about, what does make them tick?

The old Jewish gossips can spy and eavesdrop all they want, but they would never understand a word of these new topics. So in order to calm themselves down somehow, they take a different approach altogether. They purse their lips and ask one another, "How could it happen that such a respectable Jew like Ephraim would have such degenerate grandchildren? Since when do grandsons threaten their grandfather with some 'Committee'? Those thugs! Those degenerates! And look at their father: all he does is sit there and suck on his cigar, like a goy! Why would Meyer's daughter have such a long conversation with this thug? It's odd!"

Meanwhile, the wine had brought joy to the soul of old Ephraim.

"Oy vey! Young people today are such weaklings! Is this how we used to have fun in the old days? At a wedding, no less! Just watch these dancing couples rotate: one, two, three; one, two, three. . . . It's ridiculous!"

With that, he waved his red handkerchief, calling on the guests to join hands and make a big circle that filled the whole room. Then he waved his handkerchief again, tilted his yarmulke to one side, and stepped into the center of the circle. "Come on, you women, show us how you can dance, show us how we used to have fun back in the old days!"

The old women didn't need another invitation to show what they could do. They started clapping their hands and broke into *Scherele*, an old Jewish dancing song. As they clapped and sang, the circle went round and round, with Reb Ephraim standing in the center and moving his legs with such gusto that it put the younger men to shame. He whirled around, stretching his limbs so that his body seemed to grow taller, then froze in bliss. His legs appeared as one for a moment, then separated again. Look at this Jew: he is old, but he is so light on his feet, he really knows how to dance!

Those who said that bit their tongues promptly and spit three times not to jinx it. But just then, Reb Ephraim suddenly turned pale and staggered. Luckily, the circle immediately broke up. People quickly brought him a chair and sprinkled cold water on him. The old gossips changed their tune in an instant, saying,

"Mark our words: he won't last long, he's an old man. He is past seventy, after all, that Reb Ephraim."

Some people remembered their words and later said, "Those wedding gossips were right! They know everything before it happens! God endowed them with sharp eyes."

Those who remembered the women's words said this. Others were blindsided by the news; it struck them like a bolt of lightning.

9

The Raskin family had expanded.

Dubovoye was a small farm within the Telyatichi estate, about two miles away. This is where the newly married Ilya and Rachel chose to settle.

Let no one think that their choice had any special meaning. It did not signify any division, separation, or anything like that. It's just that Ilya thought that it would be better for his work if he stayed on the farm. As before, he continued to gallop through the fields and meadows on his paunchy little mare from dawn till dusk. He was as diligent as ever.

Before long, the Raskins fully realized how wise and perceptive Kratz had been: they could not have wished for a better wife for Ilya. Rachel brought peace and harmony to the Raskin household. She visited Telyatichi almost every day. Now, nine people sat down for dinner instead of eight. Good-natured and cheerful, she developed unique friendships with every member of the family. All of them, without exception, came to love her.

Back at Dubovoye, she had started her own small farmyard. Hens clucked, chicks peeped, turkeys strutted, geese and ducks waddled together around the large yard. When the farmhands arrived for their lunch break, Rachel fed oats to their horses herself, and weighed out bread and fatback for the men. During harvest time, she rose early and went to the fields together with her husband.

This life of hard work left little time for leisure. Winter is the only time when country people can pay attention to those around them; in all other seasons, everyone is too busy working. Only Chava spent her days at home, alone with her sadness and loneliness. As always, she wandered aimlessly from room to room. She would go to Sarah's room and sit quietly on the couch. What could Chava possibly understand of the books that absorbed Sarah day and night? Would she even notice that the novels and other fiction had been relegated to the bottom shelf, where they were slowly collecting dust? That they had been forgotten and replaced by very different literature? No, when Marx and Engels, Kropotkin and Plekhanov, Henry Thomas Buckle and Stepnyak-Kravchinsky were writing their books, they certainly did not have Chava in mind.

They probably didn't have Sarah in mind either. In some corner of her mind, Sarah could grasp that reading was not enough, that strong and courageous people know how to turn words into action. But what can you do if life itself made you an obedient daughter to your parents? Sit and wait? For what?

By now faith had been kindled and was smoldering quietly inside her. Even though it is autumn, Sarah senses that spring is in the air. Unusual dreams develop in her mind. New people will arise and change the world. And when the world is transformed, the flood will engulf her too. . . . Maybe it was naïve, maybe Moses Novogrudski would laugh at her silly dreams. Everyone's destiny is different. What can she do if her destiny is to be an obedient daughter to her parents? Only sit and wait . . .

Spring was indeed in the air. Even Meyer Raskin, that perennially busy man who seemingly couldn't care less about anything other than his work—even Meyer Raskin started paying more attention to Notovich's *News and Stock Exchange Gazette.* Even he cheered up noticeably.

"How do you like that!" he would say. "You'll see, in the end Tsar Nicky will have to remove all restrictions and let us Jews live wherever we want! England and America support it, and if these two countries are in favor . . ."

"Nonsense," Isaac would retort, shrugging his shoulders. As always, his buttons were all fastened. Everyone felt uneasy and had no idea whether "nonsense" referred to Tsar Nicholas or to England and America.

He is a strange bird, that Isaac—strange and difficult to read. He can casually drive a person to tears for no apparent reason. Take Hersh, who spends all his time drawing from life. Isaac might come up to him, crumple all his sketchbooks, throw his watercolors out the window, and scream "You useless loafer! A cobbler's helper—that's all you're good for!" Or he might grab mischievous Motya's ear and twist it so hard that it would burn and hurt for the rest of the day. Or he might lock himself up in his room, draw the curtains, and smoke incessantly. The wailing of his flute would then be heard from his room from time to time.

Ilya is the only one who is able to ignore Isaac's nastiness. If Isaac launches into an argument with him, Ilya will stand his ground without losing his composure. Once, in the fall, Ilya decided that it was imperative to order five railcars of artificial fertilizer. He sat in the "office" by the window, made notes, and talked about artificial fertilizer.

"Fertilizer?" Isaac confirmed, raising his brow and putting his quill down.

"Fertilizer?" Meyer also confirmed, but without Isaac's skepticism. He had already calculated in his mind what a fortune five railcars of artificial fertilizer would cost him.

"Yes, that's right, five railcars and not a pound less," Ilya said, and went on to explain his reasoning. But Isaac had already stopped listening, he just paced around the room and shrugged his shoulders.

Ilya didn't even bother to read newspapers. He had no idea what was going on in the world. He was too busy with his peasants and his horses, his plots and his forest parcels.

Every now and then, the Novogrudski brothers came to Telyatichi to visit their sister Rachel. Meyer Raskin, who had the ability to banter with anybody about anything, would smile through his graying beard and inquire,

"So, gentlemen socialists, how soon will you be bringing us our freedom?"

"Don't tell me you can't wait for it," Moses teased him. "Do you really need it that much?"

"But of course!" Meyer would reply. "What Jew doesn't long for freedom?"

"Well, I'm afraid that you'd hate it in no time, you won't like the taste of it—too strong."

What a prickly fellow this Moses Novogrudski was, so tough and so modern! No wonder he treated his grandfather so badly, not like family at all. In his usual affable manner, Meyer Raskin was quick to offer his opinion on this subject as well, even though no one was asking him.

"You know what I would have done if you came to me for money?" he said to Moses. "You want money? Fine! Here's a project for you, here's all the money you want—get down to work! You'd forget all your lofty ideas in no time and become true capitalists!"

Such were the thoughts of Meyer Raskin, the wise leaseholder of Telyatichi. But Ephraim Livshitz had very different thoughts and acted accordingly, even though he was no fool himself. Despite his deteriorating health, Ephraim stuck to his old ways with his grandsons: every hundred ruble subsidy from him was accompanied by much shouting and death threats.

Meanwhile, the spring of life that Sarah awaited so eagerly and that even Meyer was prepared to welcome—that spring was drawing near. Soon even Ilya, who never read newspapers and had no interest in politics, began to notice that the peasants were acting strangely. It used to be a very rare occasion when a field guard would catch a peasant's horse that had accidentally strayed into Telyatichi's pastures. When that happened, the horse's owner would be at the office within a few hours. He would fall on his knees, kiss Meyer's hand, and in the name of Jesus beg for mercy, beg not to be dragged to court and given a fine.

But now, entire herds of stray horses were appearing, and not just in the pastures, but in choice meadows and even in fields of winter crops. The peasants would not show up until the following day, as if they had nothing to do with it. They would look grim and bitter, they would not bother to remove their hats in front of the house, and even when they entered the office, would do so only reluctantly.

Ilya would start castigating them the way he always did.

"What is going on? This is not right!" he would say angrily, becoming red in the face. "You damage my property, I damage yours. What good will it do?"

The peasants would not explain what good it would do. They were grim, taciturn, and most unusually, they did not act subserviently or beg for forgiveness. This enraged even the normally calm Ilya.

"I'll take you all to court!" he shouted furiously.

"Courts don't bite, esteemed leaseholder," said one of the men, putting his warm hat back on, as if he needed to free up his hands. Even Ilya sensed something new and different in this gesture and this form of address.

What happened next made Meyer Raskin think long and hard, and furrow his brow repeatedly. He would recall the words of Moses Novogrudski—that loafer knew perfectly well what kind of seeds he and his ilk were sowing!

Peasants in nearby villages picked up "the cause" in earnest. They started grazing their animals openly in the Raskins' meadows. Not only that—they brought wooden stakes with them to guard these animals as they grazed. Once they caught a field guard, tied his old rifle behind his back with very thick ropes, smeared his face with tar, and sent him running to the Raskins in this condition.

In Telyatichi, hay was usually "quartered." A peasant would choose a lot, cut the grass, set up four stacks of hay, and in the winter, he would take three of the stacks to the estate and keep the fourth for himself as payment for the work done. But now the peasants announced in no uncertain terms that "quartering" was out of the question, that the leaseholder would be lucky to receive half of the hay, and that even this may be too much—the village people would think about it.

This is how the peasants talked now, and Meyer Raskin did not like it at all. Nevertheless, he tried to keep a cool head.

"The important thing is to stay calm," he repeated. "Patience, patience, and more patience—isn't that what some general once said?"

Well, he may not have been very calm inside, but he kept it to himself. Just the opposite—he walked around the estate with a cheerful expression on his face, leaving the farmhands to wonder what he was so happy about. He complimented his laborers and even joked with them as if they were equals.

In contrast to his father, Ilya was deeply perturbed. His face turned gaunt. He didn't have any suggestions, he just hurt inside. "The ground has not frozen yet. It's so easy to damage the winter crops if the peasants drive their herds over them day and night. And now I hear that they won't give us any hay! How are we going to feed the cows, the horses, and the rest?"

For Isaac, all these troubles were yet another reason to frown and shrug his shoulders. He acted as though he had seen this coming all along, and if he hadn't mentioned it ahead of time—well, it was just an oversight on his part.

"Do you think this is the last of it?" he would ask ominously. "Just wait, there's more to come!"

This time, Isaac was right. The unrest continued to grow. Now only Sarah could expect something positive to come out of it, and only deep in her heart. She couldn't possibly share her true feelings with her family. The events troubled the Raskins more and more, forcing them to do some serious thinking.

One day, when Meyer came home, he found a letter by the front door. He picked it up and saw that it was addressed to him, Meyer Raskin. His coachman went to Drahicyn every day, bringing back the mail and the newspapers in his sack. Meyer's first thought was that the coachman must have accidentally dropped it, but then, to his surprise, he noticed an American stamp on the back of the envelope. The envelope bore no postmarks, so the sender had probably pasted an old American stamp on it just to make a stronger impression. Sensing that this spelled trouble, Meyer went straight into the office, called Ilya and Isaac in, and only then opened the letter.

"Read it," he said to Ilya.

Now this was no ordinary letter! It contained four pages printed in block letters so as not to reveal the sender's handwriting. The letter referred to Meyer and his sons as "bloodsuckers." The anonymous author actually addressed them this way: "Bloodsuckers!" The main body of the letter was itemized. The items instructed Meyer and his family to immediately go "straight to hell." This was followed by threats of arson and murder.

"This letter never existed," Meyer said, taking the pages from Ilya. "Do you understand? Not a word to anyone about the letter. It never existed!"

"Just ignore it," he went on to assure his sons. "Some drunk wrote it. Go easy on the workers, go easy on the fines. We'll just have to wait it out. But most importantly: don't tell your mother or anyone else."

Mr. Plavski and his assistant David, who everyone continued to call by his first name, received identical instructions concerning the peasants. "That's how you handle them," Meyer said. "If they act up, you have to yield a bit and avoid riling them. That's the time-tested way of dealing with these people."

But even this approach—which used to work before—did not help this time. Other estates were already burning in the fires of the first Russian revolution. Exactly five nights after Meyer found the letter by his front door, the cowshed caught fire. The fire started on all four sides—clearly, it was arson. Even the best efforts of the farmhands and other employees failed to save fifty of the cows. They burned to death.

Peasants from nearby villages showed up to help put out the blaze only at dawn, when the logs had already turned into ashes—and only because the policeman forced them to. They were excited, as if they came to a wedding rather than a fire. Using sticks, they poked open the terrifyingly bloated bellies of the dead cows and made nasty jokes. One of them said, "I thought it wasn't only the cowshed, that there would be plenty of work to do. This is nothing. Did they have to wake us all up just for this?" Meyer acted strangely during the fire; Ilya simply couldn't understand what he was up to. In front of the peasants from the nearby villages, Meyer cursed the shepherds for being careless with fire and suggested that they may have been the culprits. Or he would suddenly mention that his insurance agent wanted more commission and hence he had insured the cows for a hundred rubles each, so now Meyer would be able to replace the fifty dead cows with at least seventy five new ones.

However, "fire talk" is one thing, and bitter reality is another. Those who paid attention could see that Meyer was deeply troubled by the fire. His face turned sallow, and Chava's loving eyes noticed even more gray in his beard. And how could it be any different? What farmer's heart would not sink at the sight of fifty dead, bloated cows? Only fools find solace in insurance policies!

That evening, Meyer held a meeting at his house. Ilya, shocked by what had happened, was close to tears whenever he thought about the cows. He did not have much to say. Mr. Plavski was in the thrall of some unnatural heroics. First, he proposed to set the village ablaze, making sure it burned from all four sides "like a candle." Then he suggested sending an urgent telegram to the governor, requesting that His Excellency dispatch three dozen ferocious fighters from the Caucasus. "They will take care of the whole thing in no time, I assure you!"

Isaac reacted to every new proposal by muttering something unintelligible under his breath. This was enough to make everyone feel uncomfortable.

Meyer did not agree to any of the suggestions.

"No, no, none of it will do. You can always summon the Caucasus fighters later, if necessary. And setting the village on fire is not a good idea whichever way you look at it—who can guarantee that the whole estate won't burn down as a result?"

"So then what shall we do?" they asked the old man. To which he replied without hesitation,

"We should wait."

This moved Isaac to set his usual gestures aside and resort to words.

"Wait for what? To be killed?"

He nearly mentioned the letter with an American stamp in front of Mr. Plavski, but was able to restrain himself before it was too late.

"Now that's another matter," Meyer replied. "I am thinking of taking the family to Antopol for a while."

After Mr. Plavski left, Meyer continued,

"In an hour, my children, we will all go to Antopol. Send the carts out a few miles ahead of us so that no one notices anything. Ilya, will you make the arrangements?"

But now, believe it or not, Ilya revolted. Yes, Ilya, of all people.

"What do you mean?" he burst out. "Leave everything to chance and flee? No, I cannot agree, I am staying!"

"But it's just for the time being," Meyer insisted. "This won't go on forever. We may be back within a few days."

"It doesn't matter. Rachel can go if she wants, but I am staying."

But Rachel refused to leave Ilya alone, no matter how much they begged her to go and no matter how much Chava cried. In the end, Ilya prevailed. The Raskins went to Antopol, while he and Rachel stayed behind at Telyatichi.

They left the house late at night. They kept saying that they should be back in a matter of days but avoided looking into each other's eyes. They dashed from room to room, turning lamps off and on and lighting candles. Everyone packed their most precious items, whether the value was sentimental or monetary. Chava was trying to wrap menorahs in a bed sheet, with little success. She sat down on the wooden couch that they had brought from the village and lowered the white bundle to the floor beside her. Ilya huddled in the doorway, stealthily glancing at his mother and biting his fingernails. Meyer briskly walked into the room, holding a folder of insurance policies and contracts in one hand and a candle in the other. The candle was flickering and dripping tallow onto Meyer's hand.

"Why are you standing here with a candle like you're at a wake?" Chava asked.

Meyer grimaced. His beard, which was lit up from below, trembled. He dropped the candle on the floor, kicked it with his shoe, and put it out.

Glancing around the room and frowning, he lowered himself heavily into a chair, like an old man. "Ilya," he said, "please play your violin. You have nothing else to do anyway."

Ilya complied without arguing. He pressed the violin between his chin and shoulder and closed his eyes. The sounds of pure Jewish melancholy came flowing from his instrument. Sarah ran into the room, breathless and concerned. Isaac stood frozen in the corner.

"Isn't it strange," the father said gloomily, "all Jewish songs are sad. Not one normal tune. Well, enough of that, it's time to get going!"

He stood up and, for some reason, stopped the wall clock. Everyone hurried outside. The house was aglow, with every window brightly lit. The estate was asleep. The wind whistled through naked tree branches. Far away, the night watchman beat his wooden clapper. First was Ilya with a lantern in his hand, then Rachel carrying little Sheva, who was asleep. It started to drizzle, and the smell of potatoes from the field grew stronger.

For more than half an hour, they walked single file in morose silence, getting wet from drizzle and perspiration. Only Chava sighed occasionally, but, of course, Chava could always find a reason to sigh. "Why are you sighing? We're not going to America, thank God," Meyer grumbled.

"Well, hurry up," the old man said, when he heard the snorting of the restless horses and the rattling of the glass in the carriages' lanterns. Ivan, the senior coachman, was saying something in his stern voice. "Say your goodbyes quickly . . . ," Meyer continued. "Best to all!"

But the family took their time saying their goodbyes and crying, paying no heed to Ivan and his men. Then the horses set off abruptly and raced forward noisily. The hunched backs of the Raskins were visible for a short while, but they soon disappeared, leaving only golden dots wavering in the rainy mist.

The only remaining light started moving in the opposite direction. It slowly swayed in the air, leaving red, green, and blue reflections on the wet road. Ilya and Rachel were returning home to Dubovoye.

10

Who could have ever imagined that Antopol would become the site of some kind of revolution? Antopol! Maybe St. Petersburg, maybe Moscow, maybe even some provincial capital. . . . But Antopol? That sleepy shtetl in Kobryn District of Grodno Province?

And yet there was a revolution in Antopol. It wasn't just old women and busybodies gossiping—everyone knew it was happening. By the time the Raskin family arrived in Antopol, the revolution was already in full swing.

"These are different times," the old Jews at the synagogue commented, and promptly offered their analysis of the situation.

"Would any decent man act so brazenly and engage in the devil knows what? Clearly, all this rioting and unrest only appeals to tailors, shoemakers, and loafers! 'Freedom', you say? Just hang on a minute. Hold your horses! The government ministers and officials have not lost their minds yet. They'll show you freedom!"

So grumbled the old Jews at the synagogue between prayers.

Of course, many people knew that the local "rabble," the young tailors' and shoemakers' helpers, gathered at Malka's, a widowed seamstress who lived on the outskirts of town. But who gave it another thought? Who knew or cared why they gathered there! Even Yartsev, Antopol's magistrate, did not think much about it. But when he had one too many at the home of a wealthy Jew, he would wave his index finger in front of his fat, red nose and pronounce,

"I know that there is a secret cabal in your Jewish community. It's called the Bund![4] Oh yes, Yartsev knows everything!"

No one was sure whether he was joking or not. But when they poured him yet another shot, he would change his tune,

---

4   A Jewish socialist party in the Russian Empire.

"So let them gather, I don't give a damn. No reason to get my hands dirty over this."

And he studied his index finger in bewilderment, as if he himself couldn't fathom why he had such a long finger.

But now a new wind was blowing. The government ministers and officials had briefly loosened their grip on the reins of power, and the common people of Antopol promptly raised their heads. Later, jokesters insisted that it was Baruch, a local bookbinder, who one day ran into the sick, frail Ephraim Livshitz on the street. Baruch, a man who had never before showed any interest in politics, strode boldly up to the old man and either forgot or deliberately neglected to greet him properly. Instead, he poked his finger into Ephraim's expansive belly and exclaimed,

"Do you really think that this is your stomach? Excuse me, but this is our stomach!"

This quip spread rapidly throughout Russia. Later, you could hear it in Kobryn and Brest-Litovsk, in Pinsk and Grodno, and even in Warsaw. It is hard to tell who the author was, especially since Baruch himself swore up and down that he had nothing to do with it. But the local jokesters continued to insist that it was him.

Be that as it may, the Jewish working people raised their heads and, just like the peasants of Telyatichi, took matters into their own hands in earnest. The owners of the tailoring and shoemaking shops were the first to be affected. One sad autumn day, they received a strict directive concerning their apprentices. It prescribed raises, an eight-hour workday, and. . . . There were so many things that those loafers demanded! They even invented a name for themselves—Bundists! At first, the shop owners took it as a joke, but these "new people," these Bundists were in no mood to joke. They set a three-day deadline, and after it had passed, glass started shattering in the owners' windows. The owners caved in.

And that was just the beginning . . .

A malicious rumor had it that Yartsev was either bribed by the Bundists directly, or scared of the revolutionaries, or maybe even had orders from above to loosen the reins for a while. Whatever the case, Yartsev did not interfere in anything and turned a blind eye to what was going on. Meanwhile, Jews continued to act up.

And the things they did! Of course, they had never been taught good manners or proper conduct, and they showed their true nature from the start. The language they used! Tsar Nicholas II was "the bloody tsar," "the last tsar." The police were "bribe-takers" and "butchers." The citizens of Antopol were "disgusting bourgeoisie," "bloodsuckers," and "parasites on working people."

The poor grew ever more brazen by the day. "Give them an inch and they'll take a mile," said the old Jews at the synagogue. "Those loafers grasped right away that their time has come."

By then, two important events had transpired.

First, Ephraim's Polushen had burned to the ground. And not just a single structure like a cowshed, but all of its buildings together! The Jewish manager was barely able to save his family and flee to Antopol at dawn. Old sick Ephraim was so shaken that, without further delay, he said a final prayer and expired by the end of the day.

Second, his notorious grandsons, the Novogrudski brothers, arrived in Antopol on the same day. How might one expect the Livshitz grand-children to behave on such an unfortunate, sad day? The lowest Jew would know in his heart exactly what to do. Just think of it: all the shopkeepers of Antopol, as if by arrangement, closed their stores out of respect. But apparently, the rules of propriety were not for the likes of the Novogrudski brothers. They came to Antopol, checked into Isaac Rubinstein's boarding house, and immediately—without even washing their faces—went to a meeting. Their grandfather, their own flesh and blood, is lying dead on the floor; the whole town is mourning and wailing over this terrible loss—and they are off to a meeting!

Meetings were held in the open now. The Bundists were defiant. They announced that within an hour, a general meeting of the entire shtetl would be held at the main synagogue. Crowds of layabouts, those who were simply curious, and all sorts of other people started gathering at the synagogue.

"Couldn't they find another place for it?" the old men grumbled, hast-ily vacating the premises nonetheless. "These loafers have gotten completely out of hand; there may very well be trouble!"

We shall refrain from describing the meeting at the synagogue that fea-tured the Novogrudski brothers. For now, suffice it to say that the speeches, which Yartsev had recorded "from eyewitness accounts," were later incor-porated into the formal charges against Ephraim's grandsons. In the end, the court exiled the Novogrudski brothers to Siberia.

Naïve people might assume that the speeches the brothers gave at the synagogue on the day of their grandfather's death marked the end of their provocative behavior toward the dearly departed. Far from it!

After the gathering at the synagogue, after the "committee" meeting at the home of Malka the seamstress, after spreading and pasting leaflets all over town, the Novogrudski brothers headed for Ephraim Livshitz's house.

The two entered the dining room, where the wealthy man's body lay in rest surrounded by his devoted sons, daughters-in-law, and grandchildren. They all raised their tearful eyes, expecting to see tears in the brothers' eyes as well.

The Novogrudskis, however, had no intention of crying. They walked up to their uncle, Ephraim's eldest son, and loudly announced,

"In three hours, you are to deliver six thousand rubles to us, three thousand each. In the event of "nonpayment," Ephraim's funeral will not take place."

Later, when life had returned to normal and the disturbances had subsided, the people at the synagogues were quite incredulous. After all, dozens of family members were present in the dining room that day. How come there wasn't a single brave soul among them who would have taken the shameless troublemakers by their collars and thrown them out of the house?

Be that as it may, the brothers presented their demands to Ephraim's eldest heir and slammed the door as they left. Exactly three hours later, one of them returned for the response. But there was no money and no response for him—only tears, which didn't really count. The body had been washed, wrapped in a shroud, and carried out of the house with much crying and wailing. Ephraim's heirs were so overwhelmed with grief that they had completely forgotten about the threats.

Yet the threats were no empty words. The house was already surrounded by the local "organization," which did not allow the funeral to proceed. So, instead of tearing up their clothes in mourning for the dearly departed, Ephraim's sons had to dash around the shtetl, trying to collect the required six thousand. While they were at it, the body remained unburied for three days, in clear violation of Jewish law.

It was right after the funeral that the Raskins arrived in Antopol. They had completely missed all the preceding events, but had any of them still wished to observe the Antopol revolution in progress, their curiosity could easily have been satisfied.

During those troublesome days, people were too preoccupied with their own affairs to pay much attention to others. Yet the nosiest among them could not help but notice that Sarah Raskin showed inappropriate interest in the outrageous antics of the local "loafers." Eyewitnesses insisted that they had seen Sarah in the streets in the company of "demonstrators and protesters," and that she was in the thick of them, right next to the standard-bearers. Not only that, she was said to have frequented their meetings, both in the center of town and on the outskirts, and if anyone had bothered to look inside her jacket, they would have found quite a few leaflets and brochures there. But our people are not informers, God forbid, and it is nobody's business what exactly Sarah Raskin was doing or what she took an interest in. After all, when "our hooligans" were arrested, Sarah was not among them. The only thing that the Jewish women did say was that when an epidemic arrives—"may God spare our land!"—everyone catches it. Either way, nothing bad could be said about Sarah Raskin, who remained an obedient daughter to her parents. That's just the way she was.

The first Russian revolution was drawing to a close. Spring is naturally followed by summer, but this human spring was followed by a cold, dead autumn. The old Jews at the synagogue were absolutely right—the government ministers and officials had not lost their minds, and in the end, they did "show people their freedom."

A firm hand had once again taken hold of the reins of power and pulled them in. It was as if the magistrate Yartsev had suddenly awakened from his sleep: he rolled up his sleeves, set all reservations aside, and got down to work. The Novogrudski brothers were arrested, along with many others. The two were taken to Warsaw and later put on trial. It turned out that they had stirred up plenty of trouble in the capital as well, and that all the money which they had been extorting from Ephraim had gone straight to the "Committee."

Some wise heads claimed that they knew all along how this was going to end.

"Jews should never get involved in riots or start revolutions," the wise heads said. "This is not the end of it, you'll see!"

The end of "it" was very sad. One city in Grodno Province—Bialystok—was hit especially hard, paying for the misdeeds of the "Jewish rabble" with Jewish blood.

The first Russian revolution was over.

PART TWO

PART TWO

1

Life slowly returns to normal and sorts people out, like the winnower sorts grains—some will spend just three months a year in Telyatichi, living in the twenty-room mansion; others will manage the leased estate, spreading their roots every which way; still others will bow low to the landowner, doffing their hats within hundreds of feet of the manor house, and digging through the poor Belarusian soil.

In the spot where the cowshed once stood, marked by piles of ash, and brick pillars blackened by fire, axes echo cheerfully and chips fly like birds over the carpenters' heads. And once again, as before, the distillery puffs and squawks in the winter, yeast bubbling in enormous vats. The yeast gives off such a smell that one cannot help but think of warm wheat bread. Two-horse carts loaded with potatoes arrive at the trolley one after another. A thin, smooth stream of alcohol, shiny as a mirror, runs through the counter inside a glass cabinet. Three times a day, the tall pipe on the distillery's roof emits a long whistle together with clouds of vapor. Then preparations begin in the ox barn: baskets of chaff fly into cement pits. Soon the pungent mash, yellow as pea soup, will gush out in a thick, boiling current.

The threshing barn is busy too. Even from a distance, you can hear the thresher's strained panting and clanging. Women and girls stomp around in a golden cloud of dust; they work in tandem because the machine controls their pace. David, Mr. Plavski's assistant, has nothing to do; he sits hidden among the sheaves and pensively removes bark from a piece of wood, making himself a walking stick for the summer. Seeing Ilya hurrying toward him on his short, crooked legs, he gets up, clears his throat solemnly, and strokes his red mustache.

"Hey, dames and damsels!" he shouts sternly but jovially. "Chop-chop! You, girl, are you sleeping there?"

And, like someone who is privy to a great enterprise and a great mystery, he buries his arm in the mountain of grain, grabs a whole handful, pours the grain from hand to hand, and declares earnestly and confidently,

"Good threshing, thorough! The grain is dry . . . as a bone!"

In the cowshed, calves are already mooing. They feel cold, they shiver on their thin legs and seek their mothers' teats with their slimy, knobby muzzles. Meyer Raskin walks through the cowshed briskly. He doesn't pay attention to minor details, he is more interested in numbers: how many gallons of milk today? Wouldn't it be better to stop making Swiss cheese and switch to butter alone until all the cows are calved and the milk yields have gone up? What would the cheesemaker say to that? How many cows have calved during the last twenty-four hours? How about adding oat straw to bog hay?

Only sad Chava remains inside the four walls of the Telyatichi house. Lucky are the busy people: their chests breathe easily, their hearts beat evenly, and the winter respite is a joy for them. The Raskins' seven rooms are warm in the evening, kerosene lamps with milk-white glass shades burn cheerfully. . . . Is Meyer even capable of realizing that the evening was preceded by a long dusk, when blue shadows slowly descended on the painted floors, growing thicker and thicker with time. . . . Crows caw behind the double windows, they fall on the branches like big lumps, knocking off the snow. Suddenly a dog howls woefully, raising its head to the chilling skies—God knows what kind of trouble it forebodes. Konon, the one-armed caretaker, traipses forlornly through the rooms, moving slowly from one stove to the next and poking inside with a metal rod. From time to time a log crackles angrily, hundreds of sparks burst out inside the fiery traps, and the room lights up like a blood-red sunset. Oh, how she wishes the lights were turned on already, that Meyer and Ilya had returned from work, that Rachel, her cheeks red from the cold, had flown in on her light sleigh, and moody Isaac had stepped out of his office.

Meyer doesn't want to know about any of it. Life sets its own milestones, you can think all you want—to no avail. That's how it is, dear Chava.

When Meyer comes home, he kisses her on the forehead, pulls her closer, and gives her a hug, as if feeling guilty toward her.

"It's evening now," he says. "Evenings are long in winter, we'll have plenty of time to talk, to play sixty-six, to have some tea, or maybe even remember our younger days . . ."

He doesn't dwell on the subject of memories, sparing Chava's melancholy soul. Smart people don't like to dwell on the past, especially if the present is better. Life sets its own milestones, there's no need to get ahead of yourself and try to guess what the future holds. Time assigns roles to people and no man can do it any better.

Who, for instance, would take it upon himself to tell Isaac, that gloomy, perennially disgruntled Isaac, that his hair keeps getting grayer, that his heart keeps hardening, and that it's time for him to learn the joys of female companionship? That certainly wouldn't be Chava, who is a bit afraid of Isaac, and it wouldn't be Meyer, forthright with everyone else but sheepish with his own children. Meanwhile, Telyatichi is ripe for new weddings. Let's not forget: Sarah comes after Isaac. Time waits for no one, especially for a girl. What's a girl worth after she turns twenty-five?

First Sarah read books of one kind, then of another, then all of them became covered with dust. . . . Sarah no longer pays much attention even to the younger three: Hersh, Motya, and Sheva. All is fickle, all is a dream, all is unsettled. She has again started to watch how other people live, to imitate them—maybe some of them do know how to handle their days, weeks, and years?

Take Rachel, for example. She knows what she's doing, futile thoughts don't torment her. Her days are filled with duties and chores, and that's why her cheeks are so rosy. Take a peek into the low-ceilinged rooms of Dubovoye. A frail calf rests in the kitchen. Geese, ducks, and hens sit on their round baskets in dark pens, preparing a new generation for the spring. Tubs of fatback fill the mudroom. It's true that the fatback has a whiff of tallow and pickling salt, but it's better than leaving the tubs in the barn where rats will get to them. Rachel doesn't do anything for show or to impress other people—only for herself. She is a bit cagey when it comes to her own affairs. When Ilya goes to see his family, she sits hunched under a lampshade and sews. Sometimes she'll listen to the wind howling outside and shake her head, a smile on her lips. She'll secure the needle in the tablecloth, smooth out the seam with her fingernail, and stretch a baby's shirt out on the table. Why talk ahead of time about someone who is living in your belly?

Sarah watches Rachel. Sarah will work, too, and work will bring her peace. She rises at the crack of dawn and hurries to the pigpen. The powerful smell of manure assails her nose, incessant oinking gives her a headache. Women in skirts tucked up to their knees shriek, hit the animals, pour whey into tubs. Seeing Sarah, they give her friendly nods and tuck the locks of hair that have fallen on their faces under their kerchiefs.

"Good morning, Miss!" they shout cheerfully. Sarah frowns: perhaps, deep inside, the women are making fun of her?

But still she asks, "What's new? Do the pigs like the whey? Maybe they need something else?"

"They're fine, they eat it all right. We wouldn't feed them sugar, would we? Look, Miss, Sanka has just farrowed. There were seven piglets, but she already gobbled up two, that bitch. It would be good to take them into a house and feed them milk for a week or so, or else she'll finish off the rest of them."

So Sarah makes a quick decision: she'll take the animals in, she'll nurse them. She throws them into a bag, pink and squealing, and drags her stirring load home. But on the way, she runs into Mr. Plavski. He respectfully removes his hat, waves it, and shouts, "Good morning, Miss! What is the young lady carrying?"

This is enough to make Sarah blush and lower her eyes sheepishly. What was she thinking? What on earth is she going to do with these pigs?

What had just seemed like a good idea no longer appeals to her. The piglets crawl and slide on the floor, they oink disgustingly, they poop ten times a day and slurp repugnantly with their shiny little snouts. No, no, that's enough, they are going back to the pigpen!

In addition to the Jewish melamed who stays at the house, a country teacher from a nearby village comes to work with the younger three. She is a healthy-looking young woman with dimples on her cheeks and a long braid of light-brown hair hanging down to her waist. She wears loose Ukrainian folk dresses embroidered with tiny red and black crosses; brightly colored beads exchange whispers around her smooth neck. When she energetically walks around the room and dictates to the children Krylov's fable about the crafty fox in a staged, didactic voice, glasses and saucers tinkle on the table. Her lithe figure exudes rosy-cheeked joy and quiet bliss; even Isaac inadvertently glances at the teacher's rounded curves. Sarah tries to read the country girl's soul: what, what is it that she has in her life that Sarah doesn't?

Sarah puts on her rubber boots and a coat and says to her, "Would you like me to walk with you? Or better yet—give you a ride home?"

The teacher jumps to her feet in excitement. Soon the two of them drive off. It's so beautiful! It's dusk. Shrubs throw funny shadows onto the white snow. When the horse jerks the sleigh forward, little horseshoes of snow fly into their faces. Here's a dry stalk—it's so long! Take a deep breath. The air smells of burning firewood, frosty snow, and soup. Don't wrap yourself up too tightly at such a delightful moment. Breathe! Breathe deeply! Don't close your mouth. It's so tempting to jump out of the sleigh and run up to that drifter over there, losing your overshoes on the way! The drifter is wearing bast shoes and carries a sack of alms on his shoulders. He hurries to stop for the night, making holes in the snow with his pole. Good evening, holy man! May peace be with you! Have some rest, look around, forget the hustle and bustle. The world is so wonderful, life is so wonderful!

"Sophia Meyerovna," says the teacher, rubbing her cold cheek against Sarah's shoulder. "This is so wonderful, so lovely! If I were you, I'd be riding every evening. I'd be going to Drahicyn, having a million dresses made for me. I'd invite young men over sometimes. Gramophone, dancing, pancakes, tea with jam. Or I'd go to Brest for two weeks. Please don't think I envy you, dearest! Not at all, my life is good too."

"I envy you," Sarah replies. "You breathe so freely."

"The whole world breathes freely," says the teacher with conviction and laughs. "Oh, isn't that wonderful! My mother is so old—but you should hear the songs she sings! You know what? Let's stop by my house. I have so many house plants you'd lose count! They even make the air greenish: ficus; cactus; lemons. . . . I'll fire up the samovar."

A week or two passes. Sarah stops more and more in front of the mirror. A bottle of freckle remover appears on her dressing table. She orders a hat from Pinsk. She goes to Drahicyn and studies fashion magazines. She sits in a sleigh or a carriage looking nonchalant—she is "breathing deeply." Shtetl Jews exchange whispers behind her back—it doesn't bother her one bit. Time sorts things out, rest assured, and no one will do it any better.

And then, when the ground is ready, the figure of Abramovich, the red-bearded freight forwarder from the train station, appears on the Telyatichi horizon. The time is ripe for new weddings at Telyatichi.

2

Abramovich has been to Telyatichi before on freight business, and the Raskins were always happy to see him. He is not a rich man, but everyday concerns somehow bypass him without touching his soul. He knows who to talk to and what about, and he has a soothing effect on everyone.

Chava likes Abramovich; she sees him as the opposite of Meyer, who is always in a hurry, always overworked. Encouraged by the forwarder's words, she says to him,

"Tell my husband that no one is going to erect a gold statue of him anyway. The man knows neither rest nor sleep! Tell him that he's not a young man of twenty anymore and that it's God who counts our days."

"Actually, we shouldn't be talking too much about it," suggests Abramovich. "The best thing is to be happy with what is, was, and will be."

"Happy?" Chava repeats and smiles wistfully. "But what is there to be happy about? Maybe that our Sarah is already twenty-three? That I don't get to see anything beyond these walls? Reb Abramovich, have you ever tried to talk to the walls?"

"Don't talk to the walls, talk to the soul. What is it that you lack? May God give so much to each and every Jew! Your husband is in good health and are you; your children are healthy, knock on wood, they are growing well. Before Sarah there's Isaac—why are you ignoring him? First we need to find a bride for Isaac, and then we'll marry Sarah off."

So says Abramovich, a wise Jew who doesn't like to fuss, doesn't care for empty or unnecessary words. He notices everything and knows how to keep quiet. He feels at home at the Raskins', and everyone is frank with him. He discusses the matter with his wife and, when everything is ready, he drives his sleigh to Telyatichi. He drinks tea with Chava, chats with her about this and that, and then goes to see Sarah.

"I have a match for Isaac," he says. "How long is he going to remain a bachelor? It's a good match, I did talk it over with my wife. As long as Isaac agrees, Reb Arye Kagan, the bride's father, will come "to look him over.""

"Why are you telling me this?" Sarah asks without pausing to think.

Abramovich could have given Sarah an exhaustive answer. But not everyone has the gift of conveying the truth directly.

"You are young and so is he," says the forwarder. "Who'd better understand one another than two young people? Listen to me: just talk to him quietly, I don't need to tell you how."

The next day Sarah goes to see Isaac in his office. She talks to him about Rachel's qualities, about how miserable Ilya would have been without his wife. . . . She talks about loneliness, too. And about the daughter of Kagan, a timber merchant from Brest-Litovsk.

"Kagan?" Isaac puts down his quill and hunches his shoulders. "Arye Kagan? Never heard of him."

So Sarah continues talking about a nice girl who she knows absolutely nothing about. Her voice breaks at times, she is ashamed of herself, but she keeps talking, talking, talking . . .

"Her father will be coming here in a week, you'll have a chance to meet him."

"What do I care about her father?"

"But you wouldn't have anything against him coming here?" Sarah keeps pressing.

"I don't care. All kinds of people come to Telyatichi."

With that, Sarah concludes this difficult and uncomfortable conversation. People are whispering around the house. What if Isaac finds out about the plan and makes a scene? People look at him with apprehension and disguised alarm, and the one most alarmed is Sarah.

Isaac, for his part, continues to pace nervously and smoke incessantly; the sound of his wailing flute wafts from the room.

A week later, Arye Kagan, a timber merchant from Brest-Litovsk, arrives at the train station. It's very cold, and a two-horse sleigh with a wonderful thick bearskin for his legs is dispatched to pick him up. The bay stallions from Telyatichi are covered with a red net, but they still send lumps of snow flying into the sleigh. All this puts the timber merchant from the city in a solemn mood. When the stallions come to an abrupt stop at the Telyatichi house, one can see a gray-bearded Jew in a bowler hat, his ears red from the cold, sitting in the sleigh like a statue. He enters the house and at first doesn't know what he is supposed to do. He wants to keep his hat on, but the Raskins are all hatless, so he promptly removes his. What is it with this Jewish gentry?

When he has to, Meyer knows how to conduct a conversation. It's just not clear where he learned it and whose example he is following. The Telyatichi wealth is not conspicuous or flashy—one would think the Raskins have been rich and comfortable for hundreds of years, their fortune passing from generation to generation. After dinner, tea, jam, and pastries are served in the living room.

"Well, children," Meyer says genially, "Why don't you play something for us?"

The children pick up their instruments. The music is not bad at all. They play the *Kol Nidre* prayer, then some Gypsy dance music, then a march. Arye Kagan cannot overcome his discomfort and talks exclusively about credit.

"The Merchant Bank of Mutual Credit," he says, forgetting why he actually came to Telyatichi, forgetting that the only reason he brought up the bank was to mention that he had been recently elected to its board. "The Merchant Bank . . ."

But he doesn't get a chance to come to his senses. After the march, Motya jumps forward and recites Russian poems. He does it with a Jewish accent, however. His friends, Belarusian boys, have significantly distorted his vocabulary: for instance, he uses Belarusian words for "hut" or "quickly." But no one notices. Then the gramophone is turned on. Then comes the tour of the office.

"Isaac does all the books," Meyer whispers into Kagan's ear. It's not his habit to brag about his children, he just mentions it in passing. Kagan opens a ledger tentatively and asks Isaac deferentially,

"Do you write all this?"

"Yes," Isaac replies, "Why?"

"Nothing," the Jew mumbles. "Very nice handwriting."

Then he returns to harping about mutual credit. "My wife should have come," he thinks to himself. "I have no idea how to handle this. Should I try talking about firewood?"

Kagan departs. He doesn't need to worry too much, Abramovich is on the case. A week later, the forwarder sends Meyer a note. Abramovich reports that everything is fine, thank God: in three days Luba Kagan and her mother will be at the Drahicyn train station. This wasn't easy for him to set up—for him or his wife. Since when does the bride come to "look over" the groom and not the other way around? At least for the first few days the Kagans will stay with the Abramovichs, at the station. In the meantime, Isaac should take advantage of the break and get himself a gold tooth—he is missing a front tooth. That's what Abramovich and his practical wife have concluded.

Meyer furrows his brow and frets as if the note from Abramovich concerns a major, critical issue. He'd rather sell ten railcars of alcohol, sign any kind of contract with the Poles, take a trip to Warsaw or even Berlin, if necessary—than talk to Isaac about things like this. "A gold tooth," he whispers, pacing around the room. "I have work to do, and now there's this tooth. Why?"

"Sarah," he says, mangling his words in embarrassment, "Sarah dear, read this note . . . and do what you think is best. I'm very busy, Sarah . . ."

Sarah, of course, doesn't talk to Isaac about the gold tooth—forget it! But she again engages in that difficult and unpleasant task. Her ears turn red, her hands become as cold as ice. No one is trying to tell Isaac what to do, but why won't he and Sarah go to the station together? These people came all the way from Brest-Litovsk for a reason! Isaac will finally take a look, make his acquaintance, and go back. Who says that he will necessarily like the girl?

Isaac is sulking, he is annoyed. He hunches his shoulders and sends the cellaring journal flying. He is ready to send all timber merchants to hell. He will think of something that will make the Kagans flee in no time. What will he talk about with this princess from Brest-Litovsk?

Nevertheless, he goes. He insults everybody, he spars with everybody. The Raskins themselves are sorry that they got into all this. Sarah gets the worst of it, she sits in the sleigh like a martyr. A five-mile journey feels like an eternity. The time spent at the Abramovich's also feels like an eternity. Isaac keeps turning abruptly to the window and falling silent. Sarah has to fill in the pauses. In the evening, brother and sister return to Telyatichi, with the understanding that they will be back at the Abramovich's the following day.

"What do you think of Luba Kagan?" Sarah asks Isaac, bracing herself.

"Who the hell knows," replies Isaac and hunches his shoulders, as is his habit.

Sarah makes an effort and says,

"I like her. . . . Honestly, she's not bad. Not bad at all. They must be a very good family."

Gradually, the initiative moves into Sarah's hands. She becomes used to Isaac's brashness. Perhaps he is being brash just to disguise his embarrassment and lack of willpower?

"We should invite the Kagans to Telyatichi and send a four-horse sleigh for them," she says to her father and then adds quickly, without waiting for the question, "What kind of a girl is she? A nice girl. A cultivated family. Her mother goes to Wiesbaden every year."

Isaac turns around like an over-drilled soldier and goes into his office. Everyone looks at his back with alarm, but the horses do get dispatched to retrieve the Kagans.

Old Mrs. Kagan does indeed go to Wiesbaden for treatments every year and breathes like a pike. She has tired, motionless black eyes and false teeth; she looks as if she knows someone wants to dupe her, while she herself would happily take the Telyatichi leaseholder for a ride. And Luba? She is tall and dark, her eyes are small and mocking. She brings a box of candy for the kids, gives each servant a ruble as a tip, and says "Mahlzeit"[5] after dinner. Everyone in Telyatichi repeats this mysterious word after her. She wears a formal gray dress and mentions to Isaac that it is her everyday outfit. She says that Telyatichi is a wonderful summer cottage, that it's probably nice here in the summer but boring in the winter. She would never agree to spend the winter in Telyatichi. She has an air of coldness about her, even though she sings a romance song after dinner in a wooden voice and, squinting her mocking eyes and feigning interest, asks Raskin's youngest daughter, "What is your name?"

Yet she neglects to listen to the girl's answer.

Old Mrs. Kagan finally achieves an understanding with Meyer on all the details. The engagement has to be arranged. Meyer runs around the house like a madman. Chores, chores! He has never felt this lost before.

And so Sarah gets back to work. Wine, desserts, and delicacies are brought from Drahicyn. Chava puts on her best dress and cries just in case—she is always happy to find a reason to tear up. Mr. Plavski arrives, and David, and the distiller, and the foresters. They are offered wine, so they become cheery and propose toasts. They say that bachelors should get married and that the married ones should have kids. "That's right, Mr. Isaac, there's nothing to be mad about here, nothing to be ashamed of, this is absolutely true and right." Ilya picks up a violin and plays something cheerful.

"Well, Isaac," he says, patting his wife on the back of the neck, "you are a bridegroom now. Remember how we used to go to the village school

5   German mealtime salutation.

together? I sold you a sparrow for three half-kopeck coins—and you never paid me back. So, my dear brother, you owe me money, you ought to pay up right now. God knows what might come back to you after a mere twenty years!"

Isaac pretends that Ilya's words have nothing to do with him. Bringing this up now?! He frowns and waits for all these Plavskis and foresters to leave.

After the engagement, Isaac goes to Brest-Litovsk for a few weeks and, just like when he returned from Pinsk, he comes back a changed man. In the summer, his future wife and her family will be staying at Telyatichi instead of renting a cottage in the country. He will need three separate rooms—and luckily, the house does have two kitchens. They'll have their own help, and their own meals. He paces around the room and casually chides his mother. "Why do we eat on an oilcloth instead of a real tablecloth? Why do they put a whole loaf on the table here instead of a basket with thin slices of bread? Why does Chava wear a wig instead of having her hair done? Why are the children allowed into the dining room instead of keeping them in their own special room?"

Then he compiles a list of relatives who can be invited to the wedding. Uncle Kadesh? No, he is poor, he'll bring countless children with him, they would grab pastries from the table and bring everyone to shame. . . . Uncle Leybe from Gorovakha? Father must write to him and hint at a new frock coat; he wore some ridiculous jacket to Ilya's wedding. Daniel Yaglom? But is it appropriate for him to bring his Rachel?

All this gets on people's nerves and gives Chava one more reason to shed a few tears. Oh my God, Isaac is planning to turn it into a display of some sort! Since when do you not invite all your relatives to a wedding? Maybe she herself should stay at Telyatichi instead of going to Brest-Litovsk?

She talks about her concerns at night in her marriage bed. Meyer pretends he is desperate to go to sleep. He tosses and turns, puts his hand under his cheek, begins to snore quietly and sigh, and then finally says,

"Enough, enough of that, old woman! Do you think I like it? Me neither. . . . But if you blow on a small flame, you'll create a big fire. It is what it is. The main thing is that it's such a relief. It clears the way for Sarah—now we can start thinking about her. All right, please go to sleep, don't worry about little things!"

3

That's how easily they lose their wits at Telyatichi, and before you know it, everyone focuses on something unpleasant. On the surface, nothing terrible has happened. The moment you leave the house at the crack of dawn, there's so much to do. Your chores make you forget unpleasant thoughts, but then you come home and the world shrinks again, and again something is happening with Isaac. One day he leaves for Brest-Litovsk without saying a word to anybody. Another time he starts bugging Sarah, driving the girl to tears, "Write to those Kagans and tell them to forget about the wedding, the wedding is off, Isaac has changed his mind."

So Chava sits by the window listlessly, Meyer furrows his brow and sighs, while Sarah locks her door from the inside and torments herself with reproach. It's all her fault: out of her desire to get married, she has put a burden on her brother that he cannot bear.

Only Ilya is blessed with the ability to fully control his thoughts and moods. He won't be thrown off by any tantrums. He listens to yet another Isaac story and a minute later reports that the potatoes in one of the storage rooms have frozen.

"That's right," he says, noisily sucking tea from his saucer. "Frozen—imagine that. If we hadn't caught it in time, thirty-two tons of potatoes would have turned into mush. The potatoes were covered with straw and began to rot. They must have been put into storage on a wet day."

He is, however, capable of talking not just about potatoes and thinking not just about work. His ideas are well-thought-out and unshakable, but for a while they ripen deep in his soul. And only after he hashes everything out down to the last detail, he says, "No question about it," proves his point—and he won't budge no matter what.

For a while now he's been paying closer attention to his younger brothers. He would join them at the table and listen to the melamed who, having mastered the arrogant contempt of the prophets, derides loathsome reality in a melodious voice, swaying and rolling his eyes. The village teacher does something complicated with barrels, pouring "a certain number" of gallons from one into another, diluting wine with water, mixing together different kinds of tea: two boxes; three boxes; five boxes. . . . When Ilya was Hersh's age, he probably lived in Adryzyn; back then, the Raskins' entire fortune would fit into one pocket. Times were different, too. How could a Jew go to a gymnasium back then? But now there are private schools in Brest-Litovsk, and in Bialystok, and even in Slonim; they accept Jews without any quotas, all you need is money.

Along with blue and yellow price lists for artificial fertilizers, agricultural machinery, and premium seeds, Ilya starts receiving school prospectuses in the mail. He reads them when he has time, tracing the lines with his finger, not missing a single word—he has had great respect for the printed word ever since he was a child. When everything is clear to him, he announces, "Entrance exams at the Brest-Litovsk commercial school begin in two weeks. As it happens, it's not very busy right now, so I can take Hersh and Motya there."

"How do you like that?" grumbles Isaac. "Why the commercial school? Why Brest-Litovsk? These swineherds won't amount to much anyway."

He paces around the room and doesn't hear what Ilya has to say.

"What an odd idea," he keeps grumbling. 'they are slackers, all they care about is chasing sparrows. Brest-Litovsk! The Kagans don't have anybody to watch over them."

But when Isaac realizes that Ilya never meant to send them to the Kagans anyway, he quiets down. Ilya has no desire to bicker with his brother. Ilya is right and that's why he is calm. He has even calculated how much the children's education would cost, and Meyer is fine with it.

"What will they become?" the father wonders. "Engineers? Doctors? Lawyers? Oh yes, that is a guaranteed livelihood. One can be a leaseholder and still have a profession just in case. If business is not going well—you can thump your patients' chests and give them enemas. You can always make a living that way."

The scent of goodbyes now permeates Telyatichi. Chava, who cannot understand many things about life, doesn't understand this either. Is it really true that life is all about sadness? Motya is still a boy, featherweight and pale. When peasants in the village became unruly, when the tax inspector was screaming about excise stamps, he would crawl under the couch, shut his eyes and cover his ears, and tears the size of beans would roll down his cheeks. When he came down with typhoid fever and the doctor said he wasn't going to make it, his mother sat alone by his bedside all night long, every night. Delirious, he was trying to fend off the taxman. Chava poured tea into his mouth with a teaspoon; the tea bubbled and dripped through the corners of his mouth. His father was away, the older kids went into other rooms and listened anxiously, waiting for their mother to start wailing.

The lamp was burning, a fly darted under the lampshade. The silly thing couldn't figure out how to escape from the enchanted golden circle, so Chava had to raise the shade to let the fly out. At that point, a frozen lump of manure exploded outside and hit the wall, and simultaneously a tree cracked from the cold. The mother was waiting for sunrise. And at sunrise, her little boy woke up happy, with cold sweat on his brow. Rays of sun shone into the room through the window pane which was pale blue from the cold.

It was such a joy when her child stretched out his hands and said, "I want black bread with herring!" Dearest child, may God bless you, how can one describe such joyous moments? All one can do is shed an extra tear over the Sabbath candles and tuck the little boy in even tighter when he goes to bed—and say a prayer with him. Who would do this in a strange city? Sit down with your mother, sonny, yes, like that, give me your hands. You don't know yet what living apart is like. Take a closer look at these rooms, at these faces, and remember what everybody looks like for the rest of your life, don't forget, don't forget . . .

The child's heart beats faster, the boy begins to feel his mother's sadness. He wanders around the rooms and thinks, "How odd! The dining room has polka dot, chocolate-colored wallpaper, the living room has stripes, I hadn't noticed that before. Flowering houseplants sit in the living room. One can secretly plant a seed in a pot and not tell anybody. And then, living in a strange city, it would be nice to think about this seed growing and germinating; it would make life less dull. The seed will be a link to my home, the secret seed that nobody else would know about . . ."

His older brother Hersh, a serious and secretive fellow with eyeglasses, has lost his cheer too. He spends a lot of time putting his drawings together, packing up his collections of butterflies and of lizards preserved in glass tubes with alcohol. His hands are definitely trembling, but he frowns, adjusts his eyeglasses, remains morosely silent, and can't decide whether to bring his violin with him. If yes, then he needs to order a case for it from the cabinetmaker.

Finally the day comes when Ilya puts on shoes instead of his usual boots and scrubs his blond stubble with a razor in front of the mirror. He attaches a tie to his cotton shirt and recalls in passing that the tie was bought for the wedding, his own wedding; he hasn't worn it ever since.

"In short," he says, "in short . . . the train leaves in three hours. There's no need for all these pastries, rolls, and cooked chickens. I'm putting the children on full board."

"Oh, God!" Their mother can't bear it anymore. "Don't you know that Motya likes crumbly shortbread cookies? Who will make those for him in the city? Maybe they will also eat dinner in restaurants so that they can ruin their stomachs, God forbid?"

She is unnaturally sprightly, she runs from room to room. Then she suddenly stops in bewilderment, forgetting what she was hurrying to do. Or she lowers herself into an armchair and drops her arms by her sides in exhaustion. Her heart beats so hard that it looks as if the printed flowers on her dress have come to life and started moving. She spots Meyer hurrying somewhere, and calls out to him quietly, pointing at the armchair next to hers.

"Meyer," she says, barely moving her dry lips. "Our small children are being torn away from my heart. . . . Don't look at me with big eyes. Just tell me one thing: is it really necessary?"

"Yes it is," Meyer replies, stroking her hand. He has answered her question, now he can get up and go, but he is staying put.

"Someone always thinks something is necessary, but I don't understand why," Chava sighs. "All Jews live in shtetls, yet we are here at Telyatichi because it's necessary. Now it is necessary to have the children live in a strange city like orphans. . . . Go, Meyer, go, I thought you were in a hurry . . ."

But suddenly Meyer furrows his brow and gets mad at the "silly broad."

"Yes, that's right, it is necessary! The cheesemaker in Zakoziel earns just five hundred rubles a year—yet even he sends his son to school. He sells the shirt off his back, he goes into debt, but he does send his boy to school. And he is right! Who says that they absolutely have to be engineers? They could be businessmen with college degrees. They could even be leaseholders with college degrees. Is Telyatichi ours for good? The lease will expire—and who knows what will happen then? The Peasant Bank is buying up estates. Żuk may get an attractive offer and then he won't go for another lease, he will simply sell Telyatichi. Then what? Well, this is silly, of course, everything will be fine. If you really love the children, put on a happy face and let's go eat dinner."

Chava tries to do as Meyer says but it doesn't work out too well. What can you expect from a "silly broad?" Motya's lips start shaking. If it weren't so shameful, he would have hidden himself in a corner and cried his heart out. He will have to take entrance exams, but he knows nothing. So he will tell them right away: "I know nothing, what do you want from me?"

Well, carefree childhood, farewell to you! Nothing in life repeats itself, but that doesn't mean that one has to freeze and stop the clocks. The servants carry sacks and baskets outside. Ilya dons a leaseholder's sheepskin jacket and gets into the carriage. Chava gives each boy a ruble.

"If the food is bad there, buy yourselves a bagel to eat," she says. "If nasty children are mean to you, better tough it out for a while."

"But not for too long," Meyer clarifies. "Fight back! Although it's better to live in peace. Well, Godspeed . . ."

Farewell, carefree childhood! The blue house with white shutters has already disappeared behind the trees, the plant with the sign that the children know by heart—"Telyatichi Distillery No. 114"—has flashed by on the right, the horse stables and the cheese factory have flown by, and the forge has appeared after the gates. The blacksmiths wearing goggles—they are Polish noblemen—bang on crimson-hot iron with their heavy hammers. They juggle the hammers from hand to hand, remove their caps, and bow. Farewell, young gentlemen! Behind the hill, the windmill emerges as if it grew out of the earth; it flails its broad vestment-like sleeves. Farewell to you, windmill, we might see you again someday!

After the windmill come the Kobryn sands with flints in the ruts. Here's a roadside cross with an apron, ribbons, and a bunch of dried rowan twigs on the crossbar. A ramshackle graveyard bristles with scrawny crosses. Why is the graveyard moving like flames of a bonfire burning in front of you? Well . . . farewell, graveyard! You will remain as you are, though there may be a few more crosses, and someone might steal a plank for firewood. A peasant is traipsing forward on his horse. Lucky peasant! He doesn't need to go to school; he'll live and die among his people. Farewell, peasant! Perhaps, as we are coming back, you will be riding the same way, dangling your feet in your bast shoes and urging your nag on while beating its skinny ribs with your fist. It's not that hard to remember you, you will stay in our memory forever. Farewell!

Nothing repeats itself, but that doesn't mean that one has to freeze and stop the clocks. This tranquil page—life on the estate—has been turned over, the children are in Brest-Litovsk, they go to school. One can think of the past, even be a bit sad. One can pick up a calendar every evening before going to bed and cross off another day. The school holidays are now one day closer. Young people, however, do not live by memories alone. There are new friends, new interests, encounters, conflicts. One keeps growing up, starts liking some things and disliking others. His first steps are timid and unsure, but then the path is cleared and off he goes . . .

"The quiet children"—for now that's what they call Hersh and Motya, the new Raskin generation. On Sundays they visit the Kagans. In the dining room, they sit next to each other motionlessly on a needlepoint sofa; the younger one is afraid even to stir or cough properly. Kagan appears, preoccupied, absentminded. He blows his nose loudly and then notices the children; now he has to talk to them.

"Which grade are you in?" he asks Hersh.

"Second," Hersh answers.

"And you?"

"Senior preparatory."

"I see. And what's your name?"

"Motya."

"And yours?'

"Hersh."

A week later, the following Sunday, he will ask them exactly the same questions, but they don't find it funny. Rather, it puts them into some kind of dusty, deadly gloom, like everything in the house: the furniture in slipcovers, the blown-up photographs of relatives on the walls, the pharmaceutical smells. Sometimes they get to see Luba or her mother, a sick woman who has difficulty breathing. None of them cares to talk, even the way they open their mouths seems particularly dull. So the boys hurry to leave.

"Here's ten kopecks for you," the older brother says to the younger. "Go to the cinema."

This means that Hersh will have company and doesn't want Motya to be around and get in the way. The brothers are not really friends, they are cagey, they don't share any pals or any interests—perhaps the difference in age is the reason. Hersh looks a bit sullen. He has already drawn a large portrait of Nekrasov for the poet's anniversary; the portrait now hangs in the teachers' lounge. He has two friends: Sarver and Wiener. Sarver draws too. He is somehow restless, nervous, he doesn't look like a regular school-boy. He uses thick notebooks, makes do without textbooks, and when he is called upon, he offers instead to cover the material for the entire quarter during the final exam and gets away with it. His older brother has moved to Philadelphia, and Sarver dreams of going to America himself. Wiener is the son of a melamed; he is a smart, diligent fellow with doleful eyes. He has trouble paying the tuition. He makes monthly payments, he uses ink to mask the holes in his shoes, and he can talk about a gold medal with great excitement. He will finish the commercial school with a gold medal!

In addition to these two, Hersh is also friends with some "ladies," that is, girls. He doesn't stroll with them on Chaussée Street—the "Nevsky Prospect" of Brest, he doesn't dance at student parties: the Raskins don't know how to dance. He draws portraits of them from life and talks to them about very serious matters with a very serious look. Older students don't particularly like him: he doesn't read newspapers and has no interest in current issues or politics. But his classmates don't really care for him either. They call him "the young fogey" and it's actually quite true. Put a beard on him—and nobody would guess whether he is young or old. He doesn't dream of a gold medal or a trip to Philadelphia, but he still does well in school out of self-respect and because he doesn't want to be laughed at.

Motya's life, on the other hand, consists largely of being homesick, which makes him passive and not particularly interested in what's going on around him. He doesn't even have real friends. He might confide in some-one—but then he'll notice the boy's eyes flashing when Motya gets an F, and he'll part ways. Noisiness, games, school-related interests—all this passes him by. Even when he gets involved, he does it superficially somehow, with-out putting his heart into it. He only gets excited a week before going home. Then, he hops around, chatters in class—and gets reprimanded or sent to the corner. After the cinema, he plods slowly home. He sits down on his bed and becomes engrossed in some mindless, gloomy reflections. He stares at the pattern on the wallpaper and remembers the wallpaper in Telyatichi. There, at home, a seed of wheat is germinating in a flower pot. . . . As soon as he gets home, he will immediately check on the flower pot. He closes his eyes, and the smells and voices of home all come back to him. His heart flutters out of devotion and love for his mother.

His roommate, a plump-cheeked boy from Pruzhany, pops in. He has some rare stamps from the island of Cuba that he has just purchased. A five kopeck envelope contains such valuable, rare stamps! The boy is excited, he's laughing loudly, but Motya cannot share his joy no matter how hard he tries. Motya doesn't care about his studies and goes to school reluctantly. He doesn't understand how these boys from Pruzhany, Kobryn, or Antopol can have fun here and forget about their homes.

Isaac visits the city sometimes, and then Motya goes to see him.

"So how are the two of you doing?" Isaac asks. "Got lots of Fs? If you have to do the same grade again, we will leave you in Brest for the summer, keep that in mind."

That Isaac always has something nasty to say!

"Don't pick your nose," he says, pacing the room. "Don't bite your nails. Behave like a civilized boy. Here, mama sent you some cookies and sugar. Now it's time for you to go back to the apartment."

At the bottom of the bundle the boy finds a note from his mother. She writes out every letter separately. Her notes are hesitant and pitiful; it feels as if you blew on them they would fly away and disappear like grains of sand. The content of her notes is customary: we are healthy, you be healthy, how are you doing, we are doing fine, nothing new, what's new with you? But something personal also shines through the usual dross: who is washing your hair, son? Do you change your underwear every Friday or do you forget? It's already Hanukkah, which means Christmas is coming soon, you'll be going home. We'll see you soon. Soon.

Here the letters become blurred, light-blue ink spots make them hard to read. To put his mind at ease, the boy stuffs his mouth with cookies. Then he reaches for the calendar and crosses off the finished day with a shaky hand. The day is over. Yet another day is over.

4

Meanwhile, the years pass, and events unfold slowly and quietly in the Raskin household. Winter allows time for rumination and reflection. In spring, summer, and fall there isn't a moment to spare—the best thing to do is to restrain your soul, work hard without looking over your shoulder, and avoid unnecessary thoughts. But you can't always control your heart and close your eyes. An unpleasant, unnecessary thought may strike you—and then no matter what you do, no matter how hard you try to chase it away, the uninvited thought will remain with you and lodge in your heart like a splinter, making it ache and ache. Whether in the field or in the forest, Meyer might become pensive, furrow his brow, a stalk of grass between his teeth jutting out horizontally from his graying beard.

Old Raskin is not one of those people who, in addition to working, also have the ability to mold other people's lives to their liking. As is his habit, he furrows his brow and buzzes a forlorn Jewish tune through his teeth, mosquito-like. Everyone can see that the old man is unhappy about something, but Meyer holds his tongue. For example, he doesn't care for his new relatives, the Kagans, who cling to Isaac like flies on sugar. Isaac, of all people! His own family has never dared tell him what to do, but the Kagans have put a tight rein on the young man. In the summer, the entire Kagan clan settles at Telyatichi. Their pink and lilac parasols flash under the trees, blue enamel chamber pots gleam beneath the porch, hammocks are strung up here and there. In the evening, mangling their r's unpleasantly, they carry their glasses to the cowshed to drink fresh milk. They look so odd, so out of place in the cowshed that even the cows notice and look askance at them. Or, at the busiest possible moment, the Kagans might suddenly decide to go for a ride, so Isaac, wearing light shoes and a standing collar, would rush to the stables to get the horses—the same horses that will be working just an hour later. One can overlook little things like this and try to ignore them, but apparently, little things go hand in hand with bigger ones.

Besides the daughter, Arye Kagan has two sons, Leyble and Nyomchik. Leyble is married, he lives in Bialystok and "deals" in something or other, but no one knows for sure what exactly he does. He changes occupations all the time. Arye Kagan gave up on him a long time ago; he would have been happy to forget about this son altogether. But his elder son doesn't forget about him. He might come to Brest-Litovsk with his wife and children and live in his father's house like it was his own for several months—it's "the dead season," you see. Or he would get all fired up about a new project—and his projects are too numerous to count. Typewriters, for instance. The province of Grodno has a thousand lawyers, doctors, businessmen, engineers, and contractors. Why wouldn't each one of them buy a typewriter? Kagan would earn thirty rubles on every sale. Now do the math yourself: it's thirty thousand, no less.

So Leyble gets an agent's contract, wheedles the money to pay the deposit from his father, runs around, orders forms and envelopes, nails a brass plate to his door, and buys himself a new suit. At this point, even if someone were to offer him twenty-nine thousand to buy him out—no, he wouldn't take it. But then half a year passes. Doctors and lawyers fail to buy his typewriters, the company cancels his contract, the deposit is lost—and Leyble is left high and dry. So he picks up his family and goes to stay with his father again.

His chagrin is short-lived, though; new ideas swarm in his head. Here's an idea! A brilliant idea! It's easy to find a few hundred men in the province who are bald and need money. Each is issued a top hat and, at an agreed upon time, before trains arrive or depart, the baldies come to the train station for a small fee, sit down at the station's restaurant, remove their top hats—and all will have a message on their pates! "Buy Katyk's cigarette cartridges!" for example. Everyone starts buying only these cartridges, Leyble's company grows richer and richer; it receives an exclusive license for the whole empire. . . . Can you imagine the thousands we're talking about here?

In the summer, during the "dead season," Leyble comes to Telyatichi. He sits in the office with Isaac and spits out new ideas. Do you know why his last project didn't work out? At the most decisive moment, when he needed three thousand rubles, his father Arye Kagan refused him. Leyble takes a quick, perfunctory look at the Telyatichi ledgers and smiles ironically. "Now please explain to me how it makes sense to sink a huge capital into the business and earn such piddly percentages?" Never mind the match factory that could be built in Brest-Litovsk; never mind that. Let's take an easier and more dependable way of making a living: a banking firm. First, the Raskins, like all respectable people, would live in the city and deal with people, not peasants. But most importantly, it would bring real profits, not the small change that the leaseholders are getting out of Telyatichi. Or take lottery tickets. Not everyone can afford a ticket. So special outfits purchase entire series of tickets and issue their own vouchers: one tenth of a winning ticket, one twentieth. . . . Do you know how much money people make this way?

Of course, Isaac is not so naïve as to take all of young Kagan's ideas at face value. Nevertheless, Leyble and the rest of the Kagan family do manage to sway Isaac's skepticism somewhat. He spends his winters now in Brest-Litovsk, in Arye Kagan's house. Brokers come to see him all day long. Every once in a while, he summons his father with a telegram. Meyer is not thrilled, but he still heeds his son's call and goes.

"Well, yes," he says. "All this is great, I have no doubt that one can make a profit on it. But where would the seed money come from? You know perfectly well that one can't squeeze a single kopeck out of Telyatichi."

Isaac hunches his shoulders and jumps up from his chair. Telyatichi! So it's Telyatichi that binds him hand and foot! He makes it quite clear that he is sick and tired of working in the sticks. He'd be happy to sever all his ties to this unwieldy enterprise. Who says that children must follow in their father's footsteps?

At his point Meyer furrows his brow and buzzes his mosquito-like tune. He buries his head in the newspaper and keeps quiet. In situations like this, it's better to keep quiet. His best guess is that Isaac's outburst most likely won't go much beyond talk. After all, Isaac gets a lot out of Telyatichi.

Nyomchik Kagan, too, has given the Raskins a few annoying moments. There's not much to say about him. Nyomchik is short and shriveled like a dead bedbug that has been inside a book for a few months. His tall starched collars stifle his skinny neck and hold his chin up. He finished a correspondence course in bookkeeping and took another one in mandolin; he loves playing and, apparently, that is all he does. All day long the house is filled with the tickling sound of the mandolin; it gives people headaches. When he spots Meyer, he decides for some reason that he needs to talk to him about business and demonstrate how knowledgeable he is.

"Looks like you're sowing potatoes? How many pounds?" he asks.

Meyer is always irked by these conversations. Shaking the dust off his jacket and pulling on his boots, he replies,

"Young man, potatoes are planted, not sown."

"Whatever," says Nyomchik indifferently, barely managing to suppress a yawn. "But why are you making Swiss cheese instead of Dutch?"

"Why, is Dutch cheese tastier?"

"You can make more money . . ."

"You can make even more money by milking calves. Imagine: I've got two hundred of them, and if each one produces just five glasses, then . . ."

"Is that really possible?"

Meyer roars with laughter and hurries to the porch where a light carriage is waiting for him. These young people! When Meyer was fourteen, he carried heavy bags of flax seed on his shoulders. The dowry he received was eighty silver rubles. Despite all this, he's done well for himself. But this fellow—the only thing he knows is the mandolin. Sowing potatoes! Raskin urges his horse on with the whip and tries not to think about the annoying Nyomchik. Boundless fields lie in front of him, the golden wheat bows to him, the dust of summertime settles on his face.

In the meantime, old Mrs. Kagan, with her swollen goiter, conducts diplomatic conversations with Sarah, focusing her tired, angry eyes on her. Does a country girl know about life? No, a country girl doesn't know much about life. Does Sarah know about today's young men? No, Sarah doesn't know about the young men of today, this much is clear. All shine and no spine—that's what today's young men are like. Most of them have gastritis, let alone other ailments. But those few who grew up under the watchful eye of their mothers—now that's a totally different story. While at it, Mrs. Kagan touches upon Sarah herself. What's so special about her anyway? Did she earn a college degree? No, she's just an ordinary girl. Frankly, compared to Luba . . .

At this point, Luba and Nyomchik arrive and invite Sarah to go for a walk. And it just so happens that after taking only a few steps, Luba suddenly remembers that she has some urgent matter to attend to and leaves. Sarah is left with Nyomchik . . .

This whole thing drags on for weeks, actually for a couple of months. Sarah feels like a squirrel in a wheel, her thoughts are suffocating, she wants to talk to someone, to pour her heart out. But who can she confide in? Not her mother, of course, not Ilya, not Isaac. . . . She throws a shawl around her shoulders and rushes out of the house. She hurries and stumbles, she doesn't even acknowledge the peasants bowing to her. The narrow trails snake through fields and meadows like ribbons dropped by peasant women.

The sun is descending toward the woods; people standing in the distance look like black paper cutouts. The sheaf-binder makes a steady noise; rectangular bands of rye fall and disappear into the machine. Skylarks under the shadeless blue sky are driven wild by the heat, singing monotonously, even mockingly. Everyone is working hard, no one sits idle. The wheels of the carriage make a dry patter and knock as they bounce across the lumpy meadow. Meyer pulls the reins in and stops the horse.

"If you're not in a hurry, I can give you a ride," he says to Sarah jokingly. "Are you out for a walk? That's good. Notice how the grass smells like perfume, better than all those little bottles. Get in, girl!"

He moves over and Sarah climbs in next to him. She looks at his tanned, dust-covered neck crisscrossed with wrinkles and at his broad back which is beginning to hunch up like an old man's. The curly hair on the back of his head is mostly gray. And so she tries to project her anguish and unhappiness onto her father. What good did he have in his life? Always too busy, always in a hurry, always working. He should get some rest. . . . But pity doesn't fit well with the sturdy figure of Meyer Raskin. Without turning his head, as if forgetting about his daughter, he muses aloud about his work.

"Last year," he says and waves his arm, "last year this plot was nothing but lumps, it was a meadow. When Ilya said that it could be turned into arable land, frankly I didn't believe it. Fine, let him try, I don't like to stand in people's way, but I really didn't believe it. We sank three hundred rubles worth of superphosphate alone into this field. And now look: the wheat stands up like a wall! Ilya is really good. I never thought that he would make such a fine farmer. Wait, let me pick a few ears, I want to see what kind of grain we're going to have here."

He pulls out a few ears, sticks them into his pockets, and moves on. Dark-green, almost black thickets of wildly growing potatoes attract his attention. How many tubers under each plant, I wonder? Meyer digs into the soil, skillfully throwing lumps of black earth aside. Well, look at that, the potatoes are not doing badly, not badly at all, that's right!

Father and daughter keep moving on. Meyer's thoughts take him far, far away. Suddenly, he hears some strange sounds coming from behind. He turns around abruptly. Sarah is hiding her face in her shawl, her pitifully raised shoulders are shivering. He stops the horse, gets out, comes up to Sarah, and presses her head against his chest.

"Oh my God," he says quietly and sighs. "All my life I've known exactly what I have to do, but I never know what others should be doing. . . . But I'm your father, Sarah, surely you can tell your father what's bothering you . . ."

"Dad, dear Dad, if you only knew . . . if you. . . . I detest Nyomchik Kagan. . . . I can't stand him . . ."

"Nyomchik Kagan?" her father asks perplexedly. "But why should you like him? He is a typical slacker and a fool. . . . 'Sowing potatoes'!"

He quickly grasps what's going on, tries to look into his daughter's eyes, and shakes his head reproachfully.

"My oh my," says old Raskin. "You should be ashamed, my girl. How could you even think that I would give you away to such an idiot? And generally, I prefer not to make important decisions for my children, you know that perfectly well . . ."

Meyer is telling the truth, of course—he wouldn't have given Sarah away to Nyomchik Kagan. However, it is not clear whether he would have been able to resist the pressure from all sides. Even gloomy Isaac—even he got involved in the matter; his new family must have been pushing him really hard. But then something happened in the Kagan family, something that drew their attention away from Sarah Raskin.

If the Kagans hadn't been stingy and the old woman had continued going to Wiesbaden, she might have creaked along for another ten years or so. But they coveted the Raskins' wealth, sponged off them from spring through fall, building up their health in the gardens and forests of Telyatichi—and they paid for it dearly. The weather in Belarus is not the best: the skies are often cloudy even in summer, the winds are stiff, leaves on the birches shrivel up and start rotting, and the chilly fog is so fine that you can't tell whether it's drizzle or simply dust suspended in the air. Old Mrs. Kagan came down with a cold and was taken to Brest-Litovsk. They thought it was nothing, so the Kagan family stayed behind at Telyatichi. One day, however, a telegram arrived with a single word in it: "Dying." The Kagans hastily packed their suitcases, rolled up their hammocks, and left for the city.

The disintegration of a family brought about by death invariably reveals people's true character. For a while, people take off their masks and don't bother to keep up appearances. While the old woman lay dying, the Kagan family was consumed by infighting. Kagan himself was still in good shape, he wouldn't go for long without a wife. As soon as the sick old woman dies, he would marry someone else, and all his possessions would go to her. Arye Kagan's children weren't the only ones to realize this. All close and distant relatives—aunts with barely concealed greed on their faces and warm shawls around their shoulders—realized this, too. All of them came to Brest-Litovsk, sneaking around the rooms, searching for the right keys to the dressers, stealing knickknacks and dirty sheets, and rummaging through papers. The old woman was expiring slowly; she lay in bed with a bag of ice on her head and listened to her children and relatives fighting and divvying up the loot in the rooms next door. And while they were at each other's throats, while the brothers, the sister, and the children were dividing up the possessions, Sarah Raskin became engaged to Pavel Rusevich. This is how it happened.

Meyer Raskin visited the nearby county towns quite often: Pinsk, Kobryn, Brest-Litovsk. In his spare time he would sit at a small round table in his hotel room, enjoy tea with lemon, and receive Jews with disheveled beards and tightly furled canvas umbrellas under their arms. The Jews would twirl locks of their beards around their fingers, become excited, and speak of outstanding matches for Sarah. In conclusion, they usually requested three rubles for mailing expenses. The three rubles were where these outstanding matches usually ended—but Meyer was not discouraged at all. What will be, will be, he reasoned. However, he gave more and more thought to Sarah's future, and spoke with the curly bearded Jews with increasing interest, giving them money for mailing and various other expenses. One of the matches clearly sounded promising to him. It was a young man of good standing from Lodz named Pavel Rusevich. His widowed mother lived in Kobryn and was quite an aristocratic lady. The matchmaker claimed at first that Pavel Rusevich managed a factory for someone else, then it turned out that he was not in charge of the whole operation, just the bookkeeping side of it. But even that didn't discourage Meyer Raskin.

"The important thing is that he is a man of substance," Meyer reasoned. "Fifteen years of working in factories? It means that he'd be able to run his own business as well. And I will always be happy to help out."

And so one day during the holidays, Ivan harnesses the best horses to the best carriage and rides to the train station. The Raskin house is in turmoil. Sarah, tightly corseted, her hair done, and her face powdered first thing in the morning, dashes from room to room. At times she feels that everyone is staring at her, that her role is ludicrous and pathetic—then she blushes and doesn't know where to hide. But there's still so much to do before the Rusevichs arrive from the station, so Sarah keeps dashing around, hurrying, and issuing orders. Anything is possible, you know. It is possible that Rusevich is a very decent man, a true gentleman. The fact that he couldn't find a wife in Lodz and is using a matchmaker means absolutely nothing. One never knows where one might find happiness.

Finally, Pavel Rusevich and his mother arrive. While still outside, he twists his red mustache tightly, helps his mother out of the carriage, and then heads toward the Raskin house in a measured and confident gait. There, after exchanging greetings, he finds it necessary to explain why he is coughing. He caught a cold on the way, you see, and the doctor prescribed mineral water from Bad-Ems. Of course, it's a little awkward to bring your own mineral water to someone else's house, but that's beside the point. The point is that he caught this cold by chance; otherwise, he is not usually susceptible to colds.

He brought with him large and small suitcases, the likes of which no one at Telyatichi had ever seen before. Every morning he wears a mustache guard for ten minutes; his every move is precise and well thought through. He has his own way of eating and his own way of drinking. Before taking the last sip of tea or starting dessert, he picks his teeth with a small goose quill—and the Raskins assume that this is what everyone does in the big city. He speaks a strange Yiddish, filled with puzzling German words, thus inspiring a kind of odd, timid respect. He even blows his nose in his own particular way, as if it's a sacred ritual: he slowly opens his handkerchief, always with the same motion, then bends his head slightly, covers his mustache with the handkerchief, and only then finally trumpets.

In conversation with Meyer he is very reserved. When Raskin tells him that a man should work for someone else only when he's young and that everyone should strive to run their own business, he hears the old man out and responds with something like this:

"Yes, of course, it's very hard for me not to agree with your expert opinion, you are decidedly correct. However, it is better not to rush, everything needs to be thought through."

This reply cannot but please Meyer Raskin, even though there have been times in his own life when circumstances did not leave him much room for ruminating.

In the evening, Sarah and Pavel go for a stroll. They close the glass doors of the veranda behind them. Sarah takes the first step, but Pavel Rusevich stops her.

"One moment, please," he says and sniffs the evening air. "I think it's too cold out here. Excuse me, but I will have to change my coat. In this respect—as in all others—I like to be careful."

Sarah waits until he returns wearing a warm coat.

"Well," he says, "now we can go for a walk. Of course, my feet are more used to sidewalks, but that's not crucial. Tell me something about yourself. Actually, please excuse me, but I need to explain to you what brings me to your home."

Sarah's eyes grow large in fear, muffled waves begin to sound in her ears, she doesn't hear Pavel's first words.

"Girls in big cities are spoiled," he explains in the meantime. "For you, Sophia, it is hard to imagine, but that's the way it is. They may even allow themselves to go to a cabaret with men they don't know very well. I have it on good authority, it's absolutely true."

It's late in spring and Passover is late this year. Fog is rising from the earth; the ground smells of crushed poppy seeds. Frogs hop lethargically in the overgrown alleys. The storks have already arrived and built their spacious nests on top of the thatched roofs. The silhouettes of the birds are clearly visible against the darkening sky. They stand on their long red legs, bending their necks, and rattle evenly, loudly, and clearly. Black, hundred-year-old firs break the blue canopy; you cannot see the sky around these trees. The smell of resin rises above them. A tiny nightingale hides deep in the branches—or maybe not there but somewhere completely different. He is testing his rich, full voice. He cherishes every sound, he is creative and thrifty with each one, he enjoys them himself. After a few moments, the lovely melody becomes well established. A frog emits its last croak and falls silent. Listen to the nightingale; his singing hours are limited, so listen to the nightingale!

"Amazing," says Pavel Rusevich, removing his bowler and wiping his bald pate. "Amazing," he repeats and twirls his mustache gently. "I once heard a singer at the theater; her warbling was exactly the same. Such an odd coincidence, isn't it?"

He links Sarah's arm around his, and they head for home.

"Oh yes," he says, "I forgot to tell you that I was only able to take one week off. Minus the travel time, minus the two days that I spent at home—it means that I will only be able to stay here for three days."

Then he gives a detailed account of the story line of a certain opera, then outlines his daily routine. It has to be noted in all fairness that he talks about everything with such authority that one cannot help but think that all this is incredibly important and interesting. When large bowls of clabber are brought to the table, he demonstrates how to pour it so that everyone receives the same amount of the upper layer—the sour cream. He talks to Meyer about agriculture, and even though he has no knowledge or understanding of it, his words sound nothing like Kagan's blather.

In the middle of the following day, Pavel Rusevich steps out of the house with Meyer Raskin.

"You must have guessed that I stepped out with you for a reason," he says to Meyer. "Your daughter Sophia is exactly the kind of girl I like. Of course, it would have been better if I spent a few more days here, but my time off is coming to an end. I have to leave tomorrow night. That is why I'm talking to you today. I'm starting with you because I don't want to put either you, or myself—let alone Sophia—in an awkward position. So please have your family make a decision, and tonight I shall speak to your daughter Sophia myself."

So speaks Pavel Rusevich. Easy for him: in his mind, everything is clear—as clear as his entries in the factory ledgers. Yes is yes, no is no, payable/receivable, debit/credit. But what about the Raskins? "Have your family make a decision . . ." Isaac is away, and even if he were here, you wouldn't get anything useful out of him, you'd just upset yourself. Ilya bites his nails, shrugs his shoulders and says, "Can one really give advice in such matters?" Meyer furrows his brow, his face shows pain. Chava, Sarah . . .

"Sarah dear, our beloved daughter," says the father, "what can I tell you? You know my thinking. . . . Children should do what they choose. Do you think that when I got married I knew your mother any better than you know him now? Even less. Times are different, of course. However, I do know that if a person is destined to be happy, he will be happy. I think he's a good match. As for myself, you know how I feel about my children . . ."

Oh, well. . . . A girl is not supposed to be picky, especially if she's over twenty-five. What would another girl do in her place? Another girl would cry a little and accept. After all, there aren't any particular reasons why she should decline. And since there are no such reasons . . .

So Sarah does what any other girl would do. She cries just enough, powders her face, goes to Pavel Rusevich and tells him yes. "Yes," Sarah says, "I accept." So Pavel Rusevich, trying not to disturb his mustache, kisses her on the forehead, lips, and eyes. Everyone is crying and laughing. Everyone is nervous and happy.

"Stay for another day, please, we are family now," Chava begs. "Why do you have to rush?"

"Dear mother, it is impossible," says Rusevich. The first words come as easily as the rest; apparently, he thinks nothing of calling Chava Raskin "dear mother."

Oh, well. . . . If the man's in a hurry, if he can't stay any longer, then the engagement must be arranged. In the evening, candles in heavy brass candelabra are lit, the entire living room is illuminated with candles. They crackle and flare, yet the living room is filled with soft, dim light that reflects in the mirrors as yellow swaths and twinkles. The gramophone bellows needlessly, the singer's voice seems brash, but somehow no one thinks of turning the music off. Just the opposite: the moment the singer finishes an aria, one of the family members rushes to replace him with even harsher music, noisy and deafening. Those wishing to propose a toast practice their eloquence.

Rusevich is sitting all puffed up as if at a shareholders' meeting. He stands up with a goblet in hand and acknowledges the greetings. He adjusts his mustache with a practiced gesture. At this point, a maid comes in and announces that some peasant lad and girl wish to see the young lady and her fiancé.

"Bring them in," Meyer says.

A fellow with a broad red sash around his waist and a young woman in a canvas blouse and a homespun skirt enter the living room. The fabric clings to the girl's firm breasts perked up under the blouse so that even the tips of the nipples show. The young couple bows low to the Raskins and their guests. They congratulate Sarah and Rusevich and say that they too have decided to get married in a week. They ask for twenty pounds of wheat flour as their wedding present—a custom in Belarus. The girl approaches Sarah and kisses her.

"But do you know your fiancé well enough?" asks Sarah, touched. "Don't make a mistake, you're so young, so flourishing."

The woman stops, her eyes flashing. She points a finger at her fellow, who freezes, and she bursts out laughing.

"You mean Semyon? Oh God, we've been going out for two years now, the whole village knows!"

Mr. Plavski now demonstrates how well-informed he is.

"He's nineteen, dammit," he says about the lad. "He's been 'going out' since seventeen. So the moment he was done suckling—pardon my language, madam—he, eh, . . . went for a girl. Those people, sons of bitches. To your health, Mr. Rusevich!"

But now Pavel Rusevich looks at his watch and says it's time for him to catch the train. He will be writing to Sarah every three days—on certain days she will be receiving letters from him.

And indeed, every three days Sarah receives letters from her fiancé. In his letters, he allows himself a joke on occasion, reporting that he will be wedding *Mademoiselle* Raskin in that many months and that he plans to invite her, Sophia, to the ceremony. He doesn't like the name Sarah and calls her Sophia from the first day on.

There's plenty to do at the Raskins' now. Dressmakers and seamstresses are preparing the bride's dowry. Sewing machines clatter away from morning till late at night.

"So what does your beloved fiancé write?" Meyer asks his daughter. "Oh, don't say a word, Sarah, you will have a good husband, a solid one, not some blabbermouth, rest assured. You will be a fancy Lodz lady, and mother and I will come visit you. Chava, do you hear? We're already going to visit married Sarah. What is it—does time really fly? It means, Chava, that your husband is not that young anymore. It even means that you're not such a young lady either, ha ha! Imagine, in just twelve months or so we'll be grandpa and grandma! I know what you're thinking, old woman, you probably want us to move to Jerusalem in our old age and receive letters from our grandkids every month. Really! But I won't go for it. I'm tough! I don't want to go to Jerusalem! You know what? Let's go to the fields together. What do you say, old woman? Oh, woman, woman, tearing up already! As if on cue. You know how much I love tears. So long, I'm off."

Meyer doesn't like to sit at home where some little thing always throws him off course. Let someone else deal with the little things—he doesn't want to know about them. Chava's marriage bed stories are more than enough for him. For example, she reported that Luba, Isaac's wife, is sulking. It turns out, when Isaac was a bridegroom, he received a lot fewer linens than Sarah did. What nonsense! We can make another dozen for him now—end of story! Why should Meyer worry about stuff like this?

Finally in the fall, Sarah and Pavel's wedding is held at Telyatichi. People drink and party for the usual number of days, and the Telyatichi house feels like an inn on market day in a county town. Fifteen people sit in every room and whisper to each other; Jews like to whisper at weddings as well as funerals. Fine, let them! Is this not a good wedding? Is there a single self-respecting landowner in the district who didn't feel obliged to visit Raskin, down a shot of aged rye vodka, and express his joy about the wedding? Let them whisper!

After the wedding, the house empties out like a barn in springtime. Chests and baskets are loaded onto wagons. Pavel Rusevich ties ropes around the luggage himself, numbering each "article" with a goose quill.

"Best of luck, my dears," says Meyer, pulling a handkerchief out of his pocket. His nose is bluish, but he only needs the handkerchief for waving. That's the only reason why he pulled it out.

And now Sarah is gone; she will be sending letters. Sometimes Meyer forgets this and rushes into her room. Books on the shelves, white curtains on the window, a dried-out plant in a pot . . .

"Sarah," her father calls out and only then remembers that she is gone, that she will be sending letters. Oh, absentmindedness!

After five days, a letter arrives from Lodz.

"Pass me my glasses," Meyer asks his wife and proceeds to read, muttering, "Healthy, thank God. . . . Life is good. . . . They don't have samovars here; they boil water for tea in a kettle on a Primus stove. . . . Please write, dear parents, don't forget me. . . . Pavel goes to work, I'm alone all day . . ."

"I figure she's happy," says Meyer. "What do you think, Chava? Of course she's happy . . ."

5

Chava likes to philosophize from time to time; she must have inherited this trait from her gloomy father. In summer, the children would pester her, put a cape over her shoulders almost by force, and take her for a walk in the landlord's park. The enormous park is cool and dark; Bolesław Żuk planted it back when he was young. Here and there, graceful white gazebos appear among the thickets like ghosts. Every nook, stone, or structure associate with some grim story from the past. Here a disgraced serf girl hanged herself; here a coachman who was favored by the owner's wife was mauled to death by dogs; and here a dearly beloved pooch is buried. Żuk was inconsolable; he erected a headstone on the dog's grave which said, in Latin, "Farewell, Caesar, my only true friend."

The rectangular pond is surrounded by tightly spaced firs. The water in the pond is dark green; one has to get really close to it and bend down low in order to catch a glimpse of blue sky in its center. Chava stops by the pond and watches. A row of ducklings swims over its smooth surface, lightly pushing the heavy water with their tiny feet and leaving behind long, fast disappearing ripples. They are still young and covered with brown fuzz, but the water is their element; they luxuriate in it. And nearby on the shore, a hen—the mother of the ducklings—frets and squawks plaintively, scratching the ground with her wings and puffing her feathers. She had been sitting gently on some eggs, protecting them with her motherly warmth. But then the chicks hatched from the eggs—and the hen couldn't possibly have known that they were duck eggs. She has a mother's affection for the ducklings, and the young generation may also be attached to her. But then a stretch of water appears—the hen is abandoned, and the ducklings swim across the pond.

And Chava thinks, "Life, how cruel your laws are. Doesn't the hen love her ducklings? Don't the ducklings love their hen? Is it really impossible for all of them to live their lives together until their days?"

Chava stands and thinks; the minutes tick quietly. The picture that led her to these thoughts disappears, her own life floats toward her. Ahoy, days of the past, no pity and no regrets! At a certain age you probably stop thinking about yourself and transfer the joys you haven't experienced onto your children. Your only wish is that your children will be happy, and that their lives will be easy and joyful. But . . . are they really?

The Raskin family is growing every which way. Is our Meyer emulating the late Ephraim Livshitz, by any chance? The Telyatichi house is so full in the summer that guests sleep not only in the living room and the dining room, but even on the glassed-in veranda. Rachel comes with her two children, a boy and a girl. Isaac and Luba arrive. Their new baby boy is sickly, screaming and whining all day long; a full-breasted Polish wet nurse takes care of him. Isaac and Luba bring their relatives. What Jewish man or woman wouldn't want to admire nature, breathe the healthy fresh air, and have a glass of milk "right from the cow?" Here too is Sarah with her husband, Pavel Rusevich. He comes for ten days only, no more and no less. The school break has begun, and young fellows in uniforms have started appearing at the Raskins', young Jewish fellows in commercial school uniforms. Hersh brings a friend for a few days, the son of melamed Wiener. A female teacher comes for Sheva, there's nowhere for them to study so they go into the garden. The teacher's querying voice, smooth and pleasant, carries inside.

"If a dozen apples cost fifteen kopecks, how much did the boy pay for thirty-six apples?"

They sit at a small round table under the fruit trees and work out the difficult question of how much the arithmetical boy paid to the seller. And in that instant, an apple bursting with Telyatichi juices suddenly and resonantly lands on the open pages: here I am!

The Telyatichi house is really crowded in summer; space is tight at the Raskins'. When this happens, people quickly get tired of each other and begin to notice things they would have never noticed under different circumstances. For God's sake, who could be bothered by the tidy Pavel Rusevich? One would think that every man is entitled to his quirks. The creases on his trousers, the mustache guard, the fact that he always hangs his coat in the same spot, with the exact same movements—no one should care. Incidentally, he came for exactly ten days, he doesn't stick his nose into anybody's business, he will soon be gone, back to his bookkeeping. Sophia is nauseous, so Pavel brings her a small enamel wash basin and explains that there's nothing to worry about—it is normal for a young woman to be nauseous. Luba Raskin watches him with a snide smirk; later, rolling her black Gypsy eyes, she'll say something to her husband, and before you know it, Isaac begins to watch him, too. First he makes an innocent remark, then, unrebuffed, he takes it to the next level—and a conflict flares up. Pavel Rusevich, you see, is not a terribly smart man; he can be pricked by a tongue, and he won't have a quick response. Sarah—now Sophia—is all fired up; she loses patience and replies to Isaac, also with just one sharp word, a mere hint.

Every man should live by his own wits and manage his affairs based on his own energy level. But what if a man has too much energy, enough to share with others? Then what? Then . . . Meyer Raskin watches his son-in-law closely, sizing him up. How much longer should Pavel Rusevich work to build up someone else's fortune? It is true that he has got enough to live on. He has a small apartment, and everything else a young man needs. But one has to think about the future too. And in any case, who could be happy working for others?

And so Meyer thinks up plans and projects for Pavel Rusevich. Some twenty miles from Telyatichi, there are lands that belong to Senator Skirmunt. Mr. Skirmunt owns a large textile mill. What if Pavel Rusevich were to contact Skirmunt and become his commercial agent, opening a wholesale warehouse of the Senator's textiles in Lodz?

At first, Rusevich won't hear of it. Pavel can't see how he could live without a paycheck. What if the business fails? But Meyer presses on, and one day they go off to meet Skirmunt. Pavel gets the contract.

A few months later, he is sitting behind a tall desk in his own warehouse, ordering clerks and salesmen around in a loud, new voice, the same way that others used to order him around in his younger days. He fusses, he tries hard, he twirls his mustache, but things are not going well: he is short of money. So he sends a registered letter to Raskin, arguing that a business requires capital. Could Raskin loan him—in exchange for a promissory note, of course—three thousand rubles? Not waiting for a reply, he goes to Telyatichi and repeats the request in his pretentious mixture of German and Yiddish. Isaac loses patience and reminds Meyer what Meyer himself once said—that you can't squeeze a single kopeck out of Telyatichi. Meyer furrows his brow and keeps humming his song. If push comes to shove, he can borrow the 3,000 for Pavel from the bank. Isaac is furious and becomes caustic; Luba cautiously supports him. Sarah politely remarks that the matter concerns Meyer Raskin and Pavel Rusevich alone—just the two of them and no one else.

"Then why are you meddling?" snaps Isaac.

A year passes. The business isn't paying for itself, and Pavel Rusevich is thinking about closing the warehouse. The owner of the factory where he used to work offers him his old job back, even promises a raise. But Pavel Rusevich was stung by his father-in-law's opinions. At some point, Meyer had loaned him three thousand rubles. Why shouldn't Rusevich borrow another five thousand or so from him? Coupled with the dowry, this will make a tidy sum. With money like this, he could start his own business making textiles on leased machines. Or would it be better to return to his good old job? As a bookkeeper, he understands that working for a factory owner is safer. But he can't get Meyer Raskin's wealth off his mind. . . . What to do?

We can leave him to ruminate over this for the time being and turn to the two younger sons, the Raskins' second generation. Pavel Rusevich's plans will later fall in line with what one of the Raskins wanted—and things will take a very different turn.

When someone is growing up right in front of you, you can follow his development casually, without much effort. His eyes slowly acquire a different expression, his voice changes and breaks. The boy stands in front of the mirror and feels despondent about his freckles. Every day he applies water and cologne to his unruly, springy hair ever more thoroughly. But what if this is happening out of your sight? What if you only get the chance to take a good look at these young men once a year—and only during the busiest time of the year at that?

In that case, a man appears in front of you without warning. The boy is now a man. The duckling has seen the water's gleaming surface, flapped its still weak wings, not yet covered with stiffened feathers, touched the water with its feet—and now it is swimming, swimming, swimming . . .

What can one say about the Raskin boys? The younger one, Motya, has at least retained his affectionate nature. He has a strong and tender, yearning love for his aging parents. He'll come home, run inside without taking his coat off, dash to his mother, hug her, and for a few minutes kiss her and regard her intently. A lock of gray hair sticking out from under her wig will make his heart sink. He'll look away and ask in a changed voice,

"How are you feeling?"

"Not too bad," his mother will reply, agitatedly going through her pockets in search of a handkerchief. "Not too bad. It's just that this thirst is getting the better of me. I am so thirsty. The other night I woke up, walked over to the dresser, saw a glass of water, and started drinking. Well, it turned out that Meyer had prepared some boric acid for his inflamed finger. I drank it up and didn't even notice . . ." Seeing her son's face fall, she adds hastily,

"It's fine, it's nothing. . . . The thirst is already going away, it's fine . . ."

The boy is concerned. Oh my God, how many times did he say that she needed to see a doctor! It's outrageous!

In the evening he sits by his father and muses,

"Remember, when I was little, you used to give me a kopeck for every white hair I pulled from your head? Back then, I could barely earn a dime. But now I could get rich this way. . . . Maybe now you'll pay me for every black one? Wait, wait. Last year, when you frowned, your forehead showed six wrinkles. You used to say, 'One wrinkle for each child.' Now you've got seven, and look, here's the eighth. It crosses the fifth and the sixth—that is, me and Sheva. Do you remember what I used to call you when I was little? I called you Kamelik. Why Kamelik? I don't know, I swear; isn't that funny?"

On the very first day, Motya manages to survey the whole house and the estate. He is lively and impressionable, he notices all the changes and remembers everything. This room wasn't wallpapered; a spider had woven his transparent nest in the corner. I wonder if it's still there. Yes, yes, it is! So the maid remembered Motya's request not to remove the spider. Good for her! There's mail on the triangular corner table. Well, look at that! A letter from America to a local woman has been lying here since Christmas. Did she die, or is it just that nobody has bothered to pass on to her the unhappy lines from her husband living across the ocean? Motya flies around the estate like a whirlwind, young men greet him, he nods at everyone, finding a few minutes for each.

"Hey, Semyon, greetings!" he shouts, "How are you, my friend? How is Pashka?"

Semyon sits on a tall wagon, on top of a moving mountain of straw.

"With God's help. He's already a shepherd boy, the owner pays him fifteen rubles for the summer. Kindly climb up here, Master!"

He yells, "Whoa!" and the horses stop. Motya looks at him from below and wonders aloud in Belarusian,

"How can I reach you from here, my brother?"

Lame Semyon, puffing away on top of the straw and urging the horses on, relates his farmhand's troubles with a calmness and indifference that Motya cannot fathom. His wife fell ill, you see; at the busiest time of year she just went ahead and fell ill. She needs to be taken to the district hospital in Drahicyn; there's no way she can walk there, his wife. He asked mister leaseholder for a horse to take his wife there, that is. But the owner, Motya's father, that is, was very busy, so he says, "Wait till the fall," he says, "can't do it now, harvest time." Well, it's true, of course, harvest time, but the wife won't make it to the fall, she'll die, that's what.

"Then why don't you get mad and quit?" Motya suggests.

"Eh, Master, what's the point, that is? Nobody would hire me in mid-summer, and even if they do? Working for Kantorov is even worse, and in Zakoziel the manager is a German, he'd never hire anyone with a limp. So that's it then, time for the old woman to die."

"You'll get a wagon tomorrow," says the boy, agitated. "Definitely!"

There's still much Motya doesn't understand about life. How could his father, his kindly father, treat Semyon like this? Semyon has been at Telyatichi for five years—nothing to sneeze at!

"Semyon," Motya asks the man after some contemplation, "is my father a good man? Tell me the truth—is he?"

"But of course," Semyon replies. "He's a good master, a true master, may God keep him in good health."

Hersh is very different. He probably doesn't know the farmhands' names or who lives where. He's still sulky and secretive, although his sulkiness is nothing like Isaac's melancholy and unhappiness. He's reserved with the family, he'd never have a heart-to-heart with anyone. People hear about him from others, but nobody dares to check the rumors with Hersh himself—is this true or not? Perhaps his classmates were right when they said that he looked like an old man, too bad he didn't have a beard. He draws pretty well, paints from life with oils, makes a self-portrait with a palette in his hand. Then the green background around his figure feels too open and empty, so he imitates Böcklin, adding a skeleton with a violin in its bony hands standing behind him. Mother sees the portrait, gasps, and becomes agitated.

"What's the matter with you? How can you paint a thing like that?"

The portrait hangs in the living room for a few weeks, spooking Sheva and the servants. Gradually, Hersh begins to notice flaws in his own work. The complexion is not right, the folds of the suit look like pig iron, the brush strokes are uncertain and timid. The portrait needs to be redone, but Hersh doesn't feel like doing it. He takes the canvas off the wall and paints it over with white.

When Hersh comes to Telyatichi for vacations, his room feels like a museum and a zoo all at once. He nurses a wounded hare until it dies. Then he stuffs it. A squirrel constantly scampers and circles inside a wheel. A lizard whizzes under a glass cover.

"It'll bite you!" a peasant warns him, watching the young man trying to catch a lizard with his hands. "Get it with a stick, the tail will fall off right away!"

But Hersh doesn't listen, he doesn't even bother to explain to the man that a lizard's bite isn't poisonous.

He often wanders around the woods and fields, avoiding places where he might run into other people. He'll come home and rush to the triangular table, asking glumly and seriously,

"Any letters for me?"

He does receive letters, and it begins to alarm his father. Meyer looks at his son warily, furrowing his brow, not daring to ask directly who exactly his son is corresponding with. He prefers to surprise Motya with questions, but it's hard to get anything useful out of his younger son.

—Does Hersh have a lot of acquaintances?

—Lots.

—Boys?

—Boys.

—And girls?

—And girls.

—Who is he corresponding with? A boy or a girl?

—I don't know.

Soon everything becomes clear—there are new worries and concerns for his old parents! Just when he starts receiving letters, Hersh begins to muse about how he needs to prepare for living independently. He is supposed to start a new grade at the commercial school, but he's not even planning to finish it. Why on earth would he waste two more years? Say he finishes this school and gets his piece of paper. What would he do with it? He can't go to university. That leaves the Higher School of Commerce. He would spend several years there, and then what? Become a bookkeeper in a bank?

Anticipating an answer that he won't like, Meyer furrows his brow in advance and asks, "So what are you going to do?"

The young man frowns, adjusts his gold eyeglasses, and replies, "In the fall, I'd like to go to Krakow, to the Academy of Fine Arts."

Krakow? Academy of Fine Arts? Become a painter for life?

Meyer Raskin's son will be a dauber, he will be poor—of course he will be poor, all these "artists" are poor, always dying of hunger. Oh, man. . . . Small children—small troubles; big children—big troubles. As is his nature, Meyer can only hint—hint that he doesn't like Hersh's plan one bit. And Chava? Another mother would have talked to her son, she would have explained to him . . .

"And you, why aren't you saying anything?" Chava asks Meyer, who responds only with a sigh. Can't Chava imagine that he doesn't, simply doesn't have the time to deal with this? He is busy, you know.

That is the excuse that Meyer Raskin offers.

Soon the whole story with Hersh's correspondence comes into the open. Suddenly in the summer, without saying anything, he begins to pack for a trip. Meyer makes a huge effort and asks him where he is going.

"I'm going to see some friends," Hersh replies. "They are in Domachev near Brest-Litovsk, at their summer cottage, so that's where I'm going."

He leaves for about ten days and then returns with a gymnasium girl of about sixteen. The day before, he informs his parents that he will be bringing his friends' daughter named Fanya for a visit. So that's why Hersh needs his independence!

"I don't understand people, I just don't," Meyer tells his wife while tossing and turning in bed restlessly. "Another father would have kicked this young lady out of the house. Or he would have gone to her parents and made a scene: why are you bothering a seventeen-year-old boy with this 'independence?' Why aren't you letting him study peacefully? You like my money, don't you? But you're not getting any of it. Another father . . ."

"Another father, another mother . . . ," Chava mocks him. "I have a secret to tell you. The secret is that you are a doormat. And since you are a doormat, then you should keep quiet."

And so Meyer keeps quiet. The girl stays in Telyatichi for as long as she and Hersh want. If during this time a curious Jew drops in, Raskin mumbles sheepishly that the young lady is their distant kin. My oh my! Meyer Raskin married off the first three, but it looks like the last three will do it on their own. New times, new times! Good thing Hersh doesn't seem to be in a hurry with the wedding. Give thanks for small blessings.

Hersh is determined, however, to make his idea of independence a reality. He talks about Krakow more and more; he's preparing to go. And Meyer begins to yield. Why should Hersh be a dauber and not a first-class artist like Repin or Antokolsky? Even Mr. Żuk's daughter, who knows something about all this artistry, says that Hersh will go far, that one senses a God-given gift in his work. Let him do what he wants. We'll see, we'll see!

But that brings the issue of Motya to the fore. What to do about Motya? You can't leave the boy alone in Brest-Litovsk. Besides, he is having problems with the French teacher who is forcing him to retake tests repeatedly. Motya is unhappy with his studies, he finds no joy in the commercial school.

"Maybe you too should think about independence?" Meyer loses his patience. "When will you bring a young lady to Telyatichi?"

The boy flushes and looks down. That's not it, that's not what he's thinking about. But Meyer is glad to have his younger son answer for the troubles brought by the older one.

"That's all I need now," says the old man. "'Don't you dare. . . . A boy must do what his parents want him to do."

But what do his parents want? Could Meyer answer his own question?

And this is when Pavel Rusevich arrives at Telyatichi to negotiate the loan of five thousand rubles. He practices his German/Jewish dialect, he schemes, he assures that his plan is solid. In a few days he has a stroke of genius. Lodz has textile schools. Even the richest mill owners in Lodz send their kids to these schools that train real experts, true aces. Why wouldn't Meyer send Motya to Lodz? He'd stay with Rusevich and go to such a school. In a few years he would become an expert. He'd be able to open his own mill. Or we could open a mill together: Motya, with his new knowledge would later join Pavel Rusevich's business, Pavel Rusevich's profitable business for which Pavel is now asking for a loan of 5,000 rubles.

Meyer likes this project better than Hersh's "independence." Motya is blown away by the idea, it's all he can talk about. He'll go to Lodz, he'll go to Lodz! Lodz and nowhere else!

"Say, what's your take on this?" Meyer asks Ilya tentatively.

Ilya starts fretting and hesitating, the quiet Ilya who is always busy and doesn't meddle in other people's affairs. Why are they asking him about such outlandish things? Since when do boys do whatever they please?

Meyer tries to drop the topic. He was hoping that Ilya would approve of the idea. Let's just not talk about it.

But life goes on, and Ilya's words cannot stop that. Brest-Litovsk is no more. In the fall, Hersh leaves for Krakow and Motya for Lodz.

6

The Raskin house grows quiet and sad when everyone leaves in the fall. Time, it seems, stretches lazily and sleepily on the couch under the large brass pendulum of the wall clock. And the pendulum itself slows down, feeling tired. Its shiny disk becomes covered with inconspicuous dust. A lazy tomcat bats the glass with his paw and kills the last busily buzzing fly. The gardeners have dismantled their branch huts and departed. The garden has emptied out; touched by autumnal freshness, its scarlet foliage falls away. A flame red apple has survived at the top of a tree, hidden from greedy human eyes. The leaves have thinned out, revealing the fruit which now gleams in the sunlight. Wild geese appear drawn in the sky like little arrows. The gloom of the Belarusian fields doesn't suit them; the geese are flying south. A shepherd continues playing his bleak melody on a long birch trumpet, and suddenly the glasses in the cupboard start to resonate. It's as if life itself is completing its cycle; old, tired life moves its legs slowly, choosing a warm and comfortable spot in which to fall asleep forever. The hour will strike and the old will vanish, yielding its place to something new and different.

Chava is very thirsty. She wanders from corner to corner, wraps a shawl around her shoulders, and tries to think about her children and what awaits them. Her own life must be coming to an end; this is certainly her last decade. But her thoughts circle back to the mysterious ailment that dries her out on the inside. Chava drinks water and tea glass after glass. She hardly eats anything. Not wanting to alarm Meyer, she tells him that she couldn't wait for him any longer and ate dinner without him, but she'd be happy to have some tea. While he sits and eats, she slips into the kitchen several times, sinks her trembling lips into a dipper of water, and drinks it down. Then she quietly returns, sits down next to her husband, puts her hands on his broad shoulders, and lovingly looks into his eyes.

"Meyer," she says, "you are getting older, you know . . ."

"Am I?" Raskin wipes his beard with his hand and strokes his mustache. "And I thought it was just the opposite—I'm getting younger, and soon you'll be sewing me those kid's pants, like you do for our grandson, Ilya's Moses."

He suddenly becomes serious. His faithful glance registers drops of water on his wife's blouse. He furrows his brow and asks with alarm, "Have you been drinking water again? Tell me honestly, have you been drinking?"

Without waiting for an answer, he abruptly pushes his plate away, kicks his chair back, and starts racing around the room.

"No, no, it's all my fault!" he shouts harshly and pulls on his beard. "A person is practically expiring in front of me, and I just keep asking questions. It's like the Lord has punished me by taking my mind away. . . . Oh! . . . What's the matter?"

Tears roll slowly down Chava's face like two translucent beads. But her expression is serene, and her eyes, refreshed by tears, hint at a forlorn and tender smile.

"You're a grownup, Meyer," she says quietly, "but sometimes I feel that you're like a boy. A boy who has suddenly become stubborn: I don't want to go to cheder, I don't want to and that's that! But, my dear husband, a boy needs to go to cheder."

"Please, no philosophizing!" retorts Meyer, wincing. "I don't like it and I'm not good at it. What does a boy have to do with anything? Stop it, please! I've listened to you—enough of that, now you listen to me. Tomorrow we're going to Brest to see some doctors—end of discussion. If you love me, even just a bit, please don't argue; it won't help anyway."

"You should have taken me to Brest last year, when the younger kids were there. . . . But it didn't occur to you back then . . ."

"'Didn't occur, didn't occur. . . .' We're not going there to have fun. Well, enough of that, I've made up my mind, we're going to Brest tomorrow."

The next day the old couple sets out. They huddle together and hunch over in their open buggy. Meyer holds an umbrella over their heads. Drops of heavy, driving rain play an intricate beat on the tightly stretched silk. The road has already turned into muck, it quivers like dough in a bread trough. Ivan has tied up the horses' tails. Green winter crops sprout on both sides of the road. Wet jackdaws waddle around the stubbled fields like elderly peasants. Caw!—and suddenly they take off in an angled line, awkwardly raising their crooked legs. Caw! Small leafless trees caped in mist can be seen farther out. During the first year of the lease, mast pines grew here. They were sold to a tenant and cut down. Now, in the ninth year of the lease, young trees are rising up in the same spot. So there!

In the city, the old couple goes to see specialists.

"Money is not an issue," Meyer jokes with the doctors, "just fix my old woman, please. I think anything can be fixed. The Telyatichi distillery is as old as a torn shoe—and even it can be fixed, and it'll be good for another year. After that—more fixing."

As the doctors wearing gold eyeglasses put their hairy ears to the old woman's chest, Meyer watches them with alarm.

"Maybe she needs to go to some resort?" he queries. "Maybe some spa? Go abroad, perhaps? Never mind that my lady is not wearing a hat, I've got enough money."

He pays them generously, they thank him respectfully and look at the old man carefully. One of them, an old Jew with a shaved head, wearing a colonel's uniform, asks,

"And you, Mr. Raskin, how is your health?"

Meyer gets up and with one broad downward motion points at his whole body,

"See for yourself. I wish my old woman was this healthy."

"I don't see anything," says the old colonel with a shaved head. "The fact that you are fat doesn't mean anything. Kindly step behind the screen, I'll use a little hammer on you."

Hidden by the screen, he feels and probes the leaseholder of Telyatichi.

"Do you drink milk?" asks the doctor.

"I do."

"And you like fried chicken, don't you?"

"Yes."

"With white bread, of course?"

"Well, occasionally . . ."

"Congratulations then. You have cardiac obesity. You need to eat less, and your wife needs to eat more."

He thinks that Meyer is about to object, so blood rushes to the old doctor's head. He still has his habits from the military and treats patients as if they were soldiers.

"What's that?" he shouts. "Quiet! No objections! Jewish food? None of this stupid kosher! You wife must eat ham! As much caviar as she can, a pound of butter each day! What? Push it down her throat, end of discussion!

What? You two sit in your lair and develop ailments! Quiet! Your wife has high blood sugar, she has diabetes, you understand? She should drink Vichy water and go to Carlsbad in the summer. You—to Marienbad, to lose weight, she—to Carlsbad, to gain some."

He calms down, stops shouting, and switches to Yiddish.

"Do you understand me, my dear oldsters?"

Hearing her native tongue, Chava replies, "I don't understand anything of your medical matters. But I do understand. Sugar schmugar—those are just empty words. I think my heart has gone bad. And you're not going to give me a new heart, are you? Just tell me what's wrong with my Meyer, I'm really worried . . ."

"No worries! You will take care of yourselves—and you will live. Do you think I'm healthy? I'm sick, too. All people are sick."

No worries. Meyer comforts Chava, Chava comforts Meyer, but their eyes increasingly show alarm. Pretty soon Meyer forgets about his ailment. What is this cardiac obesity anyway? He will eat less, and there will be no obesity. He is worried about Chava growing weaker. Meyer spends more and more time at home. He has learned to write long letters to his children, he writes them for hours on end, then he reads them to his wife out loud. Here's the rule: if she won't eat, Meyer won't read to her. She should have mercy on his old age and eat one more morsel, just one extra morsel. Without the silliness and the philosophizing, sick people live on for decades. He knows for a fact that diabetes is dangerous when you're young, but old people can live with it to a hundred years. No worries!

Meyer can afford the luxury of spending an extra hour at home. But he is still very busy all around, it's hard for him to sit idly. He was told not to walk fast, but he forgets about it the moment he leaves the house. He is convinced that any ailment can be cured with work. It's only work, duties, constant drive that bring peace to the soul. If only Chava could understand that!

As soon as the springtime sowing is finished, Meyer applies for foreign passports. Personally, he would much rather stay home, but you can't send Chava abroad on her own. He cannot even imagine how she could possibly live alone in Carlsbad!

"Ilya," he says to his son, "you'll be in charge here. Look, Ilya, I don't need to tell you what to do, you know these things better than I do. Please send me a registered letter every three days and tell me about everything. Don't forget to send the lease payment to St. Petersburg on the first of the month."

"Of course," says Ilya in the same tone he used many years ago when the old man asked if he would be able to handle the plots in Adryzyn. "Of course," he repeats, biting his fingernail, "it goes without saying. There's one thing, though: the lease expires a year from now. Żuk has no obligation whatsoever to talk about the future with us until the lease is over. But we need to know what to do. Are we to sow the fields the same way we did in the first year of the lease, as the contract requires, or at twice the rate? During these nine years, the seeding rate has doubled."

"Oh yes, yes," Meyer replies absentmindedly. "As soon as I get back, I'll talk to Żuk. I most certainly will."

During many a sleepless night, Meyer has already been thinking about the future. Now he feels uncomfortable: it's as if someone has put into words something very intimate, something he himself has not quite formulated yet. He has learned from very reliable sources that a son of the long-deceased Ephraim Livshitz—now an old man himself—went to see the landowner in St. Petersburg and offered to lease Telyatichi from him not for twelve but for twenty thousand per year. More than once last year Meyer, with a cheerful face, tried to talk to Żuk about the lease. Isn't it time for old friends to discuss the future over a glass of good old wine? What are his Lordship's thoughts on the subject of another decade? But each time Żuk got away with meaningless words.

"We'll see, we'll see," he mumbled, puffing on his cigar. "What's the rush? Time will tell."

Now, talking to Ilya, Meyer repeats the landowner's words.

"We'll see, we'll see," he says. "Why worry ahead of time? Time will tell."

But Meyer himself is already brimming with questions. He has had quite a few sleepless nights thinking about what is coming. Life never draws lines on the surface only. Each stage of life has its own mood. Ten years ago he was full of vigor. He used to make business decisions for everyone. He liked to take risks: without risking, Meyer would have never made it in the field he chose. He is still vigorous; by no means does he want to sit on his hands or, as old Jews do, put his savings into bonds and live off the interest. He knows himself well—he wouldn't survive a single month that way. No, one has to work, one has to strive, a man has no right to stop, to slow down, or else he'd immediately fall apart and grow old in a single week.

Meyer Raskin knows all this perfectly well; he feels it. But his agility and decisiveness are gone without a trace. These days, when thinking about the future, he has to take into account all kinds of circumstances. He has to remember that Isaac got cold feet and has repeatedly stated that for him, continuing to work at Telyatichi is out of the question. Isaac is an adult of course, he can be bought out, let him try to make it in the city. But what if he runs out of luck there and loses everything, God forbid? Then what?

There are other circumstances that Meyer has to take into account as well. Clearly the younger children will do something else in life. They certainly won't become leaseholders. So who will be running Telyatichi when he, Meyer, grows old?

There's yet another question, painful and worrisome: Chava's illness. The old woman needs care, she needs to be visited by a doctor at least once a week. So might it indeed be better to move to a city, say Brest, buy a house, settle down, and then get involved in something else?

So reflects Meyer, tossing and turning and weighing all the circumstances, overwhelmed with doubt. Like a cat, a man becomes accustomed to a place, to a house, and at times Meyer feels that he won't find peace outside of Telyatichi, that he won't find anything to apply his energies to.

These thoughts are reinforced by what he learned from the Jews he met at Marienbad, a foreign resort. What does a Jew do for a living?

He owns a wholesale warehouse or a wholesale food distributor. For a minute Meyer pictures himself in the place of such a Jew and cannot contain a bitter chuckle. A great line of work! What does a Jew do? He does big business in commissions, he goes to cafes, he fiddles with his walking stick—and money somehow flows into his coffers without any effort. What a lovely occupation!

Don't you ever want to do some real work? See the fruits of your labor? Take pleasure in them? Odd! Yes, very, very odd!

Meyer is bored with these fat, bloated resort-goers. He has nothing to talk to them about. He is drawn away from them, so he goes to the fields and watches the German peasants. They work hard, their work is beautiful, and so is their rest. They sit between the plots during lunchtime and engage in lively discussion. Their blonde-haired daughters bring them lunch from the village. The peasants spread their snow-white napkins, eat, drink their beer, which makes them turn pink, and read their newspapers. Peasants read newspapers at lunch! Meyer can't resist approaching them and sits down next to them. People start talking, total strangers start talking. They have common interests, common thoughts: their work. Meanwhile, the letters from Ilya are more and more troubling. Ilya is clearly nervous, worried. Żuk came to Telyatichi for the summer; he is besieged with offers. The Peasant Land Bank wants to purchase Telyatichi, split it into small farms, and sell those to peasants. Countess Bobrinski, the owner of Zakoziel, also wants to buy the estate.

Countess Bobrinski! Ilya cannot help but sound sarcastic in his letter, even though he is not acerbic at all. German managers, numbered outbuildings, yeast factories and distilleries, medical checkups for farmhands, veterinarians, phone lines between different units, their own shipping offices—and in the end, an estate three times the size of Telyatichi generates fifty thousand rubles per year in losses! The general manager makes a thousand rubles a month! "And how much does he steal?" Ilya asks in his letter, forgetting that this is beside the point and is none of Ilya's business. Does the Countess visit the estate at least once a year? Do farmhands stay at Zakoziel for more than one season?

Meyer reads the letter, his hands trembling imperceptibly. All of sudden he feels the urge to share with someone. He suddenly notices the four walls of his Austrian hotel room, the metal bed, the quilted blanket, the curtains, the electric bells near the door, the switches. He wants to ring these bells all at once, turn on the lights, gather all the hotel guests. . . . Exhausted, he cannot help but lay down on his bed. Some Germans are talking in the hallway. Water is slowly dripping into the sink. The clock ticks resonantly next to his heart. Meyer gets up, hastily stuffs a towel and a bar of soap into his pocket, and leaves the room without looking. He hurries to the station and takes the first train to Carlsbad to see his wife.

And how is Chava doing?

Chava is happy to see him. Chava is bored. Chava wears her dressing gown to the mineral spring and everyone notices. What's so terrible about wearing a cotton dressing gown to the spring?

"Nothing, nothing terrible," Meyer agrees, "although it wouldn't hurt you to put a decent dress on. But you better tell me: what are we going to do with our lives? Where would you like to live next?"

So Chava starts with her allegories—apparently she cannot do it any other way. A man built a house and put a metal roof on it. And then, when everything is done, he begins to ask how to build the house, what color to paint the roof? But the house is already built, the color of the roof will make no difference whatsoever.

"You've become impossible, you've become absolutely impossible," Meyer grumbles.

Then he remembers that he's dealing with a sick person and changes his tone immediately.

"Oh, forget it, there is no reason to sulk and overthink things. Do I really need to conquer the world? Our old age is secure, thank God. And you are better now, you look really good, Chava. Look at the test results— just a mere half a percent of sugar left to go. We'll have a great life, old woman! Let's go buy you some presents. Chop-chop!"

But a sad smile touches Chava's lips. He's a big child, that Meyer, just a big child, may God give him many more years. And if he gets married after she dies—may God send him an honest woman.

Now she feels that she overdid it. She hugs her husband and says,

"Yes, you're right, I'm much better now. If that is God's will, I will keep on living, He'll give us a happy old age. How are you feeling? What do the children write?"

7

By the time the old couple returns from their foreign trip, Telyatichi resembles a disturbed anthill. Things are coming to a head too quickly! The future of Telyatichi doesn't need to be decided until a year from now, but in all likelihood it will happen earlier. Ilya was right: Żuk is accosted from all sides. The landowner has no emotional ties to Telyatichi, so his reasoning is simple. How much rent does he get? Twelve thousand. Let us assume that the next leaseholder will pay him twenty thousand. Let us further assume that he can make another ten thousand a year by selling timber without damaging the estate. Altogether thirty thousand—and that's very optimistic. And now he has an offer to sell the estate for eight hundred thousand. Even if he just puts the money in the bank at six percent—that's forty-eight thousand annually. Forty-eight thousand without lifting a finger.

Żuk wouldn't even discuss leasing at this point. Meyer Raskin has a ten-year lease, and only nine of the ten years have passed thus far. But that's small potatoes. Countess Bobrinski will come to an agreement with Meyer, she will take care of dealing with him. She'll buy all the implements from Meyer down to the smallest trinket, she will offer him compensation, and if he doesn't agree—it will be his loss.

An unsettling wind rushes across Telyatichi and moves on, disturbing the nearby thatched-roof villages. The peasants are in the grip of worry and fear, bodily fear for their scant livelihoods. Old men sit on a bench and hash out their lamentable fate. Then they put on their best kaftans, polish their tall boots with tar, tie sashes around their waists, and go to see his Lordship Żuk at Telyatichi. They stand by the white columns of the mansion for hours until his Lordship comes out to meet them. Then, as if on cue, they kneel and plead for mercy—that is, "not to sell" them.

Mr. Żuk doesn't quite understand. He claps, and a chair is brought out for him. He sits down and tries to explain that the old men must have gotten something wrong. Serfdom has long been abolished, so he cannot sell them even if he wanted to.

But the peasants persist, old peasants with greenish-gray beards in boots that reek unpleasantly of tar. They even begin to argue that life was better under serfdom. Yes, indeed. Back then, a landowner was supposed to take at least some care of the souls he owned. And now? So Mr. Żuk is selling the estate to Countess Bobrinski. The peasants don't own any pastures, they pay to use Telyatichi land. But the Countess does not rent out pastures on any of her estates. So what are they supposed to do? What would happen to the livestock? So it does mean that Mr. Żuk is selling the peasants down the river. "It's total ruin, your Lordship, by God it's ruin." All of them, and their fathers, and their grandfathers have worked this land, so may his Lordship have mercy.

They pause, spell out their complaints, and start the whole story anew. His Lordship gets tired of this gloomy tune, and on top of that, the reek of tar from the peasants' boots is unbearable. Do these fools really think that he would turn down 800,000 rubles? Why don't they tell him right now, this very moment, what is better: 30,000 or forty-eight? He pulls a five ruble bill out of his vest pocket, gives it to them to buy themselves some vodka, and looks into the distance. The old men thank him for listening and shake their beards. Their eyes are moist. May his Lordship have mercy and not sell his peasants. Żuk abruptly turns around and goes back inside. Lackeys chase the peasants away, "Look, they flattened all the flower beds with their boots, they stunk up the air—what boors!"

An unsettling wind is blowing through Telyatichi. Peasants with younger and more restless blood hear the elders out. Their eyes turn red, and they propose to put the estate to the torch. Maybe that will make the Countess give up her plans? But the oldsters have long memories, they remember that eight years earlier things like that brought about floggings, hangings, and firing squads. "We've got nothing to lose," the young ones argue. "We're finished either way."

Learning about this, Meyer hurries to accept the offer from Countess Bobrinski. Young foreign-looking men—in breeches, spats, and starched collars—roam the estate, the fields, and the woods. They measure, they examine, they record. They enter the house without knocking, count the rooms, inventory the furnishings. The farmhands have completely lost their minds: they don't know whose orders to follow or who the boss is. Old managers, lawyers, foresters run around like mad. One day they sneak in to see the Countess's representative to show their loyalty to the new master, reporting secrets and gossip. The next day, they go to see Meyer Raskin, the former boss. Will Raskin really abandon them just like that? Telyatichi is "finished." But there are other estates out there! Maybe Meyer can lease another estate and take all his staff with him?

During these few weeks, Meyer has lost more weight than he did in Marienbad. People pester him from morning till night, but he's got nothing to tell them. Nothing! Meyer is confused, stunned, floored; he did not expect the end to come so quickly. He looks at Ilya, he notices his rounder, larger eyes, his longer, thinner nose, and he tries to console his oldest son. What's the problem? Actually, there isn't much of a problem. Nine years ago, the Raskins had very limited means. During these nine years, Meyer married off the first three children. All are doing well. All have money. Not counting his sons' money, Meyer has seventy-five thousand rubles. Ilya also has at least twenty-five and maybe even thirty thousand. Same for Isaac. So what's the problem? Now they will take a break, look around, and start something else. There are other fish in the sea, plenty of things to do besides Telyatichi. Cheer up!

Meyer's comforting words have exactly the opposite effect on Ilya. He wakes up at the crack of dawn and rushes outside. The air above Dubovoye is pale blue and clear, the sun is not quite up yet. As is his habit, Ilya hurries to the stables, then stops halfway. The stables are no longer his. If he wants to take a horse out he has to ask permission from the new manager. The manager has taken over two rooms in his quarters in Dubovoye even before Ilya has moved out. No, he doesn't need a horse now. And he has nowhere to hurry either. Ilya has nowhere to hurry! He walks slowly into the field, thinking depressing thoughts. The curse of his people is upon him. The ground that he walks on, the same ground that has absorbed more than a few drops of his sweat—this ground doesn't belong to him. A hard worker, he is nevertheless being booted out like some lazy shepherd.

He stands there for a long time. The sun rises over the earth. Its golden orb is reflected in a splash of dew. Young peasants are going to work, shepherds are driving a herd. Everyone looks grim. The boys whip the oxen with all their might. "What did the oxen do?" Ilya wants to yell to them. But his throat only produces a hoarse sound: his voice, his word doesn't carry much weight anymore. Ilya turns around and hurries home. He is ashamed, he is desperately ashamed. He prays to God that he doesn't run into anybody on his way back. Ilya is ashamed—but of what?

An unsettling wind is blowing through Telyatichi. Meyer has become talkative, he keeps telling everyone that everything is great, but it's obvious that he doesn't really believe his own words. A person gets accustomed to a house the way a cat does. Even Chava is quietly crying. One would think she would be the least sad of all of them. She'll find hundreds of Jewish women in the city, and Brest has a synagogue on every corner. Take your pick, Mrs. Raskin! But no, she sits by the window and bids farewell to everything in sight. Farewell trees; farewell outbuildings; farewell strangers. A new chapter is beginning in the life of the Raskins. Let Meyer brag about his assets. He approaches his old woman at his brisk, somewhat agitated gait and starts telling her lies. Everything is fine, everything is great. For the time being, he has rented an apartment in Brest for himself and Ilya. We'll rest, we'll have a good rest. We'll sleep until noon and in the evening we'll go to the cinema or the Jewish theater. Plenty of time, plenty of money. He is more than certain that those slick brokers have already come up with hundreds of business opportunities for him. They will come to Meyer and offer more and more opportunities. But there's no rush, this is not an auction. We'll look around carefully, and then we'll get involved in something if we wish to. We have money, we have free time, God has plenty of available opportunities. Isn't that right?

"Right," old Chava agrees, "of course that's right." But maybe Meyer could explain to her why the luggage is being taken to the station in the evening, why they themselves have decided to take the evening train when there's one at midday? Maybe Meyer could explain to her why is it that when peasants come to say goodbye to him, he anxiously hides in the back rooms and asks everyone to tell them that the master isn't home. Maybe Meyer could truthfully confess why he pretends to be asleep at night when he really isn't? Oh, well, here comes Ilya. Chava doesn't need Meyer's excuses. Better that the old man put on a happy face; she too will wipe off her tears, and they'll talk about something more cheerful.

Ilya enters the house and takes a few minutes to realize that it wouldn't hurt to say hello to his parents. What is it that he wanted to tell them? Oh yes! The luggage is on its way. All the luggage is gone. No reason to sit here and wait. Time to go. Why sit here with nothing to do? He cannot understand it and he doesn't want to. He shouts, his voice has been strained all this time. He shouts and flails his arms in front of his nose. He simply cannot understand it!

Fine, going means going. So the lamp with the white shade, which has already been packed and shipped to Brest-Litovsk, is replaced with an oil lamp from the kitchen, an unbearably smoky one. Squares and rectangles are visible where portraits used to hang on the walls. The rooms behind the dining room have already been vacated for good. All that is left is debris, empty medicine bottles, some boxes, some powders, tins, pages torn from missing books, cobwebs on the walls—the kind of refuse that is left behind in an abandoned house. Nearly ten years, a long stretch of life is being left behind. Chava thinks she hears a noise from behind a closed door.

"What noise?" Meyer asks irritably. His own voice spooks him so he repeats in whisper, "What noise?"

Chava opens the door, picks up the oil lamp, and starts walking through the rooms. Cold shivers run through her body. A cat scampers around the room. It has drunk some forgotten valerian extract and is now beside itself. It jumps up the walls, swings its tail, meows, knocks on the window glass. It doesn't hear Chava's voice, it has lost its mind. How did it happen that the cat has been left behind?

Ilya races into the room. He is short, with crooked legs, and his shadow swings across the walls and the ceiling like the sails of a windmill. He pulls at his hair, which is curly and light like goose down, and frets loudly. The horses have already been waiting for half an hour, people are gathering. If the Raskins don't leave right now, all of Telyatichi will converge at the porch. Can someone explain this regal departure to him? Do we really have to miss the train?

A coat is held open for Chava; she thrusts her arms into the burrows of the sleeves. The maids start wailing in the kitchen. Young men standing in the kitchen with their hats on puff on their smokes. Children collect the boxes that are lying around, get carried away, and start a fight. Meyer removes his bowler and mops his forehead. Large and massive, he looks like a monument now. He wanted to say something, he wanted to say something very important. But he has lost the thought. Ilya circles around him like a whirlwind. They will miss the train, Ilya simply cannot understand this regal departure at all.

"Best of luck!" Ilya quickly says goodbye to everyone on behalf of his whole family. "Best of luck, remember us kindly. We are in a hurry, we have to catch a train."

"I wanted to say something," Meyer utters one more time, continuing to mop his forehead. "Yes, I wanted to say what Ilya said. . . . Best of luck, remember us kindly, we have to go now . . ."

8

This is a new, third stage in the life of the Raskins: they are city dwellers now. They live in Brest-Litovsk. Through the windows and the glass door they watch people walking on the wooden sidewalks. All day long people walk on the sidewalks. When do they work? Or is it true that all these contractors, brokers, wholesalers, and agents really do nothing, that their work consists exclusively of walking?

In the beginning, they spend some time on bringing the apartment up to par. While at it, Luba Raskin can clearly see that her sister-in-law Rachel has no understanding of anything. For example, she doesn't understand what she needs a living room for. One can sit in the dining room or some other room. Similarly, Rachel refuses to wear a hat. No, she doesn't need a hat.

"But it's unseemly!" Luba, Isaac's wife, bursts out and winks at her husband sarcastically. "You're not a maid or something!"

It is hard, it is really hard for country people to get used to the city, with its measured pace and noise. They cannot even imagine that a maid would be sent to the store just for a pound of butter. The cobblestones hurt Ilya's feet, and by the second week his toes develop calluses. Then he kicks off his shoes, finds his old boots, rubs them with castor oil, and puts them on. During more or less the same week he loses patience with his tie and angrily tears it off his neck. Ilya becomes irritable. The new day confronts him like a vicious enemy; it drags on and on without end. Ilya wanders the streets aimlessly, he drops in on his father, goes to see his brother. He cannot get used to sidewalks and walks in the middle of the street for some reason, slouching and constantly glancing over his shoulder. Then summer begins, the sun softens the asphalt, clouds of dust waft through the city, the dust gets into your throat, plugs your nose and ears. Ilya looks at the sun and realizes that this is a good time for mowing hay. The weather has settled, the grass will dry out in three days, and then you can start piling it.

"What do you care if it's mowing or sowing?" asks Isaac.

"What do you mean? Can't you see what the weather is like?" says Ilya.

"Who cares?" grumbles Isaac.

Now Isaac pesters his father and brother daily: it's time to get involved with something appropriate for the city. Leyble Kagan discovers a new America every day—and Isaac gets all excited about his brother-in-law's ideas. Finally, Meyer loses patience with all this. He furrows his brow and says,

"Well, why don't you start, we'll see how it goes."

"And you? And Ilya?"

"In due course. It's your idea, so you start. We'll join you later."

But Isaac doesn't have the guts for bold, large-scale projects. He would make a move and then immediately start dithering—what if something is not right? Turns out, he's timid, that Isaac, he holds on to his father like a child to his mother's skirt. For now, he's only good for spelling out his conditions. They should take up something in the city, they will no longer handle any country estates.

"Why decide in advance?" Ilya asks naïvely.

Gloom, gloom is the order of the day in the Raskin household. Meyer still rises at the crack of dawn, he can't sleep. He should be doing something, but there's nothing to do. He pulls out his briefcase, goes through his papers under the light of a lamp, and sorts through them. His old notebooks are all there; the numbers in them reflect the various stages of his entire life. Each number describes a certain period. Then Meyer puts the papers away and goes into the kitchen. The city servants are still asleep, they couldn't care less, they are not used to rising early. Meyer starts the samovar, pours a glass of tea, and carries it to the bedroom for his wife.

Brokers, ne'er-do-wells, men full of hot air besiege Meyer from dawn till dusk. Their constant chatter gives him a headache. Meyer is elected to all kinds of charitable societies, all the synagogues set their best seats aside for him, rabbis and cantors invite themselves to his house. But Raskin is bored with them, he's got nothing to talk to them about. They openly court and flatter him, which he finds unpleasant. So much for city life, who knew!

Finally Isaac makes up his mind and starts a new undertaking. What is it? The Brest Fortress is selling a large batch of defective artillery shells. The shells need to be exploded and recast. A mob of brokers swarms around this project. Isaac picks up Meyer and Ilya, and they go to the fortress together. Ilya examines the shells and wonders out loud: what kind of work is involved here? Fine, the shells will be bought, then turned into metal and sold. Is that it?

"What else do you need?" Isaac hisses.

"I need real work," Ilya answers bluntly.

However, Ilya does not come to regret this trip to the fortress. Old Raskin did not put his hopes on the brokers for nothing. Brokers have an acute sense, they immediately grasp who needs what. One of them—tall and lanky, with a large Adam's apple and an umbrella under his arm—takes Ilya aside and asks,

"Mr. Raskin, how would you feel about leasing a small estate?"

"I would feel good about leasing a small estate," Ilya answers promptly. "What? Where? How?"

Isaac catches the conversation with one ear. He is livid, he curses Ilya and the broker in front of everybody. They came to look at the artillery shells, and these two are busy with the devil knows what. Ilya answers calmly that it is not yet clear who exactly is busy "with the devil knows what," it is not clear at all. The discord between the two brothers keeps getting worse. Meyer Raskin, the former Telyatichi leaseholder, is caught in the middle. He is a man of peace, he'd much rather the brothers weren't fighting. Actually, all their quarreling is not worth wasting one's breath on. They should look into every opportunity and then choose what's best. There is no rush. It's only been six weeks since they left Telyatichi.

But Isaac won't let it go. "It's a matter of principle: no more dealings with landowners or peasants. Enough is enough!"

Ilya, however, has suffered enough during these six torturous weeks of idleness. Ilya is an adult; he has no interest in sticking to Isaac's principles, they are not his. Meyer furrows his brow. He senses discord, division, and disintegration in the Raskin family; the children must have thoroughly forgotten the old fable about the bundle of sticks.

A few days later Ilya puts on his dustcoat, picks up a small travel bag, and goes on a reconnaissance trip with the broker. Well, take a good look at this unique estate, the Zelovo estate that belongs to Princess Dolgorukova. You can see through the barns and sheds as if they're made of matches, everything is decrepit—but the lavish park features a two-story castle with thirty-five rooms, complete with fountains and a winter garden. The furnishings alone are probably worth 25,000—but who needs them? In the past three years, the Princess has visited Zelovo just once, and for one week only. Some people are blessed with riches that they have no use for!

Carts sit in the middle of the courtyard, pigs dig through the vegetable garden, the fields are overgrown with burdock, little boys pull hairs out of the horses' tails in the stables. The manager of the estate is Andrey, the Princess's coachman, a literate peasant with a dazzling mustache, who wears a dark-blue coat. He has heard about the Raskins before and greets Ilya genially.

"There's nothing one can do here," he says, yawning slightly. "The fields are no good, the meadows are no good, the horses are no good, the cows don't produce milk, the hens don't lay eggs. The place is only good for sleeping."

Ilya spends three days in Zelovo. He walks up and down all the fields and meadows and fills his notebook with numbers. On the fourth day, he summons his father. Meyer must listen to all sorts of reproaches from Isaac, but nevertheless he heeds the call of his oldest son and goes.

"Everything has been completely neglected here," Meyer says. "The estate is in bad shape." But the old man's voice sounds cheery. Again, as at Telyatichi, he puts his tall boots on, he bobs around in a single-horse carriage, and gray dust covers him from head to toe.

At lunch time, father and son buy a jar of milk and a loaf of bread. They sit together, split the loaf, and take turns drinking from the same jar.

"But it has good potential," Ilya hurries to sway him. "Having their own forest means that the outbuildings can be repaired. A milk farm is a distinct possibility."

"Now wait a minute," Meyer moves the jar aside and uses his fingers to fish bread crumbs out of his beard. Wrinkles instantly crisscross his brow. "We need to think this through. Telyatichi was five times the size of Zelovo, there was enough work for all of us down there. But here. . . . You do understand what I'm getting at?"

"I am not arguing," says Ilya, biting his fingernails. "In short: everyone gets an equal share."

"God forbid! First of all, Isaac has no intention of being a partner in this. As for me—I don't need it. What I'm trying to say is. . . . This is perfect for one man. So you're the one who needs to do some thinking. Meaning you'll be on your own . . ."

But Ilya doesn't even want to listen to his father's evasions.

"Absolutely not!" he says with conviction. "You can't refuse. I'm not saying that you should move to Zelovo; there is no proper housing here anyway, and on top of that, mother is sick. But you must have a share in this business. If you feel bad about Isaac—well, he doesn't have to know about this . . ."

He is aware that he has touched on a very delicate subject, and he hurries to correct himself.

"I'm not refusing to give him an equal share, not at all. But if he doesn't want to. . . . You see, I can't sit idle anymore, I will lose my mind in that stupid Brest. Zelovo would be a salvation for me . . ."

"I understand, I really do," replies Meyer, shaking his gray head. "I do understand. . . . I hope you do really well here, with God's help."

And so life goes. Once again, Ilya Raskin's tables, chairs, and beds are turned upside down, while carts carrying his possessions travel from the city to the estate. Ilya is no longer playing second fiddle, he is his own man now. Instead of his large house in Dubovoye or a comfortable apartment in Brest-Litovsk he now occupies one room in Andrey's house. But that doesn't bother him. Zelovo is now filled with joyous sounds: the blows of axes, the cracking of pines, the dry stony rustle of bricks. Soon Ilya will be moving into a new house. Soon the steel plows, shiny like silver, will dig deep into the earth, and the cows will stand in their warm, new, comfortable sheds. Ilya is restoring a web torn into pieces by other people's hands. His life has meaning again. His days are once again too short. Ilya barely manages to write to his father once a week.

He writes to him about whatever is going on, five or six pages of stationery filled with his straight and rounded script—a report rather than a letter. Meyer goes to his wife, sits down in front of her, puts on his gold eyeglasses, and reads to her the letter from their oldest son. He reads slowly, savoring every word. After each letter, he feels his solitude and the empty hours in this bourgeois city even more acutely. He has already tried out several projects, some of which have even proved profitable. A few lucrative schemes energized even Isaac for a few days. He would emerge from his closed, gloomy existence and even try to make jokes—but none of it was the real thing! Out of sheer idleness, Meyer has once again applied for a foreign passport, but he keeps dragging his feet on the trip even though the month of May has already passed.

"You know what," Meyer says to his wife while quickly folding up the letter, "I'd like to go see Ilya. . . . You won't be too bored if I go there for a week, just one week?"

Ailing Chava understands him and says,

"Of course. By all means, go. And please say hello to everyone for me."

A week passes, then ten days, and Meyer is still away. He watches Ilya work for one day, then gradually joins in himself.

"Well, well," he says, smiling into his gray beard. "I still remember how to work, I'm still good for something."

The way he was spending his time in Brest was so hard on Meyer that he himself was surprised that he didn't lose his capacity for real work. Little by little he starts to boast as old men do.

"Give me an estate five times the size of Telyatichi," he says, "and I'd still manage. I know how to work. I've been at it since the age of thirteen. I did it all by the sweat of my brow. I . . . what do you think?"

"Of course," Ilya replies. "It goes without saying. Of course!"

9

When Motya was a child, he was prone to anxiety, which later turned into dissatisfaction. School didn't leave him with a single happy or joyful memory. Classmates with whom he tried to be friends quickly disappointed him: they were greedy and disloyal.

He immediately seized upon the offer from his brother-in-law Pavel Rusevich. He didn't know what awaited him in Lodz, but he was convinced that nothing good would come from staying in Brest.

The change of scenery provided by Lodz did not last him very long.

By then, Rusevich had a two-bedroom apartment. It was appointed like the apartments of all fledgling business owners. A completely useless upright piano in the dining room, with Böcklin's *Isle of the Dead* on the wall above it, a cabinet with glass doors, the ubiquitous settee with removable mirror that shakes with every step, figurines on the shelves. . . . In his spare time, Rusevich would twirl his mustache, remove invisible specks from his impeccable suit, and instruct Motya in the art of living.

"Look at me," he would say in a flat tone. "You must forget that your father is wealthy. It will only get in the way of your own work. For pocket money, I will issue you a half-ruble every week. You must record all your expenses in a notebook and show it to me at the end of the week. You spend your half-ruble—you get another one."

He would then yawn, remind his wife that dinner was to be served in exactly ten minutes, and conclude,

"The letters that you write and send home—show them to Sophia first. It is very important."

Sarah would lower her gaze and, dangling her keys, remark with slight hesitation,

"Believe it or not, Motya, it is very important, that's right. Upbringing is tremendously important. You can't even imagine how important upbringing is."

Sarah has developed a new habit of adding commentary to what her husband says. She has completely closed herself off, so it is hard to tell what she feels and whether she is happy with her life. Preparing to go to Telyatichi for the summer, she ordered the best suits and dresses for herself, she bought extra hats—all, presumably, to show how happy and comfortable her life was. Luba Raskin, with the expression of a connoisseur, would examine Sarah's new purchases and try to comment, but it always fell flat. What can you do? They follow fashion in Lodz more closely than in Brest-Litovsk. Sarah easily countered Isaac's gibes with equally sly and scathing barbs. In fact, she was quick to embrace her husband's interests in Lodz and became a "Lodzian" in the full sense of the word.

The Rusevichs entertained almost every night. The men would immediately seat themselves around a green table to play Préférence, while the ladies sat on the sofa, drank tea, and engaged in conversation. Sarah kept up with them.

They forced a suit on Motya, complete with wide, stiff cuffs that dangled around his wrists. Sarah attempted to introduce him into "society," but nothing came of it. His mistrustful stare, morose, inquisitive, and shy all at once, did not bode well. Some ladies brought their sons with them. These were dashing young men. Since the age of sixteen, they wore tuxedoes and orange vests. Brightly colored handkerchiefs showed their notched corners from the side pockets. They emulated the grown-ups in everything, and the better they did it, the more popular they were. They looked down on Motya: skinny and clumsy, in an awkward suit—he was indeed a laughable sight.

At the same time, Motya was secretly pleased to notice that these dashing fellows didn't amount to much. They could dance, they hummed popular tunes, they chatted in Polish—but they were ignorant and hardly read anything at all. Their favorite activities were playing billiards on weekdays and pursuing pretty working girls or going to brothels on weekends. Motya was annoyed with their double game—elegant reverence with the adults and laxity in their own company. He was happy to get back at them in any way he could. At the most inopportune moment, when one of them was in the process of putting his charms on those present, Motya would suddenly ask him a tricky question.

"I don't read what those Russians write," the flustered and annoyed youngster would mutter, staring at Motya with hostility.

"Pardon me," Motya would reply, barely able to contain his glee. "It's from Stefan Żeromski. He's a Polish writer . . ."

Ambushes like this, however, did not give him much satisfaction. He soon realized that the Rusevichs lived a dull and empty life. He often entertained himself with nasty thoughts. Wouldn't it be good if Pavel Rusevich's affairs went downhill and he was forced to sell the piano? One wonders if that would disrupt his balanced and placid disposition and force him to think about something new . . .

Motya's dissatisfaction grew stronger every month. So this is the life they are preparing him for! In ten years they will turn him into another Pavel Rusevich. He will have a portly wife, he will play Préférence at a green table. . . . He came to feel that he had made a terrible mistake by dropping out of the commercial school. But pride would not allow him to return to Brest-Litovsk. He could clearly picture his former classmates making fun of him. Where had he been, what had he done? It was uncommon to hear Russian speech in the Kingdom of Poland: people spoke Polish, Yiddish, or German. The young Raskin started worrying that he would forget everything he knew, that he would become an ignoramus. He threw himself at his books and read all night long. He had made a mistake, and it was Rusevich's fault. Pavel needed money, so he came up with that textile school scheme. Motya's dislike for Rusevich was turning into anger.

Now Motya vehemently hated everything around him. Whatever he did was informed by his anger toward his brother-in-law and his friends. He sensed that he was becoming petty but he couldn't help it. He didn't wash on purpose, he would sit down at the table with dirty hands. He responded to admonitions with unabashed rudeness. He started smoking. He really wanted his sister to think that he was meeting with street walkers. He terrified Sarah with his opinions so much that she became wary of him.

Three years passed in this way. Motya finished textile school, and it was time for him to get involved in something real. But the thought disgusted Motya. Besides, he wasn't too familiar with the manufacturing process. How about working as an ordinary weaver for a year or so?

He uttered this thought out loud. Pavel Rusevich looked away. He didn't say anything—he had given up on his brother-in-law a long time ago. Sarah opened her mouth—and a flood of reproaches poured out. The more outraged she grew, the firmer was Motya's determination to pursue his plans. He was a grownup now and he would do as he pleased.

He bought a dark-blue worker's outfit and acquired a small pipe. He even changed his gait to underscore his otherness. His loneliness was now a source of delight for him.

And so Motya Raskin finds himself in an entirely different world. The clanging machinery, the spinning wheels flickering with silvery flares, the transmission belts wriggling like snakes—all this overwhelms him at first. It is hard for him to concentrate, to keep his feet firmly on the ground—it feels as if some thundering force has torn him away from the earth and continues to carry him through the air.

The mill wasn't large: fifty power looms altogether. A moving beater would thunderously separate from the tightly woven fabric and then slide back to the frame as if in free fall. The shuttle, glistening with its metal appendages, would dart from roller to roller like a mouse. The control thread, measuring the amount of work done, extended along the fabric. A worker standing at the loom would start counting every few minutes. He would earn five kopecks for every 1,000 cross threads. Work began at sunrise. Raskin had the impression that all the workers concentrated on was the control thread: how many thousands done? Not wanting to fall behind, he was among the first to arrive at the mill and would go straight to the loom. He even managed to eat breakfast while working so as not to lose time.

Now he ate lunch not at home but at the lunchroom near the mill. At noon, the cool, low-ceilinged spaces of the eatery filled up quickly with merrily chirping spooler girls in brightly colored kerchiefs and men in caps and oil-stained jackets. A music box boomed in many voices, canaries invisible in the smoke warbled during the pauses. The patrons, used to the clanging machines, spoke loudly, so the noise did not abate even for a moment. After lunch, Raskin, like almost all of the workers, would get a bottle of beer and constantly look at his watch: was it time to go back to work?

Later, on his quiet days off, Motya Raskin would think back to his first months at the mill, and he would feel that the measured pace of the machines, the belts running on the wheels, the thunderous noise—all this had completely consumed his thoughts and feelings and turned him into an appendage of the tightly fitted mechanisms. He didn't think about anything other than work, which he approached like an athletic contest. Even at home, he still heard the thumping of the beater and saw the control thread slowly moving through the flow of the warp.

As he grew accustomed to the noise, he once again became curious and observant. Those hundreds and thousands of people who, at the crack of dawn, while rats were still digging through cesspits, hurried to work only to return in the dark of night—what was it that made them tick? Raskin himself embraced this life only superficially. The control thread couldn't be the sole purpose of life. Granted, it had enthralled him too for a while, but that enthrallment had passed, and more and more often he cast a curious eye around the mill.

Many times, he tried to start a conversation, but nothing came of it. The workers kept their distance from him and brushed him off with generalities. He knew from books and from the conversations of Rusevich's guests that workers had common interests, but here at the mill he did not see it no matter how hard he looked. Quite the opposite: different ethnic groups didn't mix, the Poles did not make friends with the Jews, nor the Germans with the Poles. Old Jewish workers went to the tavern only to drink tea and brought kosher tidbits with them. Young Poles secretly swapped Jewish sausage for the Krakow variety. Many found it funny. Some of the weavers brought to the mill and read *Dwa grosze*—a dirty little tabloid that incited ethnic groups against each other. Then immediately some Jews would flash copies of the nationalist *Lodzer Tageblatt*. During their important holidays, old Jewish workers stayed home and their looms went idle. Others kept teasing them long after the holidays, asking how much matzo they ate and how many hours they fasted. Reality was not what Raskin had thought it to be. The peasants at Telyatichi meekly obeyed their masters, while the workers in Lodz quarreled among themselves.

The daily grind was consuming the life of sixteen-year-old Raskin.

It was only meeting Król, and the events that followed, that opened the road to political struggle for him. Motya never forgot his brief association with Król because it determined the direction of his entire life.

10

Król worked right next to Motya: the bases of their looms touched. Raskin often noticed his neighbor watching him—and always saw a sneer in Król's eyes. It made Motya uneasy: he would begin to putter, pulling out the shuttle, changing a spool, restarting his loom—but the man's brown eyes continued to follow him. They had a spark of irony in them. Motya would shrink under his glance, frown, flush, and get flustered. His antipathy toward Król kept growing. At the same time, he noticed that workers of all ethnic backgrounds treated Król with particular respect. Raskin would occasionally make an effort to strike up a conversation with Król, but he was always sorry when he did: Król was clearly making fun of him.

"Aren't you sorry that your hands are getting rough?" Król would ask Motya. "No toilet water will fix that."

Motya was tempted to cut him off rudely but instead he always felt an irresistible urge to explain himself.

"I don't care what my hands look like."

"Really?" Król would say doubtfully.

Raskin wanted to embarrass the man, to confuse him, to put him in his place, to make him change his tone and explain himself somehow, even defend himself. The thoughts that Król made him think were complicated and confused. Motya was losing his balance. He had a feeling that Król embraced all the workers, while Motya couldn't condone the way some of them behaved.

One evening in March they were walking home from work together. The sky was dark blue. Thin ice crunched under their feet, streetcar cables sent silver sparks crackling and flying. Król was walking fast. Motya did not want to fall behind. He knew that Król's eyes were mocking and watchful in the dark, as always. He couldn't see them now, so they didn't bother him.

"Today, several workers almost came to blows outside," said Raskin. "They picked on an old Jew and tried to force him to eat fatback."

Król said nothing for a while, then calmly responded,

"Well. . . . The owners are now training replacements for the workers, and those people won't be doing that . . ."

Raskin pricked up his ears.

"What replacements?"

"People like yourself—Daddy's boys from their own ranks. They will train their own army of workers and then they will throw out everyone they find objectionable, whether they eat pork or not . . ."

Instead of the usual irritation, Motya felt a wave of anger run through his entire body. He no longer wanted to explain himself, he wanted to fight. Motya clenched his fists; his steps began sounding sharper, his heels cut into the ice making a springtime tinkling sound.

"I've been meaning to have a serious talk with you for a long time, but you are either rude to me or just joke around. I'm not a little boy. What gives you the right to talk to me like this? You don't know me at all, you don't know what brought me to the mill, and yet . . ."

He was choking on angry words, he was agitated, but gradually his speech leveled off. He spoke emotionally and at length, mostly about himself and his own grievances. Król walked next to him in silence. Out of habit they would slow down at the streetcar stops, then start walking again as if on cue. Street followed street, one after the other. They reached the city center from the suburb where the mill was located. Then the streetlights became more scarce and the streets emptier. The workers' neighborhood, densely populated and dark, slowly opened its alleys before them.

"Well, goodbye now," Król said. "I'm already home."

They shook hands and parted ways. Raskin felt relieved. The wind was blowing into his hot face, cabbies' horses clinked their shoes on the cobblestone pavement. Raskin walked against the wind, breathing deeply. The next day he and Król met like pals, and Raskin was not surprised when after work—and it was a Saturday—Król casually said to him, "Tomorrow is a day off, come over for a talk." They became friends. Each day of this friendship opened more and more horizons before Raskin. Life was acquiring new, exciting meaning. It was as if it was freeing itself from its old shell. Waves were crashing under a surface that appeared smooth, but they were breaking through with increasing frequency. A crisis was brewing. Many factories had switched from a six-day workweek to five days. The old mechanism that supported Telyatichi's prosperity was sputtering, gasping in the throes of death.

Spring brought with it hopes for renewal. Cossacks rode through the arrow-straight streets of Lodz. Spirited Russian songs sounded out of place in the Polish city. Threat lurked behind the blasting of factory whistles. Small antipathies, disagreements, and misunderstandings retreated into the background under the fresh breath of spring. Instead of the yellow press, leaflets of a different kind began to appear. People hid them from the foremen and passed them from hand to hand. Raskin was excited when workers shared leaflets with him without hesitating, as though he was one of them. Tense anticipation was everywhere. It traveled without words, as if through the air, and not only the workers felt it—the foremen, their assistants, the warehousemen all felt it too. They spoke less harshly, and their steps sounded less determined and firm. Policemen often appeared at the mill's entrance. In the evening, Cossacks rode single file through the streets; songs of the Don River steppes rose above them, echoed by the rhythmical clinking of horseshoes against the cobblestones.

The First of May passed. It was a false alarm. Wheels spun as always, shuttles darted, heavy iron parts moved as if they were alive. A steady, invisible hand controlled the gates, restraining the force and holding back the human floods that were ready to surge forth at any moment. Where was the center that directed the workers' will? Few knew the answer, but everyone felt its presence. It was the same for the whole country. The hand was on the steering wheel. Everyone was waiting for it to move.

It came later, starting in St. Petersburg. Imperceptible waves then spread to the working class centers of the once and future country of Poland.

The initial trigger was the arrival in St. Petersburg of the French delegation headed by Poincaré. The delegation was greeted with the workers' primeval weapon—cobblestones. The steady hand that until then had been waiting for the right hour now turned the wheel.

The day began as usual. The June sun had been streaming through the panes of the mill's glass roof since early morning, forming squares on the stone floor. Thick smoke from the mill's smokestacks crisscrossed the blue sky. Clanging and thunderous noise was shaking the building. Gears rotated at their usual speed, flashing their metal parts. They would slow down and break tempo only a minute before the lunch break.

There was no sign of anything unusual until ten in the morning. But at ten o'clock sharp, the thunder of the machines faltered. The wheels started slowing down. The shattered silence was returning and growing. It was as if the machines themselves were surprised by this unusual stoppage. Some of them had enough time to move their beaters close to the base and then froze with their open jaws full of thread.

At a firm and steady gait—now, in this sudden silence, footsteps resounded clearly on the mill's stone floor—everyone was heading for the exit. The gate was locked. A policeman was kicked aside like a football. The gate snapped open in a terrifying way: not inwards, as was usual, but outwards, onto the street. A cohesive group of seventy-five people spilled onto the sidewalk. A few mounted Cossacks moved aside. A rock whooshed over one of the Cossacks' heads. He ducked and the rock missed him.

At the same moment, the whistle on top of the multistory building of a nearby mill started blaring piercingly. Here, the gate had been locked, too, as at Raskin's mill. Waiting for their comrades to appear, the workers threw the gate wide open. The new arrivals were met with shouts of "hurrah." A thin line of Cossacks slowly and reluctantly moved aside. The two streams of dark-blue tunics, jackets, caps, and bright-colored kerchiefs merged into one and continued to move forward. The Cossacks followed a few hundred feet behind. The bright sun made them squint, the wind disheveled their light-brown forelocks. Here and there, a song rose above the crowd. It was hard to make out the words: people were singing in several different languages, but the tune was the same. It rose and hung above the marchers. Reams of leaflets flew up occasionally like flocks of birds. Frightened passersby scattered. More and more streams of people from the side streets were joining the broad current. Skimpy detachments of Cossacks manned a few intersections. They moved away reluctantly as the marching ranks of workers approached. However, after letting the crowd through, they would join the cavalry that casually followed the crowd. Streetcars had stopped running. Abandoned by motormen and conductors, they immediately filled with street children. Small red banners flashed in a few spots like flames.

The marchers were moving toward the center, to Piotrkowska Street.

The street rose, slumped, and ended against the large building of the city hall. The sight of the city hall raised the workers' spirits. They picked up the pace. And just then, Cossacks emerged from cross streets and alleys and rushed the crowd. From a distance, with spears at the ready, they looked terrifying. The human expanse faltered and then moved forward even faster. Gunfire rang out from all sides. Shots flashed in the hot air. Women were screaming hysterically. A man with a gray beard who was marching next to Raskin lurched forward, jerked his head a few times in a frightening way, and slowly prostrated himself on the cobblestones right before Raskin.

"What are you doing?" Motya screamed, trying to help him up.

Only then did he notice that the old man's mouth was filled with a squishy red ooze. Stones were flying over their heads. It all turned into mayhem . . .

And so Motya Raskin found himself in prison. The cell was filled with strangers, who kept quiet. He had a dull pain in his chest—did the gendarmes beat him up in the fracas, or did he fall down while backing away? Motya had no idea what happened after he had been trampled by the crowd and lost consciousness. He walked up and down the cell several times, stopping by the long and narrow window with metal bars. What an odd thing! He had heard and read a lot about prisons. All of it was bleak, even frightening. But now he felt neither fear nor dread. Youthful verve, inexplicable joy streamed through his veins. He stretched, spread out his arms, and smiled at the old man who kept watching him. The man's face darkened even more, and he looked away.

"He clearly thinks I'm an informer," Raskin thought. "Of course!"

He didn't find the thought insulting, though. His joyful mood persisted.

Two weeks later, Motya Raskin was dispatched, under guard, to internal exile at his parents' place of residence, Brest-Litovsk.

That summer, the sun was relentless. It would appear in the sky at the crack of dawn, then float and melt away all day long. The railcar smelled of paint, the toilet, and the sun; eggshells littered the seats. Conductors in short canvas jackets with colored signals on their belts walked by. A little baby was learning to walk in the space between two benches, one of which was occupied by Raskin and the policeman who escorted him. The baby grabbed on to the boards heated by the sun with his tiny hands and squinted at the luminous pillars of dust in the air. His mother's steady hand guided him from behind without touching his shirt. The woman shielded her eyes from the sun with her other hand, squinted, and smiled at Raskin, the policeman, and the fields that were sliding past the windows. Bright printed flowers lit her loose dress. A tin kettle clanged on the shelf. It clanged rhythmically, in tune with the clattering wheels. Raskin listened to the clatter for a while, looked at the baby cheerfully, smiled at the baby's mother, and started whispering in tune with the wheels,

"We shall go on with our fight, we shall go on with our fight, we shall go on with our fight!"

PART THREE

1

In June 1914, after toiling to his heart's content at Zelovo, Ilya's estate, toasting himself in the sun and becoming almost younger—or at least more agile, Meyer Raskin finally returned to Brest-Litovsk. He decided to rest for a few days and convince Chava—who lately needed convincing about everything—to go abroad with him. While still at Zelovo, he received an angry letter from Motya. In terse, formal language his son reported that he had been exiled and would be forced to stay with his father. "If you don't accept, please inform me," Motya wrote, "and I will request transfer to another city."

"How do you like his tone?" Meyer grunted, passing the letter to Ilya. "'If you don't accept!' Remember the antics of your brother-in-law, Moses Novogrudski? But I'm not Ephraim Livshitz, may he rest in peace!"

He was not pleased, so he furrowed his brow as he always did in such situations. Yet beneath his displeasure one could sense a father's pride: look how time flies! Motya, a kind, skinny imp—even he has grown up and changed, he's becoming a man.

He sat in the buggy, mulling over his family, his affairs, and the latest letter from his youngest son. The night was coming to an end; tranquil mists hung above the fields. Ripe rye stood in a solid silvery mass, its heavy spikes leaning toward the ground. The mist and the predawn dew made the oat fields look matte blue. Skylarks were waking up. Horses snorted and huddled together. The driver was sliding off his box seat, his head falling to his chest—but then he would immediately wake up and take his anger out on the horses. He whipped them and, in a hoarse, sleepy voice, accused them of laziness, cursing their mothers and threatening them with wolves.

The two-story wooden train station had not yet awakened. Its second-floor windows were open, and a light wind ballooned the curtains. A guitar lay on the windowsill—someone must have forgotten it there before going to bed. The station attendant, with one foot bare and the other misshapen by an ugly, ratty felt boot, was sweeping the platform, angrily scuffling his broom. He became so immersed that he looked like a peasant mowing grass in a meadow. Sparrows kept crawling out from under the roof, looking around, and fanning their tails. A rooster was already digging through the flower beds, and a little bird was drinking from a metal barrel, raising and turning its head. One could see a droplet of water sliding down its throat. The door wheezed and slammed. A huge white samovar glistened on the dining room counter. Meyer put his hand to the samovar's belly—which was cold—and thought that they didn't need such a samovar at this godforsaken station. It only wasted coal. Tin donation boxes were nailed to the wall near the cashier's window. Who would put a coin in the slot? Perhaps only some kindhearted lady who was passing through. Everything here spoke of long-established daily routine—year after year, decade after decade.

The thought that nothing here would ever change made even Meyer Raskin somewhat uneasy. He suddenly grew restless and agitated, asked the attendant for the key to the first-class waiting room, sat down on the oilcloth sofa, drank a glass of cold "station" water, and then started examining his face in the mirror that hung askew on the wall.

"I must have a serious conversation with Motya," he thought, which made him angry. "I do have the right to talk to my son, don't I?"

All the way to the station he tried to be angry and put himself into a serious mood. He didn't have much success, though. He was sitting next to some carpenters who were headed to their distant home with axes and hand planes in their bags. Meyer quizzed them about where they worked, how well they were paid, and how good the materials were. The carpenters smoked and spat on the floor. At each stop, they would untie their bags, step out to get some boiling water, sparingly slice their appetizing white bread, and munch on it. An old, gray-haired Jew turned away to the window. Giving Raskin a chilly stare, he donned his *tallith* and started to pray loudly. Through the windows one could see people who had risen at the crack of dawn to work in the fields and meadows. The carpenters forgot about their trade and started a lively discussion about farming.

The train arrived in Brest-Litovsk at eight o'clock. It still felt like morning here. The residents were sweeping the streets, raising clouds of dust. Rattling metal bolts, merchants were opening their shops. A group of prisoners was being led to the station, briefly delaying the horse cab in which Meyer was riding. The prisoners were both men and women; soldiers with rifles at the ready surrounded them. Raskin studied the grim, unhealthy faces of the prisoners and once again recalled his youngest son and the upcoming conversation with him. How will he talk to Motya and what about?

A disheveled young maid, taking short, quick steps in her bare white feet, opened the door for Raskin and took his small suitcase from him. Empty rooms opened up in front of Meyer one after the other. He hurried through them barely paying attention, looking for his wife and children. One of the rooms was semi-dark due to closed curtains; it still smelled of sleep. Motya lay on the bed. Chava was sitting next to him, holding a glass of hot milk and blowing on a teaspoon. She brought it to her son's lips, which eagerly opened toward it. Seeing his father, Motya became apprehensive and raised himself on his elbows. He pursed his lips and furrowed his brow. He remembered what he had written to his father and felt uncomfortable. Meyer pretended that he didn't notice his son's discomfort. He hugged his wife and stretched his lips toward Motya.

"Well . . . good morning, son," he said, kissing him. "Don't get up, it's still early."

He sat down on the bed next to his wife and looked into Motya's face closely.

"You are so skinny," he noted and hastened to add, "It's fine, it's no problem. You'll gain weight here in no time. It's not bad here in the summer."

Chava grunted and sighed for a while, then went to the next room. Meyer stayed put. He patted himself on the knees, looked sidelong at his son, and he too felt uncomfortable. "Maybe there's no need to have a serious talk," he thought. "Really, what is there to talk about? Your son is here—welcome, son! One should never add fuel to the flame—a big fire is much harder to put out." But then he remembered the letter again. He felt that Motya expected him to say something, so he couldn't remain silent.

"Ilya is doing really well," Meyer began. "I used to be the leaseholder, my children were growing up, and now he is the leaseholder, and his children are growing up. I was staying with him and somehow got drawn into his work. . . . I was so busy I didn't have a chance to respond to your letter."

He chuckled and then suddenly turned to face Motya and exclaimed half-jokingly and half-seriously,

"Why are you mad at me, Motya? What am I—your father or your enemy?"

"I'm not mad at you!" Motya replied with muffled anger.

The old man's intelligent eyes flashed with disbelief. Slowly rubbing his face, he said,

"Well, then I had the wrong impression, so there's nothing to talk about. . . . Things happen. It's actually good to make mistakes when you're young, you know . . ."

"Father, I did not make any mistakes."

"Huh? What?" Meyer lost his resolve again. "Yes, right. . . . What were we talking about here? I'm losing it . . . in my old age, ha ha. . . . I'm joking, of course, I'm not old at all! What I wanted to say is that in two or three months, I'll start working again. Something interesting will come up, so I'll start. . . . You know how I do it, don't you? Here, my son has arrived—Motya, that is. . . . So here, Mr. Motya, please take a certain percentage and get down to work . . ."

"I will not be working with you."

Meyer moved aside. Shadows played on his face, which took turns frowning angrily and lighting up, a smile ruffling his lips.

"Actually, you're right. You're still tired, you need some rest . . ."

"That's not the reason!"

Motya took a more comfortable position, his eyes suddenly flashed, his cheeks turned red. He jerked his head defiantly. Meyer glanced at his son, and the old man's heart filled with joy: this defiant gesture, this jutted-out chin reminded him of his own younger days.

"I was hoping you'd spare me this conversation," Motya said, gasping for air. "I hate pointless talk . . ." He frowned and added, as if talking to himself, "I don't think you like it that much either . . ." And then suddenly he shouted, flailing his arms awkwardly, "Why argue for nothing? You'll claim that you made your money honestly, and I'll tell you that you made it on the blood and tears of Belarusian peasants who live worse than their landlord's pigs. At least the pigs have full bellies. You'll wriggle—like you are now—and suggest that I 'drop this foolishness' and get to work. At least you aren't demanding outright repentance, thanks for that. The return of the prodigal son . . ." He suddenly grabbed his father's hand and added more calmly, "You are a smart man, I respect you for many things. But I am not stupid either, you know that. I don't believe in doing silly things, so I'm not going to try to 'convert' you. But you—please don't try to 'bring me to my senses' either—it's a waste of time. I'm forced to live with you now, I've got nowhere else to go. So let's not get in each other's way."

He grew emotional, his voice started shaking.

"Among other things, I love you very much. . . . Mother, too. . . . I feel sorry for her and I love her . . ."

These last words came out on their own somehow; Motya immediately regretted saying them and frowned again. Meyer realized that the conversation was over and got up.

"I haven't washed yet," he said. "Now get up, it's time to eat breakfast."

Motya liked the transition.

"Yes, that's right, it's breakfast time," he agreed, pushing his blanket aside. "I go to bed at ten o'clock here; it's such a sleepy, miserable little town."

"You don't like it?'

"I don't."

"I don't either."

That was the end of it.

Life here did indeed drag on slowly and tediously. The town felt sleepy and lazy. A cart would occasionally rattle past, dragging a transparent veil of dust behind it—and then silence again. Soldiers would march by, whistling and singing, their tightly rolled-up overcoats pressing against their shoulders, their mouths agape, their song surging and quavering above their heads. Children run alongside them. A Serbian man leads a bear named Masha Petrovna on a rattling chain. A boy beats the tambourine with his fist and forlornly draws out a mournful melody of the Balkan fields. When the heat breaks, residents bring chairs outside and sit by their doors. The streets liven up. A retired general walks by, puffing his chest up and slowly moving his gout-stricken legs clad in dark-blue breeches with red stripes. A dainty gymnasium girl in a funny-looking hat flashes by.

Finally, a brass band starts playing in the city park. The evening has begun. Kerosene lanterns are already hissing and casting their spells above the darkening trees. For the umpteenth time, the summer theater presents Ryzhkov's *Little Snake*. A bandmaster in a white uniform jacket makes a grand sight on his stand, nodding at acquaintances while gently waving his wand. When the music stops, one can hear hundreds of shoes crunching on the yellow sand of the alleys. The women's colorful dresses flash, their large straw hats with bright feathers and flowers sway in the air. The white jackets of students and officers flare, spurs jingle. Gymnasium boys and girls walk around in groups, as do commercial agents. On the open stage, a young woman in a low-cut dress, pressing her hands to her breast, sings her heart out about the dried bread crust that she would be happy to live on.[6] Knives and forks at the restaurant jingle in tune with her singing—dinner is already being served.

---

6   A popular Russian love song of the time.

Motya was having a difficult time, consumed by bitter thoughts.

He had no new friends, while the old ones did not bring him any joy. In the beginning, he stayed away from his former mates from the commercial school. He felt that a wall separated him from them. Actually seeing them only strengthened this feeling. His former classmates had completely different interests, but most importantly, he clearly sensed a certain condescension toward a young man who had gotten involved in something foolish, had strayed, and is now paying for his mistakes. They had a rather dim and removed view of revolutionary work. Many called Raskin a "Tolstoyan" and expressed surprise that he hadn't grown long hair and was still wearing shoes. Some inquired in a serious and conspiratorial tone whether he was collecting money for an "organization." Girls gave him puzzled looks and laughed behind his back. Gossip made him suffer, so he avoided seeing anybody. Anger and pointless hatred burdened his soul.

"It would take hundreds of years to bring this anthill to life. . . . You would need a crowbar here, to uproot everything and everyone." He would go see Isaac, but the moment he opened the door he regretted doing it. Isaac had let himself go and kept complaining about his nonexistent ailments. His house did smell of sickness. Isaac had a baby, a sickly boy with empty, tired eyes. "Even this one is already poisoned, not suitable for real, active work," Motya thought, studying his nephew's dull eyes.

"And I am supposed to spend several years here?" This thought tormented Motya the most. He gobbled up book after book, as if he had a premonition that struggle awaited him in the future, that life would boil over very soon, that the old would crash precipitously, and the new would emerge from the rubble through blood and suffering—and that all this will tear him away from quiet contemplation. Books straightened out his thoughts and filled him with energy. Clenching his fists and challenging the empty street, he often whispered the same words that he used on the train coming home,

"We shall go on with our fight! We shall go on!"

The old order was cracking, balancing on the edge of the abyss with its enormous weight and bringing fire ever closer to the wick it rested on. Shots had already rung out in Sarajevo. Imperious demands, diplomatic notes, and threats were already flying through the wires from one nation to another. But the town was still in the embrace of peace, sleep, and laziness. Sand crunched under the feet of the strolling public, and the bandmaster in a white jacket towered on his stand like a dashing, intrepid captain on the bridge of his ship. Everything was as usual.

2

A few days later, the elderly Raskins were ready to go abroad. Tightly packed suitcases in canvas slipcovers already stood in the hallway. Meyer was urgently issuing instructions to the children who were staying behind—Motya and Sheva. Motya was listening absentmindedly, while fourteen-year-old Sheva furrowed her brow and, having tossed her thick braid onto her chest, was weaving a ribbon into her hair. She was happy to be the lady of the house for the first time in her life.

Through the window panes, rays of the morning sun streamed into the room like broad golden footpaths, with barely noticeable flecks of dust playing along them. Chava sat in an armchair with her arms resting by her sides, breathing heavily and frequently licking her dry lips chapped with thirst.

"Why go anywhere?" she kept asking, glancing around the room. "To die a year later or a year earlier—what's the difference?"

The others tried to ignore her.

Isaac and Luba arrived. Isaac brought the local newspaper that still smelled of dampness and turpentine.

"Nothing of the sort," he said, looking through the latest news and rattling the page, "the telegraph woman got it all wrong. We have a neighbor who works at the telegraph. She just came home from her shift and told me in strict confidence that late at night they received a telegram announcing the call-up. But there's nothing about it in the paper."

"They will make peace," Meyer suggested. "Tsar Nicholas hasn't lost his mind yet, his bones still ache from the Japanese war. . . .[7] Isn't that right, Mr. Socialist?" he addressed Motya with a smile.

Noticing that no return smile was forthcoming, he pulled his watch from his pocket and started getting ready.

---

7   A reference to the Russo-Japanese war of 1904–1905 which Russia lost.

"Well, call-up or not, political games or not, we still have to go to Marienbad. They won't hold the train for us."

Cabbies who had received word of the trip were already waiting outside. Each was trying to get the best spot, closest to the porch, which led to much bickering. The town languished under the rays of the morning sun; it remained quiet, sleepy, and immutable. In a tiny church, the bell ringer was dreamily handling the ropes, slowly ringing the bells. Stepping awkwardly and clacking their heels, people were carrying a white coffin out of the church. The head of the deceased, who had expired during these last quiet days before the storm, swayed affably from side to side. The train station was cool and peaceful. Officers in white jackets were drinking tea in the dining room. The Raskin family also sat down for some tea. Meyer was waiting for the porter whom he had dispatched to buy the tickets.

The porter was back in no time. Instead of the tickets, however, he brought the money back. They are not selling tickets abroad, you can only go as far as the border crossing. In fact, the porter came back to ask what to do. The problem is most likely just temporary; they will issue tickets to the destination at the border. A lady in a light-gray veil, with a travel blanket in her hands, sat down right next to them. It's an outrage! Her husband is supposed to meet her in Berlin tomorrow, but now there's this new nonsense! Where's the guarantee that she won't be delayed at that goddamn border crossing? How do you like this new nonsense?

"No," Meyer said, "I'm not going. The ground isn't burning beneath me, I can wait a few days. What do you think, Chava? Well, you'll be happy to stay home, won't you? Let's wait two or three days, the clouds will blow away, and then we'll go."

This day—the last day of peace—was as quiet as any other. As Motya was returning home in the evening, he saw people with small buckets and reams of paper pasting flyers on walls and fences. Crowds gathered around, striking matches. Finally a candle appeared in someone's hand, and its flickering yellow light, shaped like a banana, fell on the freshly printed sheet of paper. The first thing that Motya managed to read was the last sentence of the tsar's manifesto:

"With a profound faith in the righteousness of Our cause and a humble confidence in Almighty Providence, We invoke in Our prayers the Divine Blessing upon Holy Russia and Our valiant troops."

A second flyer announced the call-up of reservists.

Blessed Russia was asleep. Only dogs were barking in the outskirts, and locomotives were calling out to one another, piercing the nighttime darkness and filling it with unease. Stars twinkled in the sky, and cherry-red votive lights blinked in dark windows.

The pursuit of the righteous cause began in the morning. The assembly point was in the barracks on the outskirts of town. The long dull-colored brick building was surrounded by a solid wooden fence. Reservists were gathering here, along with their families, friends, and onlookers. Carts were arriving from nearby villages. Peasant women wailed quietly, dangling their feet in shoes made of bast or rough leather that was cracked from the dust and the heat. The sun shone through their disheveled hair. Frightened children screamed. The men were grim and quiet. They held their papers in their sweaty hands and insisted on crowding around the gate. A soldier with a rifle who was stationed there was dispassionately trying to bring them to their senses:

"Don't push, people, don't push. You'll make it, for God's sake!" He kept turning his head, clad in a new camouflage cap, and, as if reasoning with himself, added with bemusement,

"What's wrong with these people!"

Someone had already unleashed the term "army wives," nasty and derogatory-sounding. "Hey you, army wives!" a drunk factory worker was yelling, winking incessantly. "Let me take a look at you! I'm a man of substance and character, so come on and love me, army girls!" Bundles had already appeared in the women's hands, woeful bundles with meager treats. The women gathered around the gate and kept trying to figure out how to pass food to their husbands. After some tears, gloomy indifference overcame them. They would stop by the carts and urinate, barely squatting, then, for lack of anything better to do, would start searching for lice in each other's hair. Large, blue-green flies landed on small brown piles. Gypsies darted through the crowd; they were shooed away. Crooks surfaced. Jewish women were selling pastries.

During the day, a procession marched through the main street. Older men in white vests carried a huge portrait of Nicholas II. The procession wrapped up promptly. Many of the women who had cried their hearts out at the assembly point in the morning now traipsed behind the portrait of the last tsar. Curious children ran ahead of the marchers and shouted hurrah. Loaded carts were heading toward the train station. Officers' orderlies sat on top of them.

Soldiers marched through, without a band or the usual singing, just with spirited whistling. Their long column, the color of pus, snaked like a muddy stream. A soldier was beating his drum monotonously. The drumbeat suggested nonchalance but also a mild sadness over farewells. Sweat was streaming down their red, agitated faces, their boots creaked in unison, their feet lifting from the pavement only to descend again with zeal. The sun and the heat pushed everyone outside, so the street began to look festive. People embraced a double life—one hidden and another for show. Grief, fear, despair, and panic were kept at home for the time being. There was no place for them in the street just yet.

The superficial side of life disappeared at sunset. Evening brought its own unease. It was as if human thinking was driven mad by the sun, the noise, and everything that had transpired earlier in the day, and thus had lost its balance and strayed from its usual path into a narrow alley of rumors. Who and what had generated them and how were they spreading? Nobody knew the answers. But when he came home, Motya sensed a new, different mood. Someone in the family had already managed to take the curtains down, which made the windows look sinister. The shutters had to be closed. Trunks stood in the middle of the room. People were filling them with whatever came to hand.

"Finally," said Meyer, glancing at Motya with displeasure. "Don't you see what's going on?"

"What is going on?" Motya asked.

"A war is going on!" his father shouted with increasing irritation, and started to relay what was now being quietly mulled over in every house: the Germans and the Austrians have crossed the border. A detachment of our border guards surrendered without a fight—it must have been treason. The front is open. All this happened so unexpectedly that the troops did not have time to get organized. People think that the army will retreat all the way to Brest-Litovsk. As early as tomorrow, they will start grabbing people and sending them to build up the defenses at the fortress. Therefore? "Therefore, we must get out of Brest-Litovsk, grab the bare necessities and go to Ilya at Zelovo. Keep quiet about this, or else everyone will realize that they have to flee, trains will be packed, tickets sold out, and we'll never make it out of here. The train to Polesia departs at eleven. If we leave in half an hour, we will certainly make it."

This is what they were saying in the Raskin household, the same as in many Jewish, Russian, and Polish households. After seeing the women scream and weep, after the procession through the town, residents of the suburbs responded to the news of war with fear, gossip, and wild, unverified rumors. People were packing quietly and secretively in almost every house. They would go anywhere rather than remain near a major fortress.

"And what if they no longer let people out?" Isaac asked.

He was sitting on a trunk in his summer coat with the collar raised, despite the heat. His ominous black shadow which resembled a crow stirred behind his back.

"And what if they no longer let people out, what if they give you a shovel instead of a ticket and send you to dig trenches? Then what?" Isaac kept asking, while the crow behind his back pecked at the wall.

Suddenly Motya reacts to this, even though Isaac's questions weren't exactly addressed to him. Motya adjusts his hair with a broad gesture, tightens his belt, and says in exactly the same tone,

"And what if we wake up tomorrow—and the Germans are already here? What if at night they set the town on fire and we all burn to death? What if they start selling laundry soap instead of bread and we all die of hunger? What if . . ."

Isaac's eyes burn with anger, he is prepared to respond in kind to this "bumptious fool," but old Meyer Raskin interrupts them. He throws a few last things into a trunk and asks,

"Can we continue this pleasant chat some other time? Isaac, tell me instead: did we get a telegram back from Hersh? A response from Sarah and Pavel?"

"No," Isaac replies. "They couldn't possibly have responded yet no matter how they tried. If Hersh is not under arrest, he'll be here in three days."

Meyer tries to signal to him, but Isaac doesn't notice, he doesn't want to notice.

"Oh my God," Chava begins to cry quietly. "Why would they put my boy under arrest?"

"Oh, never mind, he's just joking," Meyer tries to calm his wife down.

But Isaac continues to speak. He sounds as if he is deliberately trying to upset everyone, to hurt them.

"If Hersh is not under arrest . . . ," he says, "and he could be under arrest as a Russian subject of draft age. . . . The Austrians . . ."[8]

---

8   Krakow, where Hersh studied, was in the part of Poland that belonged to Austria-
      Hungary at the time.

What can you do about someone like Isaac? He's not a youngster, you can't shut him up. Meyer doesn't want to quarrel with him, he doesn't like to quarrel with his children, especially in times like this. Meyer pulls out his watch and says,

"It's time! We don't want to miss the train. Motya, go hire some cabs. But do it quietly and carefully, so that the neighbors don't notice anything. No one must know that we are leaving."

And so for the second time, the Raskin family is headed to the train station. For the time being, they will be staying at Zelovo, in Ilya's new house. One would hope things will settle down soon, and then they will be able to return to Brest-Litovsk. This is how the Raskins are thinking. This is how most people in Brest-Litovsk are thinking. But for now, they need to get out, get out of Brest without their neighbors' knowledge.

Alas! Isaac was correct, in a sense. No one, of course, had banned people from leaving the city, but doing so proved impossible. The street leading to the station was overrun by carriages, carts, and pedestrians. Traffic wasn't moving. The horses' foaming muzzles bumped against people's backs. Cabbies swore hoarsely. The draftees loitered between the carts. They had already been given a shave and a haircut, so they all looked alike. Their uniform tunics hung from their shoulders like bags, their thin necks stuck out of their collars, their caps sat low over their eyes. In beggars' voices, they asked for "a kopeck for smokes." The smarter ones offered their services to carry luggage to the station. Their services were in demand.

But the station, the platforms, the dining rooms, the lavatories, and the freight yard—all were even more crowded. Women, children, and old people sat on suitcases, bundles, and trunks. Even the better-dressed ones started spitting on other people's luggage—you can't keep swallowing your saliva forever. Frazzled porters were taking advantage of the situation, charging five rubles for each ticket delivered. Soon, however, someone hinted to the passengers—with good reason—that checking tickets in this mayhem would be impossible. Only those who actually grab a seat will be going. The crowd shifted. The queue that had started to form scattered instantly. Everyone rushed toward the entrance. A pregnant woman screamed, gasping for air. One couldn't see her face, only the convulsively trembling parasol over her head. Fathers threw their children into the open windows of the railcars; then, pushed away by the crowd, they screamed in fear. Children were crying. Perhaps for the first time since the advent of railroads, someone climbed onto the roof of a railcar and anxiously called out to his family—get up here!

"Go back, go back!" Meyer shouted, using his stout body to clear the path for his sick wife. "Children, help your mother! Someone might push her, God forbid. Hang on, Chava, we are getting out of here. Did someone push you?"

Another setback!

Finally, they made their way out of the chaos and sighed with relief.

At home, a telegram awaited them. Chava had always been wary of these white rectangles that smelled faintly of glue. Telegrams always bring worries, troubles, unexpected grief. In the dining room, Chava froze with her arm outstretched, still wearing her coat.

"I bet you it's from Hersh, his response to our telegram," said the father in a cheerful voice. "You'll see, Chava."

But the telegram wasn't from Hersh, it was from Ilya. "Carts will arrive tomorrow, come to Zelovo," Isaac read out.

"Thank God," Meyer sighed with relief.

3

And thus the Raskin family received something of a reprieve for more than a year. Plenty of grief and misfortune still await them, enough for everyone, more than enough, rest assured. But for now, Isaac doesn't need to sulk, he doesn't need to raise his shoulders or come up with some sour words in response to his older brother's hospitality. Especially since Ilya has no intention of drawing any moral capital from the situation. He presses his gnawed fingernails into the palms of his hands and wonders out loud when exactly his "parents with children" will be arriving at Zelovo. Then he saddles up a young stallion, picks up a crop, and rides off to meet them. He bobs in the saddle for a long time and, for lack of better things to do, tries to come up with a good way to greet his family. "Welcome!" he would say to them, using two fingers to raise his light cap over his perspiring head. "Welcome to our humble abode! There's enough space for everyone, thank God. Good thing I was in a hurry to finish the house. Welcome!"

The young leaseholder waits for a long time, asking peasants that he runs into whether they have seen several carts with luggage and people from the city. Their responses are rather confusing. The fact is that over the last few days, the local roads have seen all kinds of people, from the city and from the country alike. It's as if people have lost their usual impulse to stick to well-known paths and are choosing unfamiliar routes instead. Ilya waits for more than an hour, rising up in his stirrups and putting his hand above his visor—still no carts in sight. Then he rides off in a different direction. Hospitality is all very well, but work cannot wait even for an hour.

The venture he has started is not simple. The poor soil is overgrown with weeds, it is accustomed to infertility and will require a lot of hard work. The meadows and pastures are covered with low-growing shrubs and lumpy grass. But it's not the peasants' miserable, deprived cattle that walk these meadows anymore: Swiss cows have already been released here for the first time. You have to watch them daily. The fields have been plowed with an iron plow rather than an old-style wooden one. Farmhands and peasants here are accustomed to hungry idleness, they need help in learning how to eat well through hard work. So Ilya dashes from plot to plot. His stallion swings its tail and drops foam onto the dusty roads. This Ilya has never been kind to himself. If he's pressed for time, he'll have a real meal in the evening, but for now, he will ask a peasant for a piece of bread, fill his pocket with sweet peas, and munch on the green pods when he has a minute. Remember that he decided to get by without a manager—a long-neglected enterprise cannot support unnecessary hands.

Ilya rushes around like this until sundown. The cheesemaker rings his bell, the milkmaids carry brass cans to the cowshed. Ilya can't go home yet, he has to wait for the results. Are the milk yields rising at last? One would think he was going out of his way for the cows, he assigned them a plot of clover that could have been mowed down—but the yields show no improvement. What else can be done to boost milk production? Maybe the cheesemaker has some ideas?

"You have guests," the cheesemaker replies. "Congratulations!"

"Thank you, thank you," Ilya responds, and all of a sudden starts bragging about his father. Can the cheesemaker even imagine what a great entrepreneur Meyer Raskin is, what an operator, even? Ilya bites his fingernails, looks around, and praises the old leaseholder. "Oh," Ilya says, "Meyer Raskin will have an answer to the question about boosting milk production, that goes without saying. He'll have an answer on the tip of his tongue, he'll give it to you right away, no question about it."

Finally Ilya heads home, gives his boots a perfunctory shine with a fistful of hay and wipes his nose and lips. But the greeting that he came up with while in the fields has slipped his mind. His rooms, which smell of tree resin, are filled with noise, clamor, and chaos. Bundles and suitcases are everywhere. The bundles are slapdash; candlesticks and gramophone records spill out of them. Isaac's boy sits on a potty. A portable bed takes up the middle of the room; on it lies Luba. Her big-city elegance has disappeared without a trace. Isaac, in a coat and fedora, sits by the table. He is eating from a bowl. He must have been so hungry that in his haste he forgot to take off his outdoor clothing. His father is huddling in a corner, sewing a button onto his own pants in front of everyone. One cannot help but notice necks covered with grime, ears gray from dust, and dirty hands. People are changed by homelessness, something in them has snapped. Their movements are no longer calm and there is fear in their eyes. Only Chava is really happy to see her grandchildren—Ilya's kids. She stops thinking about her ailments. "God," she sighs, "please let me live to see these precious children marry. Children, do you know that I'm your grandmother? Right, some grandmother," she continues, "with all this going on, I forgot to bring you any candy!" Apparently, Chava could not remember that she had seen the grandchildren two months earlier.

"Well, it's all right," Ilya says, himself not knowing what he is referring to. "All right," he repeats after a long pause. "Things will settle down, and you will be able to go back to Brest-Litovsk."

He remembers that the call-up cost him five farmhands, and continues, "How can you have a war at this time of year? Do they think people have forgotten that the grain has not been harvested yet, and that before you know it, it will be time to plant winter crops? That's the thing! In five days everyone will be sent home." Then Ilya recalls his prepared greeting. "But for now, welcome to our humble abode! Make yourselves at home, enjoy the air and the fresh milk."

Make yourselves at home! The Raskin family will of course take advantage of their oldest son's kind offer. They will be staying at Zelovo and will try to enjoy the air and the fresh milk, as Ilya puts it. They will even try to forget what has happened—essentially, nothing has happened. People moved from Brest-Litovsk to Zelovo, from one district to another. They could just as well have come to spend the summer at Ilya's, panic or not. A Jew is used to wandering, that's what Jews do. But something is different here, it's not just the move alone. People are affected by homelessness, these several days have transformed them. Gone is their tidiness in eating and dressing. Isaac and Luba now have their own secrets, and so do Meyer and Chava. No one will pull a wad of money from a side pocket as easily as they used to, not at all. Now a man will first grunt, then put his hand in his pocket, surreptitiously separate one bill from the rest, and finally produce it as if it were his last.

Isaac lies about on the portable bed in his jacket and trousers in the middle of the day; the bed was never moved from the center of the room where it had been set up initially. Fuzz is sticking to his clothes and hair. He is miserable, unhappy with everything; this makeshift existence gives him plenty to grumble about. When Motya appears, Isaac starts needling him. But Motya does not particularly like staying at home. Then Isaac goes on to pester Sheva, a gymnasium girl. She is about to start the third grade, excellent! But does she even touch her books? No, she doesn't touch her books. She takes off her shoes and stockings and runs around the yard like a peasant girl. She collects tender nettles and chops them up with hard-boiled eggs for the geese and the ducklings. Ilya's children are younger than her, but she plays with them as if they are all the same age!

Isaac lies on the portable bed like an old paraplegic. He turns over slowly, grunts, and carps incessantly. Meyer has slowly become involved with Ilya's work. He has considered the situation, taken the times and recent developments into account, and come up with a few ideas for Ilya's operation. The former Telyatichi leaseholder has always had a broad perspective; his wits have never let him down, not once. It is wartime, which means that the operation needs to be put on wartime footing. There is absolutely no doubt that Ilya's cattle don't need nearly as much hay as Ilya has—there is a large surplus. This surplus should be sold to the military. We need to get hold of a hay press and some metal wire and urgently prepare, say, five railcars of meadow hay. We could also sell them a railcar of flour. But how can we do that? It's simple. He, Meyer, will go to Kobryn, make the needed contacts, and make the sale.

"Go to Kobryn in times like this and get mixed up with some procurement officers?"

This is Isaac talking, of course.

"What do the times have to do with it?" Meyer wonders. "Has life come to a complete stop?"

Ilya replies as if called upon in a classroom.

"No, life has not come to a complete stop. Things are a bit harder now, but we are managing."

So Meyer goes to Kobryn and pulls it off, of course. He sells both the hay and the flour, and in the meantime has yet another idea. So they pay fifty-five kopecks for forty pounds of hay? Minus five kopecks for pressing and delivery, that's fifty kopecks. He will buy up hay from the landowners of nearby estates and press it for the army. Something will be left for us, some small change can be made off this.

"What do you know!" he says, and looks at the others jubilantly. "And what did you think? Did you think that Meyer Raskin will busy himself with psalms? Excuse me, you were wrong, leave that to someone else."

So says Meyer, and Ilya looks at his father as though he is a wizard or a magician. Ilya catches Meyer's excitement. He stomps his feet and rubs his hands happily; he is ready to join his father in a vigorous "What do you know!"

"Oh yes," he says, still under the spell of his father's enthusiasm. "I almost forgot! There's an urgent telegram from Lodz. Pavel is asking for five wagons, he wants to bring the finished fabrics here and move his family to Zelovo. Yes, sure, we'll have to send the wagons, even though the whole thing will take two weeks."

In all honesty, Ilya wasn't too pleased with Pavel's telegram at first. Of course, the arrival of the Rusevich family is fine with him—there's space for everyone. But the carts! Sending five wagons away for two weeks during harvest time! But now he is infected with his father's energy, it engulfs him. What's ten horses? He is ready to pull a wagon himself!

Finally, the Rusevich family arrives at Zelovo, adding fuel to the fire of Isaac's acrimony. It's Pavel, Sophia, and their little girl with the fashionable name Sabina. The family has a mountain of luggage: they remembered to bring not only Pavel's mustache guard but even the special toilet paper on rolls. Pavel is a tidy man. When he goes to the lavatory, he takes a yard of paper with him. He cuts it up into five pieces with his pocket scissors, removes his jacket, and hangs it on a chair. He even hums a tune for the occasion, a special lavatory tune, if you will. He has no intention of changing his habits. Isaac is beside himself, he is oozing sarcasm and bitterness. Isaac is furious; he is caustic and withering.

"Well," he says, "I would love to see Pavel go to war in a mustache guard. And you, Sarah, why aren't you wearing a corset and designer hats here?"

Sarah responds to Isaac in kind. She always has the last word, she has no intention of letting her older brother get the upper hand. Pavel, however, couldn't care less, Isaac can say whatever he wants. Pavel receives letters from Moscow. The letters suggest that he is getting richer by the week. Lodz is occupied by the Germans, so the price of textiles keeps going up. If it continues like this, Pavel will become wealthy: his fabrics are sitting in Ilya's barn for good reason.

"I don't understand it," Meyer says. "If I were you, I would have sold the fabrics, bought some more, made a few deals."

"Oh, no," Pavel responds. "What for? Let the fabrics sit here in Zelovo, I earn good money every week."

Meanwhile, months go by, and the presence of war is increasingly palpable. Trains that follow no particular schedule and reek of iodoform and carbolic acid arrive at the station. Animal moaning, exhausted and hopeless, carries from these trains. Minced humanity lies numb on linen cots. The hospital stench speaks of death. The orderlies frequently carry dead bodies off the trains. Who knows who the deceased are? Some Ivans, felled by bullets on the fields of Galicia. The funeral services attract incidental people: a peasant woman with a string of dry, ring-shaped crackers that she has just splurged on to put together a parcel for her man who is a prisoner of war; Makar the drover, a lazy fibber with a bald pate covering his entire head; a very touching, sentimental young woman from the telegraph office—later, during a sleepless night, she will imagine that today she buried her nonexistent fiancé who has been brought from the battlefield; peasants, those perennial Russian train passengers who do not heed any timetable and spend their days and nights on the station's floor. A priest from a nearby village hastily dons his funeral vestments and sings the last farewell to the unknown man. The small yellow knoll will soon be level with the ground—nobody cares for a stranger's grave. The dead man, Ivan, a hero and casualty of the battles in Galicia, will be forgotten. Rest in peace, if you can. Eternal memory!

In the evening, trains of a different kind roll in the opposite direction past the crawling hospital trains. The doors of their heated boxcars are ajar. A small lantern inside provides a dim light. Rifles stand in stacks. The large, intelligent eyes of horses shine and gleam in the dark. Soldiers sit on bunks. They play cards and cheat with abandon. Every once in a while a soldier leaves the game behind, comes to the door, leans against the frame, and becomes lost in his thoughts. Fields stretch endlessly beyond the embankment. The moonlight streams from above, draping the spaces in a silver haze. It is quiet. An autumn chill is in the air. A bird will awaken and warble an anxious trill. Did it dream of something or is the night just too beautiful? An owl will respond with a frightening hoot. Behind the fields there is a forest which smells of mushrooms and bilberries, behind the forest is a village—a flock of peasant huts. It is warm and pleasantly stuffy in the huts; snoring comes from all sides.

The soldier suddenly feels a strange yearning. He tightens his belt, unbuttons the collar of his tunic, and huddles in the corner. His eyes still stare into the distance. It's quiet. Then all of a sudden, his lips open of their own volition, and sounds break the silence. What is the soldier singing about? He doesn't know yet. His soul is singing, finding its own words and sounds. The horses' bits gently chime in tune. The train will stop, its wheels sounding the last beat. It's quiet. The card game is forgotten. Everything living is listening to the soldier singing. His voice is beautiful. What is he singing about? Then another voice chimes in. It's as if a man approached the first singer, put his hand on the other's shoulder, and suggested, "Let's sing together, brother, it's better with the two of us." Now two, three, four men are singing together, and then the whole railcar is singing this melancholy song. It goes on until the wheels grind again and everything all around starts clanging. Then everyone falls silent, everyone feels awkward. "Well," says someone with a sigh, "let's play some cards here, shall we?"

Every once in a while, captured Austrians are led past like a flock of sheep. They squat behind a barn and relieve themselves. They smoke long porcelain pipes with shoulder-to-shoulder images of the Emperors Franz Joseph and Wilhelm II. A wounded Russian soldier—there are plenty of them now in the countryside—will come out to greet them and start chatting in a language that he himself has just invented. After all, they were all in the same battles, weren't they? "*Gut, zoldier?*" the wounded man will ask, which must mean something like, "Well, brother, had enough of this war? Get some rest now, take a good look at your enemies—you probably didn't know much about us. Take a look at this Russia of ours. Welcome!" The Austrian captive will take the pipe out of his mouth, exhale a puff of smoke, and reply, "*Gut, veri gut*, f--k it!" Women will turn away, old men will gasp—where did this sonofabitch learn to gab like us so good? The wounded man explains smugly, "At the front, where else?" A boy calls out to his mates, "Hey, come here! Look, Nastya's husband, the wounded one, is talking to the Austrians in French! Come here!"

Here and there, a woman will suddenly start wailing inconsolably and beating her head against the wall. This means that her Ivan, a nameless hero, has been buried at some godforsaken train station. In response to the pleading letters she sent to her husband, she received an official notice with a blue seal imprinted on it: "We regret to inform you . . . Private so-and-so . . . passed away at . . . buried at . . ." followed by illegible squiggles for signatures. Hold on to this notice, widow, it makes you eligible for an allowance, they will give you rubles for your man. Don't be too upset!

Time is crawling, moving on. Little by little, people get used to the idea that somewhere out there, in a faraway land, nations have been snarling and menacing each other with bayonets from foxholes and trenches. Autumn rains are pouring down. The woolen fabric of the soldier's overcoat is probably getting soaked in the rain, his exhausted body becomes wet. Then come the frosts. When it is this cold, it is not easy to deal with poison gas or to charge the enemy lines. But that is out there, in a faraway land. Here, a stove still gives warmth, a lamp still shines its light, it's peaceful and quiet. The *Russkoye Slovo* broadsheet provides accounts of the war by Nemirovich-Danchenko and Grigory Petrov. One needs to know how to read a newspaper out loud; Meyer Raskin has repeatedly asked Isaac to be careful. Chava takes in every word she hears, she is sick and distraught. It's been five months since Hersh disappeared without a trace. The telegrams that they sent to all corners of the earth were returned a few weeks later. Where is Hersh? How is he? If there really is hunger in Germany and Austria, what has happened to their son? There have been no answers. Meyer has been coming up with some clever theories. No, never mind, Meyer can keep quiet, it's better that he keeps quiet, his tall tales won't fool anyone.

But one day a postcard arrives in the mail along with letters and newspapers. It has no postage stamp but is covered with dozens of postmarks. Rachel reads the address, quickly turns the postcard over—and cries out with joy. It's from Hersh! Dear Chava, please get a grip on yourself. Hersh has sent us a postcard. He is alive and well, he has been interned, he is in a prisoner-of-war camp. So what does your son write after such a long hiatus? He writes about a parcel. It's probably the gray paper of the postcard that has made his message so impersonal, but all he writes about is food. Please don't cry, Hersh is fine; he is asking us to send him something to eat.

So here's a new chore—a pleasant one! Every week one needs to dry some slices of bread, put the box in a fabric slipcover, and write out the address with an ink pencil. Hersh has been able to get in touch with his family, his postcards are finally reaching Zelovo. Be thankful. Don't forget that he is old enough to be drafted here. Do you think it's better to fight than to sit in a camp? No one in the Raskin family is dead, thank God, they've all been spared. Just wait till the war is over, and everything will return to normal.

This is how the Raskins console themselves. People love to console themselves, they live on consolation and hope. But hopes aren't always answered. The Raskin family has been living in relative peace for the past few months. The heavy hammer of fate will soon fall on their heads. What is happening "out there" will soon be at their door.

It is the summer of 1915 and their year-long reprieve is coming to an end . . .

4

Sliding off the pages of newspapers that are full of white gaps left by the censors, the menacing events of the war approach ever closer. Wagons, carts, carriages, and buggies are stretched out along countless roads. One after another, whole trains of them extend for miles on end.

It's summer, but people are wearing winter coats and everything else they could possibly squeeze themselves into as they were abandoning their homes. Thick tarpaulins forming semi-circular tents shield the contents of the carts. Dirty, unkempt children covered with blisters and sores bounce around inside. The locals have one name for all of them: refugees. People are unfriendly to them the way peasants are to gypsies. The refugees are not particularly considerate of the locals either. They stop at the edges of villages and estates and immediately start acting like they own the place. They pull hay from already finished stacks, their horses stomp over the oats, adults and children lay about in the fields, damaging the ripening crops. Campfires burn at sunset. The refugees swarm the potato fields like locusts. They dig recklessly, destroying more than they harvest. The breathless owner comes running, angrily screaming and cursing in outrage. Then the travelers reluctantly step back for a while, like wolves that have been chased away from the horse they have just killed. They scowl and stare morosely.

"What is wrong with them?" say the Zelovo peasants and shrug their shoulders in bewilderment. "Where are you from, you devils?"

"From around Chelm," the refugees reply reluctantly in their mixed Polish-Belarusian dialect.

"From around Chelm,"—that's all you can draw out of them. Clearly they have been on the road for weeks now—enough to adjust to nomadic life and become changed people.

"Odd people, very odd people," Meyer Raskin mumbles, "you can't even tell what they did back home." The sight of refugees confounds him.

He walks to the road and starts asking them questions. There's something insulting and baffling about their nonchalant and derisive tone.

In the middle of the conversation, Meyer Raskin sees the travelers' horses leave the road and trample the ripe rye. The old man looks at the refugees. They look back at him as if they have nothing to do with it. They even chuckle a bit, narrow their eyes, and pause, as if trying the owner's patience.

"You horses went off the road, you probably didn't notice," Meyer Raskin says politely.

"It's all right," the refugees drawl and after a long pause add, "The horses won't eat too much, they won't burst, it's not barley."

"So they know that horses gorge on barley, which means they are peasants," Meyer Raskin concludes and explodes, the blood rushing to his face.

"Are you stupid?" he shouts hoarsely. "What's wrong with you? Get out of the field, now!"

Slowly and reluctantly, they obey.

"You won't be able to harvest it anyway," they grumble.

"How so?"

"You won't, you'll abandon it, that's how."

"How do you know?"

"We know what we're talking about. You'll drop everything."

For several weeks, the refugees "from around Chelm" crawl along the winding roads. It's as if a sea of humanity has burst through somewhere, producing dense streams as far as the eye can see. Finally, the flow starts to dwindle and thin out, the human chain breaks off. For a week, the area is granted a respite from the onslaught of uninvited guests. Life appears to be returning to normal. Ilya quickly bounces back after the invasion of refugees. He is shortsighted, that Ilya; all he cares about is work. He doesn't notice that people around him are now edgier, that their eyes shine nervously and glow feverishly. He gets up at sunrise and goes to bed right after dinner. His life is ruled by the immutable laws of nature. If the rye is ripe, then it must be harvested. If small yellow flowers appear among the oats in large numbers, then weeding is in order, some women need to be hired. It was his father Meyer who said that life cannot stop for a single moment. What is there to think about?

"We have to thresh the rye urgently," Meyer says to his son. "Thresh it and sell it for cash."

"Who threshes before everything has been harvested?" Ilya wonders. "What's the rush? One thing at a time."

"Are you sure you'll be able to harvest everything?"

"Who abandons crops? The world has not gone mad yet!"

So says Ilya and hurries on. Maybe he is right, maybe this is just a bad dream, the world has not gone mad, it just can't. The wave of refugees has passed, and it is peaceful here again. Here comes Pavel. Surrounded by nature, he can allow himself a certain degree of freedom. He wears slippers and leaves his jacket inside. He sports purple silk suspenders and a bowler that sits jauntily on his head. Seeing his father-in-law, he slows down, stops, and after a proper preamble, reports to Raskin about his successes. "The price of textiles has gone up again! This shouldn't be surprising at all, considering that the chief center of our manufacturing world, if I may say so, is under occupation." In another year, Rusevich's assets will double as a minimum, and as a maximum . . .

For a stronger effect, Pavel stops here without saying exactly how much his assets will grow as a maximum, bows elegantly, and moves on. A man should know how to take advantage of everything. If he lives in the country, on an estate, then he should build up his health. Especially since the circumstances are such that he makes good money without doing any work. Oh yes, bringing his fabrics here was not a bad idea, not at all! Not many people thought of carting their goods away. Isaac can grumble and raise his shoulders, he can bicker with Sophia all he wants—Pavel Rusevich couldn't care less.

It's peaceful again for a few days. The carefree sun is still bright and warm, skylarks are still singing their monotonous songs, crops ripen on the trees and in the ground. The droning of bees in the fields sounds busier: they sense that fall is approaching. During the hot days, dry, Indian-summer webs float and become entangled above the stubble of the harvested fields. Women start work early in the morning. They work all day, then go home, singing somberly and raising dust colored pink by the setting sun. Sickles rest on their shoulders. A wreath made of ripe stalks sways on the head of a young woman who is walking ahead of the others.

A herd slowly passes by. The sheep huddle together, moving in waves like a solid blanket of steaming wool. A young shepherd snaps his long whip. Another, an older one, wearing bast shoes and a sheepskin hat, has slowed down. He is pensively searching for the right melody on his pipe. He runs his fingers over it, covering and uncovering its holes. Finally, the song is set. Like a light breeze, like a sad "farewell" to peaceful labor, it glides over the fields and melts into the evening air. There is no need for thinking or straining now: the song flows freely from the shepherd's lips. His legs spontaneously sense the rhythm. The tempo of the song affects all living things. Everything around moves in tune with the evening melody. The sunset is crimson hot. End-of-summer smells become more intense. Grasshoppers chirp loudly in the thick grass. The lemon-colored disk of the moon emerges in the blue sky. Labor and rest still rule here, but they are counting their last days. Maybe that is why they now seem more beautiful than ever.

Enough of that! The world is on a totally different track now, the sea that burst through has not calmed down, streams continue to run. After a weeklong pause, the human flows surge through once again. In carts, wagons, and carriages, on horseback, on oxen, or on foot—they have again inundated the roads. You no longer need to ask which area they are from— it's easy to tell by their gray coats trimmed with light-blue ribbons, and by their Belarusian speech. These are peasants from the Brest area. Their faces are gaunt and dark, their every move belies haste. Torn only recently from their labors, they regard those who are still working with surprise.

"We were no different," the refugees explain. "We kept going and going—until they made us leave."

They don't talk much. When someone asks them why they didn't stay where they were, they just waive their hands and turn away.

"In Christ's name, can you spare some bread?" women plead like beggars.

After receiving pitiful leftovers, they give the local women some advice.

"You, dears, bake some bread and dry it out, you'll need it on the road."

They don't try to scare people or make fun of them—and that's probably what affects the peasants the most. The usual sequence of field work spontaneously falls apart, the Belarusians start hurrying. Instead of plowing the fields, reaping oats, or harvesting buckwheat, the peasants turn to threshing. Rumors govern their lives. The rumors come from the refugees and are spread in secret from person to person. People conceal their plans from each other. Trying not to make too much noise so as not to alert their neighbors, the peasants prepare their carts. They make rods from fresh branches and quietly stretch canvas over them. The more practical of them rise in the middle of the night, light an oil lamp, and go to the grain barn to dig a large pit in the earthen floor. They line the pits with batten and pour the "extra" grain inside. Eager to ease their own worries, the peasants lie to each other, "Can you imagine the Germans or the Austrians getting this far? It's all cheap talk! Only fools would believe it." Then they go inside and urgently prepare to leave.

Would Ilya Raskin still claim that life hasn't stopped for a single moment?

No, in situations like this, Ilya keeps quiet and glances at his father with alarm. What would wise Meyer Raskin say, with all his life experience? How would he cheer up the family?

It's difficult for a man to face the harsh truth, he is often happy to make up his own soothing lies. Meyer comes home and notices that for some reason, the curtains have been taken off the windows.

"Why are the curtains down?" he asks Rachel, the lady of the house.

"I'm washing them," Rachel replies with too much haste. It's clear that she had the answer ready well in advance.

"Oh, I see. You will, of course, iron them and hang them back up? Please excuse my meddling . . ."

"Oh, it's nothing, no need to apologize, we all live here," Rachel replies. She understood Meyer perfectly well.

Meyer says nothing. Everyone looks at him, everyone has fallen silent.

"I don't think they ever fight on country roads," Meyer Raskin says. "War moves along major highways and railroads. What I'm trying to say is that one day we may find ourselves under the Germans. The front will move past Zelovo, and we will continue as usual."

At this point Isaac—a major military strategist who studies Mikhaylovsky's columns in *Russkoye Slovo* for lack of anything else to do— chimes in.

"It doesn't happen like that," he says. "An army retreats fighting, they battle for every sliver of land."

This turn of events would be very costly to Pavel Rusevich; for him, a German invasion, even if peaceful, is highly undesirable.

"Now wait a minute!" he objects heatedly, as if the fate of the area depends upon the conversation at this table. "How can this happen? Clearly you know nothing about the textile business. Our Russian textiles could never compete with the ones from Germany. Were the Germans to take the area over, my fabrics would drop in price immediately, by a good seventy percent, if not eighty. Thank you very much!"

Others listen to Pavel absentmindedly. Everyone is preoccupied with their own thoughts, nobody even tries to smile, and even Isaac forgets to raise his shoulders. Sounds reach the house through the windows and the recently built walls. Hundreds and hundreds of carts are rattling and creaking—they have lost their way, they have broken ranks, they are spreading across the fields and the woods in disarray. People talking, children crying, horses neighing—all this mixes into a single din. The sky is covered with mournful clouds. Now, in the evening, it appears black. Campfires flicker across the plains like fireflies. People emerge from the darkness and walk past. For a while, the metallic rattling of army wagons silences the monotonous sound of civilian carts. The wagons follow one another closely without pausing even for a moment. The refugees hastily move aside—otherwise, their carts would get thrown off the road. The soldiers have accordions in their hands. The instruments wail, rumble, and compete with other sounds, finally overpowering them and reigning supreme. Spirited music is all you can hear. Every wagon carries its own tune. It's as if the accordions are speaking different languages; they don't care about the listeners, they must express themselves by spilling out the music that has accumulated in their bellows. All other sounds only add to the chaos.

The Raskins spend their last, sleepless night in their elder son's house. These noisy, uneasy hours conclude their peaceful life at Zelovo. The morning light reveals a shocking sight. Everything around has been so trampled and torn apart that it looks as if some black veins have swollen underground and burst through the surface. Dying horses, broken wheels, and overturned carts are everywhere. The crows, sensing an easy meal, caw greedily; they raise their feet and swoop to the ground. The shepherd arrives. He has tightened his belt and pulled his sheepskin hat lower. He isn't carrying his whip or his musical pipe. He leans on his walking stick and calmly asks what to do with the livestock. Should the cattle be moved to the fields or kept in the sheds? Of course, the cows "definitely cannot be" without food, so if they are not taken to pasture, they will need hay . . .

While the shepherd is still talking, the cheesemaker comes running and loudly announces that not a single milkmaid came to work this morning, which means that the cows have not been milked. Neither milked nor taken out to the pasture. So what are the milkmaids doing? The same thing as the men: they are at home, packing for the journey.

Now the rush starts in earnest, and everyone's thinking promptly changes: each one thinks of himself and his own immediate family, his suitcases and belongings. Everything in the house is upside down. Cupboards are flung open, drawers are pulled out, rags are thrown all over the floor. It suddenly becomes clear that there is no such thing as a single Raskin family.

Isaac and Luba are one family, Sarah and Pavel are another; Meyer, Chava, Motya, and Sheva—yet another. Each family tries to pack as much as they can and make their journey as comfortable as possible. Sarah is packing, while Pavel hurries to the barn to number his bags of fabrics. He dashes around the estate, grabbing people by their sleeves, promising all kinds of rewards—and still he cannot find any help. Then he rushes to see Ilya, the leaseholder of Zelovo. Rusevich needs five men for three hours, he is prepared to pay whatever they ask. Besides, he needs at least four wagons and four tarpaulins: he has made precise calculations.

"Oh, please, let it go, I can't deal with your fabrics right now," Ilya replies. His face is burning. "Can't you see that you won't be able to take them with you?"

"You're out of your mind!" Pavel hisses, forgetting all his manners. "My entire fortune is in these fabrics . . ."

He thinks for a few seconds and adds in exasperation,

"After all, I can pay you for the wagons!"

Ilya waves him off and runs away. Today, he must do everything himself, his laborers are no longer taking orders from him. Cows, horses, and their offspring have not been fed. The world has gone mad—now Ilya has no doubt about it. The self-assurance that he felt just yesterday is gone; he feels as if he is walking on shaky, swampy ground. Nothing would surprise him now. He feeds the animals and puts several padlocks on the shed's doors—in this chaos, anything could happen.

Who can calmly observe what is going on? Only those who are not yet completely melded with their belongings. Motya quickly becomes bored with the packing. His family members have revealed a new, unpalatable side. Motya wanders around the estate, then goes into the village. A broad street opens before him. Every house has a cart packed with household items waiting out front. By now, everything that could possibly be loaded onto the carts has already been loaded. People lock their doors for some reason, and sit down on a bench by the house. Now is the time to say the last goodbyes, but nobody wants to be the first to leave their home behind. At this moment, children come running and, interrupting one another, nervously report that some strangers—the refugees—have climbed over the fence and are stealing apples and pears from Princess Dolgorukova's orchard. Andrei, the Princess's coachman, couldn't stop them: they threatened him with clubs and shooed him away.

The peasants' patience runs out, and the angry tension snaps. As if on cue, they turn their heads toward their own doors that they have just locked. What on earth is going on? Today these damn refugees are stealing apples and pears; tomorrow they will come here, break the locks, and take over? Who gave them the right to barge into someone else's orchard? Let's go, fellows!

The fellows don't need much cajoling. They instantly jump to their feet, pull some stakes out of the wattle fences, and run toward the orchard of Princess Dolgorukova. Their women and children grab some empty bags for the apples that will be confiscated from the dastardly refugees and follow the men. A minute later, the fellows are standing in front of the mansion's iron fence. The gates are locked, but through the iron lattice they can see the refugees scurrying busily. The Zelovo men pause only briefly. The spirit of destruction is boiling in their veins. A moment later, the fence loudly crashes down in front of them. Hundreds of people, blind to everything around them, run through the orchard, brandishing their stakes. It looks like a fight is imminent and the stakes and fists are about to be put to use . . .

The trees appear darkened by countless plums. Heavy apples gleaming in the sun weigh branches down toward the ground. Huge green pears hang among sparse leaves. Most of the Zelovo men climb the trees themselves, grab the fruits, and stuff them into their bags and pockets. The Princess's enormous castle towers in the center of the orchard. Groomed alleyways that have not felt the steps of Her Highness in years lead to spacious verandas. Heavy drapes cover the wide windows; behind them loom the outlines of massive furnishings. A small turret made of stained glass crowns the imposing structure. The glass shines blindingly in the sun. It feels as if someone has lit the turret on fire, and now it bursts with red, blue, green, and carmine flames. The fire sends white sparks flying—these are pigeons. The men sitting in the trees feel as though they are seeing the palace of their Princess for the first time. Everyone is listening to an old stranger in a torn sheepskin coat. He is crunching on an apple and thinking out loud.

"What a huge place," he ponders, "you could build stoves for a dozen villages with all these bricks, sure thing. And the glass—there's enough for every peasant in Russia, that's right!"

He adjusts his sheepskin hat, gazes into the draped windows of the palace with a calculating eye, and continues pensively,

"And the stuff in there . . . silver, gold, five hundred yards of cotton easily . . ."

The peasants climb down from the trees, gather around the old man, and start to reminisce. After the palace was finished, dozens of carts brought thousands of boxes from the train station. The Princess sent those boxes from St. Petersburg. Some were large but lightweight, and some were small but so heavy that several men could barely handle them. One wonders what was in those boxes . . .

"We know what," the old man replies, winking. "No need to guess. We all know what!"

"Yeah," the peasants sigh. "Yes, indeed."

"Take the Germans," the old man continues, "the Germans, the Austrians, whatever. What will they do? First thing, they will pack everything into boxes and take it home, you bet they will. We here have enjoyed a few apples, and they'll get the real thing, and that's that."

"Well, we're not going to let them!" shouts one of the men angrily. "It's on our land, so it's ours! We'll divvy it up fair and square, all of us. Forget the Germans!"

"What do you mean, forget?" says the stranger with a hint of irony. He winks and waves his hands, clearly inviting everyone to join the conversation. "Nobody's going to ask you!"

"Oh, yes, they will!" the peasants yell. "You bet they will!"

"What do you mean?" the oldster wouldn't let go. "If we all flee, then what? There won't be anybody to ask . . ."

Then he describes what they themselves did, the peasants of Grushevo. At first, they were thinking exactly the same. But then the refugees arrived and gave them the idea: "You, fellas, get what you want, and we'll pick up the rest. So that's what we did."

"And the soldiers?" someone prudent asks from the crowd.

"The soldiers—oh, well, they understand. Better let us have it than put it all to the torch."

The clatter of hooves interrupts them. A detachment of soldiers rides into the orchard. The peasants cling together, someone furtively tosses apples out of his pocket. Another moment—and they would all flee. But the soldiers ignore them. They dismount and disappear into the building. The peasants, who up until now stayed away from the walkways covered with yellow sand, now run up to the windows and look up, trying to see what is going on inside. A minute later, a balcony door flies open. A soldier is holding a stack of books in calico bindings. He throws the books into the crowd and calls out,

"Here you go, fellas, roll yourselves some smokes!"

The books fall noisily to the ground, their pages whistling. No one touches them, not even the children. The peasants are still waiting. Then another soldier smashes a window with his rifle butt. Shards of glass cascade to the ground, clinking and sparkling in the sun. The smashed window says more to the peasants than the old man's cautious words. Boots thumping and bast shoes slapping, the people surge into the Princess's castle. They empty their bags and pockets of the apples as they run. The stairs creak and moan under hundreds of feet. A peasant with a pockmarked face and a full head of thick curly hair grabs a mirror hanging in the hallway by its frame and tears it off the wall. He loads it onto his back and pauses for a moment to think what to do next. Should he run with the loot to his cart as fast as he can or take full advantage and grab something else from the castle? A string of rooms attracts his attention. Holding the gleaming, precious mirror in its gilded frame over his head, he pushes other people away with his shoulders and dashes in. In the next room, cupboards have been pried open, and the peasants are pulling endless swaths of table linens out of them. The fate of the mirror is sealed—it is smashed to pieces. The man with the pockmarked face loads up on linens. White strips dangle from his hands like snakes. He stumbles over them and slips on the hardwood floor.

The rooms opening before the surging crowd are very orderly. Soft chairs on gilded legs stand in neat arrangements. There are carpets on the floors, portraits on the walls, knickknacks on the shelves. Massive bronze pieces gleam. Birds of paradise fly motionlessly on the fretwork ceilings, cherubs with little wings on their backs play flutes. For a moment, people freeze in the doorway. There's something cold about this expensive splendor. The people are overloaded with loot, but the spirit of destruction is still with them. Their eyes search for something even more valuable. What attracted their attention just a minute ago now seems cheap. Pockets and bags are being partially emptied only to be loaded with equally useless things seconds later. Loud crashing and cracking noises fill the castle. There are too many massive pieces here: you can't take them with you, and they are not easy to destroy.

A soldier hacks the mirrored surface of a large music box with his saber. A burly fellow helps him, snuffling and mopping the sweat from his brow. He sighs, takes a deep breath, and drives a stake into the ringing steel bowels of the box with all his might. Then he pulls out of it a bundle of shiny metal rolls. The box, however, still has gleaming metal parts and mahogany;

it's sturdiness is irritating. People drag it to the window with great effort and heave it outside. A Cossack sits at the grand piano. He touches the keys with his fingers, but the sounds are barely audible in the hubbub. Then he starts hitting the keys with his fist and, flying into a rage for some reason, smashes them with his rifle butt. The burly fellow shakes his head, raises his stake, squints, and aims tentatively at the strings. Soon the grand piano flies out the window too. Those who missed the beginning of the mayhem dash around the wrecked rooms. They are spooked by their own echoing voices. They rummage through the remains in a frenzy, grabbing anything in sight, and continue running. The mirrored walls multiply their reflections, so they feel like they are surrounded and are about to be rushed by the Princess's faithful servants.

So where are those who stormed through these halls just a few minutes ago? The distant roar dies down. . . . The circular room of the winter garden smells of warm humid soil, tropical plants, and flowers. A fountain splashes and bubbles. Exotic fish suffocate and die in convulsions on the stone floor. An uprooted palm tree graciously rests its branches on the floor. A frog with bulging eyes looks around in bewilderment.

The ransacking lasts for several hours. All the rooms have been rummaged through, the doors have been smashed. Now it is even clearer that of all these luxury items, the enthralled crowd grabbed the most useless ones. People return and rummage through the damaged, broken pieces and piles of torn fabrics. Two women are tearing the plush off a sofa from opposite sides, breaking their fingernails. Their movements are jerky, their eyes dart nervously, and the plush doesn't budge.

"A knife would help," sighs one of them. "Too bad I got no knife."

"Let it go," the other advises her seriously. "I'm doing it, this is my fabric."

"Fat chance, bitch!" the first one screams, pushing a candelabra deeper into her coat pocket.

They let go of the sofa, look around, and, finding no sympathy, grab each other's hair, stomping their feet heavily.

Bartering takes place right then and there. People stand amid the unusual wreckage, raving about their booty, and lying shamelessly. A crocodile desk pad with satin lining passes from hand to hand.

"Look at this leather," says an old man with protruding eyelids, removing his cap. Without the cap, he resembles Socrates. "The leather is American, for sure."

"Yeah, right!" A tall young fellow sounds mocking and incredulous. "Maybe it's not even leather?"

"Don't be silly! It's the real thing. You can make anything out of this leather."

"Yeah, right!"

The sun in the windows turns crimson. Purple shadows lie across the garden and sulk in the corners of the castle. The noise dies down, only to give way to a panicked uproar. The shadows thicken and turn into clouds of smoke. The air smells of burning wool.

"Fire!" screams somebody in a cracked voice. "They torched it, bastards!"

Hundreds of feet are suddenly rushing, rumbling through the expansive hallways. Peter the Great stares inquisitively from the wall, imperiously raising his surly face with veins on his forehead and stretching his enormous hand with a silver ring on its index finger. Carmine plumes crawl across the floors. The steps seem countless. The burly fellow, holding a bedpan in his hands, is the first one out of the building. The small turret on top of the castle is filled with fire and smoke. The fellow looks at the bedpan, turns it around, and examines it from all sides. Then he notices a shiny ball in the middle of a colorful flower bed. Flowers climb up a small green post from all sides. The bedpan flies to the ground, the fellow grabs the ball and continues running.

Only now, after the crowd has carried Motya out of the castle, does he remember his family. He didn't think of them once during all these hours. Chaotic thoughts swarm in his head; he is having a hard time making sense of it all. He is certain of only one thing: what he has just witnessed has made a deep impression on him, it will stay with him for a long time . . .

5

The Raskin family had climbed into carts many times before. Surrounded by those close to him, Meyer might recall how, as a young man, he climbed into a cart with his father, dangled his legs over the edge, took the rope reins, and set out for Antopol to meet his future wife—the sorrowful Chava. Later, Meyer Raskin switched to a light carriage, whose steel springs gently swayed his massive body. On rare occasions, four horses pulled a heavy, old-fashioned coach to the train station. Peacock feathers swept the air around the coachman's little round cap. His backside was so tight that it felt at times that the coachman might overturn. When was it? Not that long ago; any reasonable person in Zelovo remembers those times. But when Meyer Raskin was fifty-four, the lease on Telyatichi expired. Raskin closed the business gainfully: tens of thousands of rubles sat in the Merchant Bank, taking a break from agriculture-related transactions. When he moved to Brest-Litovsk, hired horse cabs replaced the carriages, even though owning his own rig would not have bankrupted Meyer Raskin. Did all this really happen? Or is the old man delirious? No, it did happen, everyone knows it.

Whatever you say, the family's patriarch can look back with satisfaction. It's not in his nature to sway over the Torah at the synagogue, and neither is clipping bond coupons and living off the interest. The Raskins have more than enough money, no question about it.

But then a storm strikes, the likes of which people's fathers or grandfathers had never seen. The Merchant Bank halts payments to its depositors. The fully furnished apartment in Brest-Litovsk has to be abandoned. The Raskins move to Ilya's at Zelovo. Everyone lives together in one house, forfeiting the comforts they had grown accustomed to. Isn't that enough? But no, fate knows no bounds, and no mercy. The decisiveness, the self-assurance—all this is gone. Thank God they were able to find a few men who agreed—for a very large fee—to drive the Zelovo herd to the nearest army field depot. The farmhands, however, had all stopped taking orders and fled. Meyer Raskin knows all too well what it means when people stop taking orders. One should be thankful that at least they aren't torching houses, taking horses, or killing . . .

All a man can rely on is himself and his own skills. Take a look! The four men—Meyer, Ilya, Isaac, and Pavel—are heading to the stables to harness the horses. Meyer is old but strong, he won't confuse the different straps; he is not harnessing a horse for the first time in his life. He also knows that he should fill up and bring with him a container of grease and a bag of oats. And Pavel? He approaches the first stable, beckons with two fingers of his left hand, and says, "*Pst, pst,*" as if he is calling a waiter in a restaurant. He calls, "*Pst, pst,*" and beckons with his fingers. The horse flicks its ears, beats the wooden floor with its hooves, shakes its head rhythmically, and shows its large teeth, intending to give Pavel a friendly tug on his sleeve. Pavel recoils and backs into another horse, which pushes its warm muzzle into the back of his head.

"Never mind, I'll do it," Ilya says.

Pavel waits, removing his bowler and blowing specs off it. He is dressed up as if he is going to a ball—all that is missing is a tailcoat and a white tie.

Ilya begins by setting up a wagon for Pavel, then puts the reins and whip into his hands: from now on, you're on your own. Pavel climbs into the wagon and immediately takes off, without waiting for the others. He has his own plans, which he chooses not to share with anyone. All of them are on their own now, he is perfectly clear about it. He urges on his horses, making them race to the barn at full speed. Then he takes his jacket off, hangs his bowler on the fence, and starts loading the wagon with his fabrics. Half an hour later, he arrives at the house. The horses can barely pull the impossibly heavy load. Pavel drags his suitcases, boxes, and trunks onto the top, then helps his wife and daughter to climb on. He is ready to go.

Other members of the Raskin family are packing too. The wagons fill up with luggage. Yes, do prepare for the journey, prepare well: as soon as you take off, you will lose your individuality, you will even lose your names. You'll be refugees!

What can you do? . . . The Raskins had climbed into their wagons under all kinds of circumstances, but never before in a situation like this. Sweat is streaming down Meyer's face, his head feels heavy, his brain is hazy, his eyes are red. He mops his brow and wipes his eyelids with his handkerchief. He is sweating so hard that even his eyes are filling with uninvited drops. Meyer has always been able to find words of comfort for his wife, but now he has nothing to say. He glances at Chava furtively. The old woman is so weak! She lowers herself onto the nearest suitcase until she is asked to move. Her dry lips are burning, her chest is heaving. Her eyes linger on each member of her family. To make things easier, fifteen-year-old Sheva has tossed her braid to her chest and removed her shoes. She grabs the luggage with her strong hands and drags it to the wagon. Her face shows no sorrow or alarm. She could burst out laughing at the most inopportune moment: it might be the red-haired Sabina sitting way up high that makes her laugh, or it might be her overwhelmed sisters-in-law. Leaving doesn't bother her: she hasn't developed a strong attachment to hearth yet. Her shoulder blades work back and forth under her brown dress.

"Lord, almighty God!" Chava thinks. "New times are coming. Lord, you chose to scatter people across the land. Why couldn't you have done it ten years later, when all my children would be standing firmly on their feet? Why are you testing the little ones, the ones not yet strong enough?"

"Hey!" Rachel shouts and spins around. "Look, an old man is dragging such a heavy suitcase. He'll break his back! Children, why aren't you helping your father?"

"Isaac," Luba tells her husband, "go help your father. It's easier together, he'll help you later."

She didn't need to say these last words, but never mind her. Now is not the time to dwell on little things, it's better to ignore them.

Chava continues with her inventory. The hardworking Ilya; Rachel; the haggard, high-strung Isaac; Luba . . . her eyes start searching around the room. Despite feeling weak, she stands up quickly, comes out onto the porch, then runs back inside.

"Meyer, Meyer!" she screams desperately. "Meyer, where is Motya, where is my son, where is he?"

Only now they remember their youngest son and brother. Yet another calamity! Where is Motya? When they get a chance, people run out onto the porch and shout into the twilight: "Motya, Motya!" There is no time for a thorough search. Carts are rattling and squeaking, people are walking by, old men are hobbling past. Where is Chava's son, her own flesh and blood?

"No!" Chava screams, grabbing a stool with both hands. "Leave me here, I'm not going without him! You want to go—go, but I am a mother! A mother!"

Another calamity! Do we need to mention that Meyer is a devoted father, that Motya's disappearance has floored him, too? He dashes around the room, searching for his bowler, which happens to be in his hands, then runs out onto the porch, takes a few steps, and promptly turns back. If they don't join the human stream right now, it will be too late. So Meyer—the devoted father!—starts arguing that Motya is not a little boy, that he is not a needle in a haystack, that there is no way he can get lost. He will realize that the family has left and he will find them, of course! We can't wait any longer!

"Do you want us all to die?" Luba screams hysterically. "You want the Cossacks to slaughter us all at night? The stupid boy went for a walk, and now we all have to perish here?"

She is spitting with anger and flailing her arms. Her countless shawls make her look like a bird cut out from a sheet of white paper—only her nose is sticking out from her wraps.

Sighing and groaning, wincing from pain and turning his face away, Meyer takes Chava by her waist and tries to twist the stool out of her hands. Her wig slides to one side, and a lock of gray hair falls on her face.

"Let me go," she croaks frantically. "I will say frightful things to you, Meyer. You're not a father. . . . You're a criminal. . . . Let me go. . . . I'll damn you. . . . Where's Hersh? It's all your fault. . . . Where's Motya?"

A minute later, she is sitting in the wagon, convulsing hysterically, howling, crying, and wailing. Meyer picks up the reins. Another moment—and the mournful caravan will be on its way. Motya will be forgotten. But then Sarah cries out joyfully. She is sitting on top of the last wagon with her back to the horses. She spots Motya amid the crowd. He is walking toward home, slowly and pensively.

"See," Meyer says, making a feeble attempt to smile. "I told you he'd make it."

But there's no time for lengthy exchanges now. They need to hurry. So Meyer, who is sitting in the first wagon, pulls in the reins and waves his whip in the air. The horses start out slowly, as if anticipating the joyless road ahead. Meyer is followed by Ilya, then Isaac, then Pavel. Pavel is pleased. How could Ilya even think of abandoning the fabrics! Of course, had it been Ilya's, he would be thinking differently. Everyone thinks of themselves now. Excellent! Pavel Rusevich will only think of his property and his family.

He sets his bowler askew on his head and cracks the whip. Giddy up! The horses strain the traces, their spines bend up, their hooves beat the ground—but they are unable to move. Pavel urges them on, then whips them. The horses dance in place and rear. Sophia and Sabina scream in terror.

"Wait, wait!" Pavel shouts to his brothers-in-law and Meyer, who are already moving. "You gave me bad horses, they don't pull!"

Ilya's owner's pride is hurt. He jumps off his wagon and comes up to Pavel.

"Oh yes," he says. "You should have piled twice as much on this wagon. . . . If you really want to get going instead of just acting silly, you need to lose two thirds of your fabrics."

The fabrics again! Why can't Ilya understand that it's just plain impossible?

"What's going on?" Isaac shouts. "Hurry up, we're leaving!"

Then Pavel lowers his tone and pleads to have his load spread equally among all wagons.

"And then nobody is going anywhere," Ilya finishes his brother-in-law's request. "We'll have to slaughter the horses after three miles, and then what? No, you do what you want. We're off."

"We're off!" That's how his relatives are. In Pavel's opinion, they kept up pretenses all along, only to show their true faces now. He runs around the wagon like mad, then finally starts removing the fabrics, roll after roll. He has really lost his mind, that Pavel: after each new roll, he timidly asks Ilya:

"Maybe that's enough? You do understand, Ilya, you're not a beast, you're a human! Think of it: if I lock the fabrics up in the house, anything could happen . . ."

People are used to locking everything up, they like to fool themselves!

"Nothing will happen," Ilya assures him. "Nothing at all. If you want to get going, the more you leave here, the better. Just lock up the house."

The Raskins finally get moving. Within a few minutes, they join the human stream. They follow and are being followed by total strangers. People are bitter and show no mercy to each other. Whenever a cart stops, it holds up the whole endless caravan. The men immediately jump off their carts and run ahead to those who are stuck.

"My wheel is cracked," a short peasant man laments, scratching his head. "Help me tie it up, pals, I've got a string right here."

"You won't make it anyway," the men around him reply with unshakable indifference. "You're just holding up everyone else."

"Keep going!" others yell from behind. "Who stopped up there?"

"But fellows, for God's sake . . ."

No one listens to him. The crowd of furious men gets thicker and thicker and surrounds the cart. Finally, hundreds of hands grab onto the wheels; dozens of whips lash the horse's bony sides. The women in the cart wail and scream. In a few seconds, the cart is off the road and the caravan starts moving again. The men run back to their carts.

The blood-red disk has sunk halfway into the earth. Pine needles crunch under wheels, feet, and hooves. Tired horses slow down and snort heavily. The refugees are beginning to think that maybe they should spend the night here in the woods. The horses halt, as if on cue. Silence falls. Then the silence is abruptly broken by strange, terrifying sounds. A distant rumble that resembles thunder rolls through the forest. People spontaneously raise their eyes to the sky. But the sky is clear. The golden dust of hundreds of stars spreads across the darkening firmament. People don't listen intently for too long.

"Those are cannons," say the refugees who have been on the road for a while.

"Keep moving!" those who became refugees just a few hours earlier scream in panic. "Go, go!"

"You can't outrun death," others counter.

The noise in the forest drowns out the frightful rumble. Exhausted horses stop more and more frequently. Their heaving nostrils acquire the blood-red hues of the sunset, their knees are trembling. In desperation, they grasp at the roadside dust with their rubbery lips. The endless caravan stops once again. You can't hear the shelling right now. Those who have just abandoned their villages try to convince themselves that the enemy is too far away, that it couldn't possibly be shelling. Maybe it really was thunder? It could be . . .

* * *

The forest is teeming with carts, campfires burn everywhere. Sparks fly toward the sky and become entangled in the black crowns of trees. Columns of smoke rise. Someone sighs heavily and dejectedly; a tired horse snorts, glancing around uncertainly, and lowers its head back to its bag of oats. A stray cow wanders around the forest; its loud mooing gives everyone the shivers. Unfamiliar noises, smoke from the fires, and human figures, black in the night, all scare the cow.

These are tough times! Meyer Raskin unharnesses the horses and starts a fire together with Motya. They carefully help Chava off the wagon and set her up near the fire on a makeshift bed of pillows and blankets. A fire, a few clothes and linens, a wagon, a couple of horses, a gramophone with cracked records, a completely useless chair tied to the back of the wagon Gypsy-style, a sick wife, and two children not yet ready to stand on their own—is this all he has to show for his sixty years of living? Why did he have to strive, to work hard, to rush? As God is my witness: old Meyer Raskin, the head of this household, has never complained about his luck. Life hasn't been easy for him, there have been some hard times. But to end up like this, to lose the roof over their heads so suddenly—this he couldn't have imagined, this is impossible to accept. Terrifying thoughts haunt him, blurring his thinking—he can't help it. Bad, really bad timing for all of this. If he were younger, then maybe . . .

"Motya, Sheva," he says, "stay with your mother and watch the wagon and the horses. I'll go see how the other children are doing."

He quickly steps out of the circle of light, and the dark night swallows him up. Now only smoky-red smudges are visible. Meyer approaches the nearest fire. The flames flicker over the human figures around it. The crackling of the fire mingles with a woman's monotonous wailing. A peasant woman sits by the fire. Her face is covered with locks of disheveled hair, her knees are raised high. A dead baby lies in the hem of her dress, which is stretched out like a windsail. The woman is swaying; plaintive words fly from her mouth, which is rounded in horror. A dark, frightful looking man with a long pipe between his lips squats next to her, poking the fire with a stick.

Raskin steps away; he doesn't need to see this right now. He stumbles into tree trunks that scratch his face. Invisible branches painfully strike his head. So where are the children? He approaches another fire. Peasants are sitting around it, solemnly smoking their pipes. They grab ambers with their chapped fingers, jog them in the palms of their hands, then toss them into their pipes, tamp the small flames down with a fingernail, and suck on the stems of their pipes. They must have eaten already, and there is nothing else to do, so they enjoy listening to the man who is talking. He was the last to leave Zelovo. He speaks slowly, his eyes are searching for those who show the greatest interest in what he has to say. Then he suddenly notices "the old master" and starts from the beginning. He was the last out of Zelovo. Cossacks took over the estate and the village. They were the ones who told him that the enemy advance had been halted. The Germans had stumbled. Tonight they will be chased back. Tomorrow we can all go home. The Cossacks assured him of it.

"So we'll spend a night here in the woods," he concludes, "it won't kill us. Right, Master?"

The peasants and Meyer Raskin are beginning to believe this implausible story; they fantasize out loud about returning to their homes and their land. It could very well happen. "The Germans are not going to push all the way through to Moscow, that's just impossible. Our soldiers were in Galicia, after all! Some fortresses were abandoned without a fight: Ivangorod, Brest-Litovsk, Kovno. . . . They can be fortified again, made impenetrable. . . . The important thing is that their advance has been halted."

Their faces turn to the west. The west is alight with a distant fire, the sky is teeming with flames. The flames tower over the forest like a red banner. The speaker falls silent and disappears into the darkness. There is no doubt about it: Zelovo is burning, the estate and the village.

"Welcome home," someone says bitterly.

The men stare at the distant glow with empty eyes. A small figure runs around in the dark, bumping into people and trees.

"Zelovo is burning, everything is burning," whispers the figure.

"Ilya, is that you?"

For a long time Ilya cannot see who is talking to him. Finally, he recognizes his father.

"Zelovo is burning," he informs him. "I can tell from the location. It's Zelovo."

"Are you all settled?" Meyer asks. "Have you eaten anything?"

"Zelovo is burning," Ilya replies. "Look at that fire. It's Zelovo."

"We need to tell the women to tuck the children in," Meyer says. "It's getting chilly, the children may catch a cold, God forbid."

"Can you see the fire? It's Zelovo, I know it."

"Let's go see how the children are doing . . ."

The children! They are doing as well as their parents, no better and no worse. They have covered themselves with pillows, duvets, and blankets, and are lying by the fire. The night chill touches their hands and faces with its damp mist. Isaac is trotting around the fire in a winter coat. The grandchildren stir, cry, and mumble in their sleep. Only a miracle can save them from colds and other ailments.

"Where is Pavel?"

"I don't know," Sarah says hoarsely. "I think he went to look for you. You haven't seen him?"

Can you really see anybody in the dark?

So where is Pavel? He is busy, of course. He has found Motya and is now conducting secret negotiations with him. Whatever you say, Pavel has helped Raskin's youngest son to stand on his feet, you can't deny it. Now Motya must pay Rusevich back for all his troubles. Motya should take a small roll of fabric from him. No one should know about it. Rusevich himself will place the fabric in the Raskins' wagon and cover it up with hay. Surely Motya can do him this small favor . . .

Dawn approaches, gray and misty. Night reluctantly parts with the earth. The campfires are dying out. It's getting chillier; even the horses' withers are shivering. The smell of pine is growing stronger. On your way! On your way!

The slow caravan of carts is in endless motion again. If one stops, it holds back everything behind it. Frazzled people fly into rage. Clouds hang overhead, the rain is pouring down, endless and heavy. Water streams off the heads of women and children, off the hats of men. Clothes stick to their bodies. Fog lies over the ground. Distinct sounds emerge and grow stronger in the fog. It feels as if a gigantic stork has spread its invisible wings across the sky and is delivering sharp blows over the thousands of carts. Women and children lower their heads and cling to the carts. Men jump to the ground and whip their horses in sheer madness. The airplane rattles and maneuvers above their heads for a long time, holding everyone under incredible strain. If this is an enemy plane up there—it could tear hundreds of carts out of the endless chain, it could mince the flesh of people and horses with the mud.

Day stretches on after night, night melts into day, one can easily lose count. How many days has it been since the Raskins left Zelovo? Which day of the week is it? No one can say. People quickly get used to the new situation. If the horses need food, the Raskins do exactly what the refugees "from around Chelm" did: they pull hay from already finished stacks and graze the horses in unharvested oat fields. If people need food, Pavel Rusevich scurries like a hare through potato fields. Sitting by the fire in the evening, his belly full of potatoes, Pavel takes off his shirt and starts searching for insects in its folds. Pavel Rusevich does it, they all do it. Everyone thinks of themselves first. Shoes get torn, clothes get worn-out and torn, too. Men grow facial hair, but no one bothers to shave. Here, on top of the moving wagons, people reveal their true nature and reach their limits. And yet they live by the past because they wish for a different, better future. They are happy to run into someone they know, someone who can vouch for their past.

After Zelovo comes Antopol, a familiar old shtetl. There isn't a single person here who doesn't know the Raskin family. But half the shtetl is already on carts, while the other half has its hands full and couldn't care less about the Raskins. Hard times are coming. The Jews fuss noisily, trying to protect their meager belongings. They need to collect several thousand rubles and pay off the Cossacks—then, reportedly, they won't burn down the shtetl and won't rape the women at the last moment. The Jews need to come up with a plan, elect smart and honest people to represent them. Clearly they have plenty to do. Can they afford to spend an hour by the Raskins' wagons mulling over private matters: "Oh yes, we have seen you in better circumstances?" No, the Raskins should keep moving.

The past unfolds before the Raskins in a totally different light. Here is Telyatichi, the place where their family took shape. Chava's tired eyes widen. Meyer furrows his brow and adjusts his position so that those in the wagon can see his back, only his back.

"Look, father, here's our house," Motya says excitedly. "Same shutters, same paint on the outside, they just added a little balcony. Why did they add this balcony? If we could stop here, I would go into the house. . . . I wonder what's in there now? Here's a tree. . . . There used to be a bench here. Where is it now?"

"The road is very good here, no reason to stop," Meyer replies to his son without turning his head, and urges the horses on with a whip.

"Strangers are living in our house, total strangers," Chava notes to herself. "Oh my God, what has happened to us, what has happened to the whole world?"

"Nothing has happened to the world!" Meyer shouts. He now shouts like a drover. "Absolutely nothing has happened to the world, just keep quiet!"

Keep quiet? Can old Raskin himself keep quiet? His eyes search around the estate. He spots a pump by the distillery. The pump is overturned. Its hoses lie in the mud like dead snakes. What's the matter? That pump moved alcohol from the barrel to the cisterns for nine years, it could have lasted another twenty. Now it's been ditched like useless junk. "Some owners! Ah, who cares!"

It's easy, of course, to carp about other people's mistakes. How hard was it to sell the alcohol a month ago and move it out of Telyatichi? One just had to choose the right moment. Now, the cellar gates are wide open. Ditches run from the cellar to the ponds, a stream of alcohol surges through the ditches. Soldiers are guarding the entrance to the cellar. They hold their rifles at the ready, they are prepared to shoot into the approaching crowd at any moment. But the crowd has lost its mind, no bullets can stop it now. The weak and the women lie down on the ground, reach for the stream, and with their hands, scoop up alcohol mixed with mud. The majority, however, head for the cellar, banging their buckets. Shots crackle amid the roar of human voices as if they come from toy pistols. Out of a cistern, the soldiers have pulled a man who drowned in the alcohol. They have placed him at the entrance: look what your madness leads to! Nobody pays attention to the dead body. Anyone who stands between them and the alcohol will be torn to pieces. Finally, the soldiers drop their guns and hurry to the cellar themselves. They don't have buckets, only pots. Drunk with anticipation, they dip their overcoats in the cisterns of alcohol. They remove their boots, fill them with alcohol, and watch with regret as it spills out.

A surprise awaits Pavel Rusevich in Drahicyn. His sister, a dentist, has a practice here. Rusevich remembers it only when they reach Drahicyn. The young woman offers tea to her niece and sister-in-law. She is hastily packing her things into cardboard boxes and preparing to leave. Where will she go? Where everyone is going: into the distance. Who will she go with? She is not even thinking about it. Pavel unharnesses the horses and leads them to a watering place. His sister, meanwhile, loads her luggage onto his wagon.

"What are these boxes?" Pavel asks with surprise.

"They are mine," his sister replies.

"Yours?"

Pavel lets go of the horses. His hands shaking, he climbs on top of the wagon and starts tossing his sisters boxes down. The dentist picks up the boxes and cries loudly. She hasn't yet been a refugee. She still finds it all unbelievable and barbarous. Sarah defends her sister-in-law. Pavel swears and doesn't want to hear anything. Ilya exchanges whispers with Rachel and finally invites Pavel's sister to take a place in his wagon.

"Don't be upset," he tells her politely, "don't be upset and please don't cry. Times are different now. You have no idea what things are like. I'm telling you this, you have to believe me. Please make yourself comfortable in my wagon, we are moving on. . ."

6

Six weeks later, the Raskins, refugees from Grodno Province, find themselves in Kremenchuk in Ukraine. While on the road, Meyer Raskin remembered that he had a cousin in Kremenchuk. Raskin hasn't seen his relative in thirty years, he probably wouldn't recognize him now. But it doesn't matter. It is important to find someone, somewhere in the world, who won't look askance at you or turn his back on you, who won't call you a refugee or think that you intend to sponge off him.

It looks as if the sad journey is over and the worst of their troubles have come to an end. The Raskins have spent two weeks in their wagons, day and night under the open sky. With much difficulty, they have made it to Pinsk. The thunder of cannons and the flare of fires followed them relentlessly. In Pinsk, they had to abandon their horses and many of their boxes and suitcases. Old Raskin went out of his way to obtain passage on a steamer. It was a leaky, old rust bucket that was pulling barges full of displaced people along the river. The steamer often ran aground. The passengers were forced to disembark. Swearing and cursing their bad luck, they would drag the ship using ropes.

Society ladies came out onto the pier. The refugees formed a line and received bread and cold kasha. While accepting the alms, the refugees told stories about their past lives, holding up the line behind them. They all made it sound like they used to lead the best of lives in the lap of luxury. It was hard to tell who was lying and who was telling the truth. Just in case, people didn't believe any of them. Come to think of it, the refugees didn't really believe each other either and paid little attention to what was said. Was there ever any past, anyway?

These are tough times! The deck is littered with people in rags. They lay on their bundles, chew bread, and scratch themselves. One of them is an old Jew with a thick, disheveled beard—Meyer Raskin. His hair has grown even grayer during these weeks, his hands are trembling. He no longer bothers with collars and neckties; a dirty shirt with trouser buttons is show-ing from under his wrinkled jacket. He, too, stands in line when he has to and talks about his glorious past, stretching out his hand for bitter pauper's bread. Oh yes, this is Raskin, the former Telyatichi leaseholder, a man who was rather well known back home. The entire Kobryn District, the entire Grodno Province. . . . Oh please, Raskin, you must have dreamed it all up, who would believe you now?

Here is an old gray-haired woman in a kerchief. Old women like this stand at the gates of Jewish cemeteries, and people whose grief has made them charitable give them some spare change. Kind, sweet Chava Raskin. She carefully chews on stale bread. Actually, she is not really hungry and could very well give her bread to her children. If only they would let her quench her thirst. . . . Why does Meyer think that fried chicken is better than black bread? It is not true: black bread is very nutritious, she hasn't had any in a long time.

Ilya's family, Isaac's family, Sarah's family, Motya, Sheva. . . . Is resurrec-tion from the dead possible? Oh, well, let people soothe themselves and live by their hopes and dreams. Let the oldsters remember the kind, all-gracious Jewish God up in heaven. The holidays are approaching: Rosh Hashanah, Yom Kippur, Sukkot. Rosh Hashanah on deck with black bread and cold kasha for a holiday dinner. Meyer gets hold of a prayer book somewhere. The Jews sit on the deck and plead with their God:

"Adonai, Adonai, you are our shepherd, we are your sheep! Do you see where the flock is going? Does the Lord remember His servants?"

Villages and towns float by, lit by magnificent sunbeams. Here, life still follows the old routine. A plowman plows, a blacksmith swings his ham-mer, a shopkeeper conducts trade.

"Children, be patient," Meyer says, his eyes lighting up. "We'll get to Kremenchuk, we'll look around. I am positive that the banks have evac-uated; maybe not in full, but surely they will pay at least something! You, Ilya, have the receipt for the cattle we sold to the government. In Ukraine, we'll find many landowners that we already know. They won't just sit idle, I assure you, and in that case, we'll find a way to make a living alongside them. The skies have not fallen yet, I assure you."

So says old Meyer, whose spirit is not yet broken. He heard a wonder-ful proverb in Germany: if you lose your money—you have lost nothing, if you lose your health—you have lost something, if you lose your spirit—you have lost everything. But no one here has lost either their health or their spirit, not at all!

After six weeks, the steamer docks in Kremenchuk. New land, please accept these outcasts eagerly and easily! The wives and the children stay on the pier, while Meyer and his sons go to find his relative. They wash themselves in the Dnieper, shake out their jackets, clean their shoes with newspapers. It's still warm here, they could have left their heavy coats on the pier. Actually, it is better to leave them behind. The Raskins can raise their collars, so that no one will notice that their shirts are not particularly fresh and their neckties are missing. After all, this isn't about dressing up, not at all.

Meyer and his sons step onto the strange land. The Raskins walk through unfamiliar streets; they look back and see a flock of street children following them and shouting, "Refugees, refugees!" They have a new dirty word here! Well! Were the enemy to come here and drive you out of your homes, then you'd know what it's like to be a refugee!

The wives and children wait for their husbands and fathers. Anything is possible. A nice carriage is about to arrive. A pleasantly surprised relative will jump out and say: "Welcome, friends, we've been waiting for you. We've heard what you've gone through and we are happy to help. . ."

An hour passes, then two, then three. The sun hides behind a distant house, but the pleasantly surprised relative is nowhere to be seen. Has something bad happened to our men? Anything can happen; they might even be arrested in a strange town. Who will be there to explain that people like them should not be arrested?

Finally, the Raskin men return and report that they have rented three rooms for the whole family on the outskirts of town, on Stolypin Street. They had a hard time finding a place. The owner didn't take Meyer Raskin's word, so Meyer had to put down his gold watch as collateral.

"I had to convince them that refugees don't bite and don't have tails," old Raskin wisecracks bitterly, furrowing his brow. This Meyer Raskin is still capable of wisecracking—it means that everything is not yet lost. He heard a proverb in Germany. . . . Well, surely he has already mentioned it.

"And the relative? Where is your relative? Where is your cousin?" Chava asks.

"What relative?" Meyer doesn't quite grasp the question right away. "Oh yes, the relative. . . . You see, he moved to Poltava fifteen years ago. Ah, who needs him!"

And now the Raskins are at their new place. Frankly, they arrived in Kremenchuk completely changed people—this is how being refugees has changed them. Meyer shouldn't have rented a single apartment for everyone—it would have been much better to find separate lodgings, however small, for each family. Some of the women are haunted by this thought: what if my husband is the first to find work? Will it mean that he will have to feed everyone, all these countless mouths?

Yes, changed people have arrived in Kremenchuk. The owner of the apartment—which is damp, dirty, and has low ceilings—used to run a brothel in his younger days. He stands in the doorway, watching the refugees, and shakes his head disapprovingly. He shouldn't have let these derelicts into his house, he really shouldn't have! Not a single decently dressed person among them, not a single cultivated gesture! Of course they lied about their past. They spit on the floor, they scratch like dirty pigs, they hammer nails into the walls like soldiers in temporary quarters. Some leaseholders!

Meanwhile, they need to consider their situation, to somehow become rooted in their new life. Members of the Raskin family, what are your suggestions?

Isaac rushes to speak first. Being a refugee has made him even more pessimistic. He has started to twitch, and his eyes have grown large and wild.

"What to do?" he asks, sounding as if he wants to yell and castigate everyone. "What to do?" he repeats. "It's simple! Tomorrow we'll go to one of the owners of the tobacco factory, throw ourselves at his feet, and beg for any job whatsoever. We will kiss his hands and feet to get anything, even if it's cleaning the outhouses. Otherwise, we'll die of hunger within the week. Here, they won't even bury us for free."

So says Isaac, who nevertheless has a few hundred rubles sewn into his long johns.

"Now, now," Meyer Raskin interrupts him. Meyer is angry now, he is tired of his son's carping and the fact that Isaac ruins everyone's mood. "Kiss their feet, die of hunger, bury us for free!' Anything else you have to say?

He defiantly rises from his chair and continues,

"The Raskins have never kissed anyone's feet. And we won't. Do you hear me? We won't!"

His father's tone encourages Ilya, who also chimes in.

"Really, Isaac, that's a bit much," he says. "What do you mean: clean the outhouses?"

"Ah, so they're about to offer you a lease? Who are the landowners here? The Miloradovichs? The Kochubeys? The Skoropadskys?[9] They can't wait for you—you and your money! Leaseholder! If it hadn't been for your Zelovo, we could have had a factory in Warsaw or something like that. We would be sitting pretty right now."

Clearly, he is talking about one of Leyble Kagan's ideas.

"Nobody was holding you back," Ilya replies. "You're not a child."

"Enough! Shame on you! You're like little boys." Meyer Raskin says. "And you really found the best time for it!"

The old man is agitated, he is full of energy. He paces around the apartment, grabbing his beard and flailing his arms. The time for groaning, for hard thinking, for moaning and doubting yourself is over: all this could be done while on the wagons or on the ship. Now is the time to act. Act! It's hard for him to imagine that people eager to work could be crushed that easily. Who needs an estate? The Raskins managed with or without estates, thank God. Nobody here inherited an estate. We need to feed our family, we need to make it through the dark days, to wait them out—that's what we need to do now. "The skies have not fallen yet, I'm telling you—I, who have seen both sides of fortune!"

For starters, Meyer Raskin heads to the bath house, then to the barber. He rummages through his luggage and finds his collars and neckties. His family members watch him, holding their breaths.

"Yes!" he exclaims from time to time. "The skies have not fallen! They have not! There's a German proverb. . . . Yes!"

He leaves home in the morning and returns in the evening. For now, he says nothing about his efforts or his setbacks. For now, Isaac sows panic and bickers with the others. He gives a particularly hard time to the youngest two—Motya and Sheva. If he were them, he would be unloading barges, sewing, fixing cargo bags. . . . If he were them . . .

But the youngest two have also changed during this period of displacement. A chipper girl who loved to laugh, who found fun and joy in absolutely everything, boarded the wagon in Zelovo. A totally different person has arrived in Kremenchuk. She found her documents in the luggage and the very next day started visiting gymnasium directors. The girl who didn't have a worry in the world, who used to be the first to pay her tuition, now visits gymnasium directors and talks about things she knew nothing about

---

9   Illustrious aristocratic families from Ukraine, major landowners.

before. They must—must!—accept her free of charge. Her parents cannot afford a single kopeck. Thirty rubles? But she has just said that they cannot come up even with thirty kopecks. The family has gone without dinner for two months. The Refugee Board? She will go to the Refugee Board, if you insist. Just give her a free ticket, she'll take a streetcar and go see the head of the Education Department. She meets gymnasium girls, borrows textbooks from them, and begins to study in the evening. She puts on her cotton dress and starts sweeping the floors. Her young lips are framed by creases now; she furrows her brow the same way her father does. Sheva's shoulder blades work under her dress. She never stops and she doesn't want to. It doesn't bother her that she sleeps on the floor under a winter coat. She has no mercy for herself or anyone else. How could someone like her grow up in Meyer Raskin's family?

And Motya?

His gaze from under his furrowed brow has become even sterner. He talks less. He watches everyone from the sidelines as if he is not a member of the Raskin family, as if he has no part in this great calamity. Pity for his declining mother mixes with gloating disdain for Isaac. He sees his younger sister in a new light. "I really don't know much about her," Motya thinks. "When we were children, I pulled on her braid; she would get mad and cry. Then, when I visited home, I saw a growing girl. She would run to school with a knapsack on her back. When she was writing, she would rest her head on the desk and diligently move the tip of her tongue. Now she is busy, putting her affairs in order, essentially building her own life. She acts like an adult tempered by hardship. And she is my sister. Does she give any thought to the past?"

The girl tears her eyes away from her book to meet her brother's gaze. "What?"

"Nothing," Motya says, failing to find the right words.

He realizes that he carefully chooses his words when talking to his sister and beats around the bush. This irks him, but he can't help it.

"It's autumn," he says, rising from his chair and walking over to the window. Through the dim glass, he can see the muddy backyard and the rippled surface of the puddles there. They reflect contorted structures and dark heavy clouds. Dried laundry hangs on the lines. The sleeves of the shirts wave and flap in the wind.

"It's autumn," Motya repeats, crackling his knuckles and pacing nervously around the room. "In Telyatichi, by now they would already be lighting the stoves."

The caretaker would be walking from room to room, the house would smell of autumn coziness, contentment, and dampness. The more impassable the mud, the heavier the rains—the more pleasant and peaceful it would be inside. The coachman would bring the mail in his leather bag: newspapers, catalogs, the illustrated *Niva* in its green wrapping. The magazine would come with yet another supplement . . .

"Don't you miss the past?"

He looks at his sister intently. Did she take the bait? Her shoulders tremble slightly. For a brief moment, Motya loses his breath. Will she really cry now, was she touched by what he said? But then a chuckling face appears from behind the book, sparkling with white, widely spaced teeth. "So she was actually laughing? At me?"

"Do you remember Uncle Kadesh?" Sheva asks suddenly.

"Why are you asking?"

"Wait. Do you remember him?"

"But of course!"

"I was five years old when he came to see us for the first time. He was funny, very funny. He liked long visits. He'd come and stay for a month. He lived twenty-five miles from Telyatichi, remember? So one day, a couple of weeks after he arrived, a peasant from his village comes to Telyatichi. He walks in and says to Kadesh, "Yesterday, your house burned down!" Just then, Kadesh was drinking tea. He raises his head, looks at the peasant, and says, "My house burned down? Impossible!" And continues to drink his tea. You should have seen his face, though. He calmed down so quickly . . . and made himself believe it—no, his house didn't burn down, it couldn't have. . . . It was so funny . . ."

She chuckles, throws her head on the back of the chair, and roars with laughter.

"I don't understand," Motya says irritably. "What does Kadesh have to do with anything?"

"Oh, I just thought about it, no reason. But let me explain. I was five years old when Uncle Kadesh came to see us for the first time. We were sitting at the round table drinking tea. A samovar was on the table. He put me in his lap and pointed his tobacco-stained finger at the samovar. "What is this?"

"A *vasomar*."

"What did you say?"

"A *vasomar*."

"Everyone was laughing their heads off, of course, but I insisted: *vasomar*, and that's that. I was five years old. Three years later, he comes for another visit."

"What is this?"

"A samovar."

"Are you sure?"

"Yes, I'm sure, it's a samovar."

"Did you mean to say *vasomar*?"

"No, I meant to say samovar. *Sa-mo-var*."

He was very disappointed and kept trying to get me to say *vasomar*. Just a year before the war, he still wanted me to make this mistake."

"And?"

"That's it. You want me to say *vasomar*, too. But I'm not five anymore."

"She expresses herself the way our mother does," Motya thought. "The same use of allegory, the same intonations. But she is not like mother at all. My God, she is so unlike our mother!"

"All right, fine," Motya said irritably, not understanding why he was so irritated. "You probably meant that I myself . . . how should I put it . . . that I left this life behind. Is that what you meant?"

Sensing that he was still unable to talk to his sister like an adult, realizing that he was digressing, and becoming angry with himself, Motya suddenly blurted out,

"But, you see . . . it's like we're castaways on an uninhabited island. Mother is very ill . . . very! I don't think she'll last more than a year under these conditions. Mother is dying, Sheva, do you understand? Mother. . . . And we . . ."

His voice shaking, he waved his hand and turned away to the window.

A few minutes later, when he resumed pacing around the room, he noticed his sister staring at him motionlessly and frowning.

"Why did you say that?" she asked emotionally. "Please don't think that I refuse to see things! I see everything, and I understand. But what can I do? I was promised a student to tutor, I'd be happy to contribute that money to the family. If it were possible. . . . I find it unpleasant when you talk to me like Isaac does."

She stood up, approached her brother, put her hands on his shoulders, looked him in the eyes, and said touchingly, like a child,

"Please don't. . . . Okay?"

A spasm gripped his throat. He didn't reply, turned, and left, slamming the door behind him.

He didn't spend much time at home these days. He caught the women's puzzled glances, and was particularly bothered by Isaac's angry, feverish eyes. He felt out of place in the family, and the more he felt that way, the harder it was for him to break away from its disintegrating ranks. Sometimes he felt gripped by despair. At moments like this, he would walk into shops, bakeries, or banking offices, and offer his services. In what capacity? He had no answer to this question. People looked at him with suspicion, so he would slowly walk out, feeling their mocking glances on his back.

The cold indifference of this alien city, busy and hectic, with freight trains running through the streets, drove Motya to desperation. The people here seemed terribly cold. If you were to fall on the sidewalk and scream in agony—even then no one would pay attention; people would walk past you as if nothing was happening. Sometimes instead of boxcars, open platforms carrying the wounded glided through the streets. Young men in white trousers and women in wide-brimmed hats stopped to look. Their faces burned with curiosity. It was a new, interesting spectacle for them, but no more than a spectacle.

Refugees passed through. Motya recognized people from home by their caps and bast shoes, by the colors of their coats. The former peasants had been readily transformed into beggars. They awkwardly accosted people on the street, slapping the ground with their torn, wet bast shoes and stretching out their hands. Sometimes they lost patience and tugged people by the flaps of their coats. The locals were wary of them and used the word "refugee" to scare their children. They truly believed that those who lost their homes and social standing, those thrown off their tracks were capable of anything.

Altruistic society ladies organized charity balls to benefit the refugees. Young people were happy to have an excuse to dance. The sanctimonious noose of charity was tightening around the necks of destitute people.

Days followed one after another. A slushy southern winter followed the golden autumn. The Russian army dug in near the town of Luninets. It seemed to have frozen in the trenches forever. The refugees continued to hope for better times ahead. They viewed living in strange towns and villages as something temporary. They didn't want to or simply couldn't believe that their houses had been burned to ashes, that their fields were pockmarked with shell craters, overgrown with weeds, and covered with rusty barbed wire entanglements. The hope that they would be able to return prevented them from living a normal life in this strange land. They washed the floors rarely, made their portable beds haphazardly, and simply covered their few remaining dresses with bed sheets.

"If you didn't lose your spirit and your health, it means you have lost nothing." An excellent saying that comes from a sturdy, hardworking, and strong nation, no question about it. But it's difficult, almost impossible to live normally in a makeshift camp. People grow accustomed to their surroundings; they get used to certain relationships, to the trust and the standing that they have achieved. When Meyer Raskin was young, he could carry bags of flax seed on his back without giving it much thought. Life lay ahead of him like a road not yet traveled. He believed in his destiny. He was lucky, and that's the way it was supposed to be. But now . . .

"To people, years are like steps on a staircase," Meyer thinks. "Sometimes they lead up, other times they take you lower and lower. Bad luck, "evil fate"—Meyer Raskin never believed any of this nonsense. "If you are out of luck, if you are a loser—it means that you don't know how to work, so it's your fault," Meyer Raskin told poor people more than once. Now he himself is beginning to believe in the magic power of bad luck. Nothing is accomplished, nothing works out. The Raskin family is marked by bad luck, by being refugees. Everything is falling apart and turning into dust. After many wonderful turns, his life is returning to where it began.

Tough times, bitter times. It is amazing how circumstances bring out the worst in people. Take Isaac, for instance. It's no secret that he has never been a particularly warm person, not at all. Even during peacetime, no one could claim that they had ever heard a kind, heartwarming word from him. But in times of trouble, he had become absolutely impossible. Everyone, everyone without exception is to blame for Isaac's misfortunes.

A month passes, then two, then three, and finally Motya Raskin gets a lucky break. The young man has suffered a lot, he hasn't had much experience of life during peace. It's time for him to break the vicious circle of adversity. He has sturdy muscles and a strong desire to make his own living. Like clockwork, he walks the streets searching for an opportunity to apply himself. Is he still hopeful? He has stopped thinking about it, he is simply looking for work with grim determination. And when it feels as though he has tried everything, lady luck finally smiles on him. It's not for nothing that he is Meyer Raskin's son!

One day, Motya is wandering the streets, as usual. A few men with sacks on their shoulders cheerfully walk by. One of them stops and pats the young Raskin on the shoulder. It's an old acquaintance, a farmhand from Telyatichi. How on earth did he end up here? Like everyone else. First on horseback, then on foot. Went hungry at times, begged at times, ate whatever the Lord provided, slept at train stations and in makeshift refugee shelters. But then somewhere in Novgorod Province, they opened an office to run the construction of a strategic road. The office is hiring earth diggers, workers, clerks. He went there, just in case. They signed contracts with him and his friends, accepted their papers, gave them an advance. He is off to work in a few days. The young Master should go there, too!

Motya Raskin tries his luck one more time. At the office, the minutes are crawling by amid smoke and nervous anticipation.

Success!

He cannot believe his own eyes and ears. Road construction requires educated people: bookkeepers, timekeepers, warehousemen. Could this be the end of his suffering? Buildings along the street fly toward him, his clouded eyes can hardly see. One thing is perfectly clear: Motya Raskin has received an advance. He crumples the bills in his pocket, keeps pulling them out—and he still cannot believe it. Farewell, unemployment! Farewell, maddening, empty days!

So how will Isaac greet his younger brother? Perhaps at least this time he will set his usual tone aside and find some kind words for Motya?

No, Isaac reads the contract, and a bitter grin twists his lips. Perhaps he too would like to try his luck at the road construction office? He won't. He buttons up his jacket and proclaims derisively,

"When the ship sinks, the rats are the first to abandon it."

That's all he has to say to his brother in the way of goodbyes.

But Isaac's verbal calisthenics are of little interest to Motya now. He is leaving the family behind, and his heart flutters for a moment. It's a good time to sum things up, and the result is rather depressing. You no longer need to travel to other cities or even cross the street to see the entire Raskin family since everyone lives in the same apartment, in its three rooms. The Raskin dwelling bears the signs of their refugee plight, signs of decrepitude that the family is not accustomed to. Portable beds stand along the walls. The oft-mended pillowcases are a dirty blue color due to poor laundry skills. Ribbons and shreds of cheap ten kopeck wallpaper hang from the walls. The walls show traces of bedbugs, those faithful companions of poverty. There are piles of junk in the corners, things that survived the collapse and were preserved inside bundles: brass door knobs, candlesticks, books, dirty laundry, a tub with cereal grains, a sugar bowl without a lid. Laundry is drying on lines that run across the room. Exhausted, depressed, frustrated people with sunken eyes, prominent chins, long-unshaven faces, and unhealthy-looking red blotches on their cheeks sit on the beds along the walls.

Here is the sad inventory.

A nice, sweet old woman, cheerless Chava Raskin. . . . Were you correct when you claimed that life is given as a punishment? With difficulty, with great strain, with agonizing effort a person struggles to plow his field and finally, exhausted and spent, he takes his last breath, closes his eyes with the final blessing, and folds his tired hands on his chest. Is that right? Were there any joys in your life? Of course there were, but you leafed through those bright pages with the same wistful smile. You sad, mournful woman, did your fears come true? Strained cords now show on your once smooth neck. You are sick; a cruel disease that knows no mercy has withered your hands. Confess: do you still think that if you were allowed to have nothing but water for even one month, you would have been able to extinguish the fire that consumes your body? But you're not assertive, not at all. You suffer pain silently, without complaining, you just wait for the end with a final prayer on your lips. The hour will strike. . . . May God bless those who you leave behind! You dreamed of a different end, of course. You wanted to be able to see all your children before the end, you wanted your fading eyes to preserve the images of those you love. All of them once pulsed beneath your heart, once fed on your blood . . .

Who could have predicted that they would be scattered across the world? Where is Hersh? Meyer sends some letters, he once even managed to mail a box of dried bread slices. He assures everyone that he will be able to reach Hersh. Yes, he does. But in the meantime, your youngest son has already packed his things. Will you be able to see him before you die?

"The Germans have a proverb . . ."

"Please, Meyer, don't."

There are moments in life when neither cries of joy nor comforting proverbs are necessary. That is when the soul speaks. . . . The soul knows no pretense and doesn't understand reason. If you don't trust your inner voice—look in the mirror. You will see an old white-haired man with cloudy, teary eyes. The former Jewish entrepreneur couldn't take it anymore, he just couldn't. Well then, turn away, pull a handkerchief out of your pocket, and wipe off your eyes. And don't say that something got into your eye, there's no need for that.

"Yes, you're right," Meyer says and blows his nose. "Who would have thought? Didn't I do all that work? Didn't I think that I would earn enough for the children, and not just the children, but the entire Raskin clan? If somebody told me ten years ago that Motya would be leaving home like this, going to work . . . to build some kind of a road. . . . I would have thrown that person out of my house. What can I do? All I can say is: good luck, son, keep in touch, life wasn't fair to us. . . . On the other hand, it is better to get a job and a deferment from military service rather than wait to be drafted. . . . Have you thought about that?" Meyer Raskin asks somewhat more cheerfully.

Here is Ilya Raskin with his wife Rachel and their two children. He has grown a small beard, this Ilya, a short light-colored beard. He wraps it around his finger, tugs on it, and sucks through his teeth. That's all he does—suck his teeth and pat himself on the knees from time to time. Who can tell what might happen tomorrow? No one can tell. In the meantime, he has enrolled his son in the first year of a technical school. Together with his father and brother, he has somehow obtained fifty pairs of shoes to sell on commission, and has taken the shoes to Minsk. He doesn't know anything about this kind of business. All Jews are taking shoes to Minsk—so he does, too.

"It's time . . ."

Meyer gets up and kisses his son. Chava also tries to get up, but it is too much for her.

"Don't bother, Mother . . ."

So says Motya, and then he kisses her on the lips with a long kiss, a kiss for eternity.

"We'll see each other again somehow," he says.

"Why 'somehow'?" his father asks sternly. "This is silly! Why did you say 'somehow'?"

"You misheard me," Motya replies, jerking oddly and shivering. "Of course we will see each other again!"

Everyone steps out into the hallway.

"Don't come to see me off," Motya says. "You are all tired, so don't come to see me off. Mother is alone in the room. Good luck and good bye!"

And they do as he asks. He walks the street alone. He takes some twenty steps and stops. He adjusts the bundle on his shoulders and looks back surreptitiously. He looks back to see how many steps he has already taken.

Sheva is hurrying toward him. She has thrown a kerchief over her shoulders and is now waving at him—wait! What does Sheva want?

"So you're leaving," she says. "I want to help you . . . the bundle . . ."

"Yes. The bundle. Never mind. I can carry it myself."

"You're leaving."

"Yes."

They walk together for a few minutes. The stiff snowy wind roars down on them. You can't hear their words. Maybe they aren't even talking. Then the sister grabs her brother's head and kisses his eyes, wet from the snow, for a long time.

"Write! For God's sake, write! Write to all of us, and to me personally!"

"Yes. . . . I also wanted to tell you something before I go . . . well, not to tell, but to ask. . . . We're not children anymore. If something happens to mother—let me know. . . . Promise?"

She kisses her brother again.

The steam locomotive lets off an agonizing scream.

It's time.

7

The story of the Raskins as one close-knit family is coming to an end. Nothing can change that. The chicks have hatched and have all wandered off in different directions. Who will bring them together again? And is it really necessary? The story of the Raskin family is coming to an end, and now a hungry, uninvited guest is knocking on their door.

"I am here," says the guest. "I am finally here. No one ever wants to see me, no one ever greets me with cries of joy. Well, such is human nature. You have to admit that I've been kind to your family, I've been sparing the Raskin household. But life itself has cleared the path for me. It's now the second generation's turn, so isn't it only fair that the first generation gradually starts to clear the premises?"

So says death, which has its own logic.

Chava sits by the window, just as she did in Telyatichi or Brest-Litovsk. Of all the joys in life, a window is the only one that she really needs. Her pursed lips form a somber crease, her eyes reflect a dreary, rainy day, her withered hands rest on her knees. It's twilight. At a time like this, thoughts and memories flow naturally.

A peasant cart rattles along a dusty Belarusian road. The pine forest exhales cool resin whose amber drops shine and sparkle on the tree trunks. A woodpecker runs up a tree, fretful and busy. The wind blows its tail to one side. Now the bird pecks on the wood purposefully. A young Jewish woman sits in a peasant cart. Through her tears, she sees her husband's broad back and his dusty neck reddened by the sun. She barely knows him. Her husband, his legs hanging out, urges the horse on with a small whip. He has no worries in the world, as if his cargo is a bag of flour rather than a living, breathing person—his wife. A few days earlier, he had arrived in Antopol as a stranger, and now he is taking a wife back home. Life sometimes weaves the strangest patterns.

The past comes back to her in warm, vivid images. Now, as Chava sees her past, she feels as if she has missed something very important, something indispensable. It would be hard for her to explain what exactly it is. But she knows that as soon as the cart stops, as soon as she places her hand on her husband's broad shoulders, the right words will come to her. After that, life will go on differently, without tears and sadness.

"Meyer," she says, choking on a multitude of words and her desire to speak. "Meyer," she asks softly, "hold the horse for a minute." Meyer is compliant as never before. The back of his head moves closer to Chava—he pulls in the reins.

"Whoa!" he says, dropping the whip onto the dusty road. He does it very skillfully and with flare, like a true drover. He turns his head to her. He has a young, rosy, sunburnt face, honest dark-blue eyes under the ink-black arches of his eyebrows, and a small, barely visible mustache.

"Yes," he says, stretching his hand out and helping her up. She can see in his eyes that he, too, is waiting for some important revelation, some words of wisdom. "Yes," he repeats with anticipation and jerks one shoulder impatiently. "Yes?"

Now they stand facing each other on the dusty road, amid the fragrant, ringing silence. The horse lowers its head, snorts heavily, sniffs the dust, and quiets down. A loud bumble bee buzzes past.

Then everything freezes.

"Yes?" The young Meyer silently moved his lips for the last time. The fateful moment was approaching. The remarkable words had not entered her head yet, but Chava was not concerned. These were the rare words that enter your soul on their own; they are remarkable and wise. The woman raised her skirt with one hand, stretched her other arm forward, and headed toward her husband. He was waiting for her patiently. He silently removed his cap and mopped his brow. While doing so, he didn't take his eyes off his wife. She approached fitfully, he didn't hear her steps. Her outstretched hand lightly touched his shoulder. The fateful moment has arrived. The strain caused sweat to appear in the furrows of the young husband's brow. Chava's hand on his shoulder grew heavier. Everything around him was anxiously waiting for the clear, prophetic words. The fateful moment swelled and lengthened. Silence rang impatiently and heavily. Terrifying confusion began to fill Meyer's eyes.

He was still trying to believe that the words would be uttered, but confusion was already bubbling up in his eyes. The skies were lowering inexorably. Had the words been uttered, the skies would have lifted again. But there were no words. The listless tongue in his mouth stuck to his palate. Meyer's eyes were filled with confusion. He was reproachful and silent.

The trees exhaled resin-filled wind, and immediately the amber drops trembled and began to flow. The whole world watched Chava reproachfully. This was the world's last glance at the sorrowful woman.

"I am here," said the uninvited guest. "I am finally here."

Chava Raskin's body formed an elongated mound on the floor. She was wrapped in a white shroud. Her toes propped up the fabric that fell in folds toward her knees. The shroud must have been made out of a bed sheet: blue trim went along her left shoulder. Candles formed a semicircle around her head. They flickered. An invisible breeze blew the flames aside. Tallow dripped on the floor. Light flowed over the mother's darkened face. Pink, lifeless blotches appeared on her cheeks. Her upper lip partially covered her lower lip. Her raised eyebrows made her face look confused.

Old Raskin sat on a chair, his back leaning against the wall, his legs spread wide. Meyer supported his chin with his hand, holding his beard tight with his fingers. The old man raised his head, his lips quietly twitched for a few moments.

"You see," he spoke in a changed, tired voice, raising his red eyes toward his children. "You see," he repeated, shifting his legs heavily. "This is it . . ."

Then suddenly he burst into a fast patter, stunning his children and combing his beard with his fingers,

"This is a relief for her. . . . She's better off now. . . . I swear it's true. . . . She needed a rest from life. . . . She fell asleep peacefully . . ."

Chava Raskin was buried that same evening. A stretcher covered with a black cloth swayed indifferently on strangers' shoulders. It was followed by the family. They formed a row, holding each other's hands and hitting the cobblestones hard with their heels, as if they were hammering nails. Behind them Luba, Isaac's wife, rode in a horse cab. She cried, fingering her hair, and blowing her nose into her hand—in other words, providing the proper ambiance of a Jewish funeral.

It was an austere funeral. No friends, no familiar faces. . . . They didn't even inform Motya of his mother's early death. The pallbearers treated the deceased irreverently: "A refugee woman died, who cares?" Lights were being lit in the windows, forming squares on the pavement. The pallbearers swayed their mournful load on their shoulders and hurried to the cemetery. Sheva felt her father's large, heavy hand in hers. It was warm; his pulse beat under his rough skin. The daughter glanced up at her father furtively. Meyer Raskin was stepping firmly, mechanically. His long coat fell open, forming broken wings behind his back. Sheva's heart fluttered, but she still made herself glance at her father's face. It was beautiful, lit up by wondrous thoughts that rarely come to a person—but when they do, they fill the heart with deep, remarkable lightness.

"In his mind, he is now recalling the best moments that he had with the only love of his life," the girl thought. "What an enormous part of his life he is now taking to the cemetery!"

Then came difficult hours and days, when even the most open members of the Raskin family felt that they had to conceal something carefully, not to think certain things through, and create an illusion of a tight-knit family.

And the more they tried, the more obvious the disintegration became. Everyone in the apartment spoke in whispers, walked on tiptoes, and avoided loud talk. They threw gauze over the mirror, and flies settled between its loose threads, preparing to die. The floor in the third room was covered with mournful traces of tallow . . .

The old family was finished.

New milestones were taking shape in the fog of the upcoming years. Some will find it too hard, lose their strength, and will be thrown off. Others will make it and complete their thorny path. For them, the sun will rise, and new life will open its embrace to them:

"Welcome! We've been waiting for you. Come and assert yourselves!"

Moscow, 1925–1928
End of volume one

IN PLACE OF AN EPILOGUE

The Raskin Family was first published in Russian in 1929, in Moscow, and was republished in 1989 and 2002. A Yiddish translation appeared in Poland in 1931.

On the last page, it says "End of volume one."

Unfortunately, my father never even tried to work on the next volume. By that time, Stalin had usurped all power. Expressing views that were at odds with official lies, whether in the press or even in a private conversation, had become mortally dangerous. Government agencies exercised full control over all printed matter.

Consequently, my father could not write the truth about what happened to the characters of *The Raskin Family* after the Bolshevik Revolution, let alone express his views on what was happening in the country. And lying was not an option for him. He used to say, "The government can shut me up, but it cannot force me to write lies."

After the revolution, the Raskin (Vlodavsky) family was scattered across many cities and countries. Here is what I know about them.

Meyer Vlodavsky (**Meyer Raskin**) remarried a few years after Chava's death, but his second wife also died in the early 1930s. He later moved to Brest-Litovsk, which was then in newly independent Poland, no longer ruled by Russia. **Isaac** and **Luba** had settled there shortly before him, along with their daughter and her husband. Together, they ran a drugstore. In 1939, Brest became part of Soviet Belarus under the provisions of the Molotov-Ribbentrop Pact. Dmitry Stonov was very eager to see his father, but the old man died in early 1940, before the newly "liberated" areas were open for travel. I think Meyer was in his eighties. In April 1940, Dmitry was able to visit Brest and see a few relatives, as well as his father's grave. The cemetery where Meyer was buried no longer exists; it was replaced by a stadium.

Ilya Vlodavsky (**Ilya Raskin**) and his wife **Rachel Novogrudski** lived in Leningrad from the 1930s onwards. Ilya was a controller at a factory and looked like a typical white-collar Soviet, but his soul remained impervious to corrosion by the state. Their oldest son Moses, a prominent railroad engineer, was good friends with my father, who was his uncle. They were very close in age.

I only saw Ilya a few times and remember him as a very reserved and dignified older man. He looked like someone who could no longer engage in his beloved physical labor and hence appeared somewhat lost, but still very much himself.

Ilya regularly corresponded with his younger brother **Hersh** in Israel, even though his son Moses urged him to stop so as not to jeopardize his high-level position. All Ilya agreed to was to receive such letters via general delivery. When my father was in labor camps, Ilya regularly sent us money that Moses passed on to my mother on the street so as to avoid entering our apartment.

Both Ilya and Rachel died when my father was still a prisoner.

Isaac Vlodavsky (**Isaac Raskin**), along with his father **Meyer**, his daughter Rosa and her husband ended up in Brest-Litovsk, where they owned a drugstore. His wife **Luba Kagan** had passed away years earlier.

His son Misha could not find work in Poland after graduating as an engineer and emigrated to Palestine in the late 1920s. There, he ran a large refrigerator factory and died in Tel Aviv in the late 1950s. As far as I know, he had no children.

In early June 1941, Isaac came to Moscow, seeking treatment for Parkinson's disease, and stayed with his younger sister Zhenia Kravchenko (**Sheva Raskin**), who was a nurse in a neurological clinic.

This trip saved Isaac's life, for on June 22, 1941, Hitler invaded the Soviet Union. All the family members who remained in Western Belarus were killed by the Nazis.

A month later, mass evacuations from Moscow began. Isaac and Zhenia with her two children moved to the Urals, where Zhenia continued as a nurse. Interestingly, my future wife Natasha and her brother were at the same children's establishment as her daughters and remember Isaac, Zhenia, and her girls very well. Isaac died in Moscow a few years after the war.

Sarah and Pavel Rusevich continued to live in Lodz until World War II. Both were killed by the Nazis, along with thousands of other prisoners of the Lodz ghetto. According to my father, sixteen other relatives of ours also perished in the Holocaust.

Their daughter **Sabina** and her husband fled from Nazi-occupied Lodz to Brest. When Germany invaded the Soviet Union, they left Brest on foot. Later, they managed to board a train going east, but at one of the stations the train was attacked by German planes. The train abruptly took off while Sabina's husband was still outside trying to get hot water. She never saw him again, so he must have perished in the bombing. Sabina spent the rest of the war in Siberia, but in 1946, when Stalin allowed former Polish citizens to return home, Dmitry advised her that it would be easier to reach Palestine through Poland. After arriving in Poland, Sabina immediately started making her way to Palestine. On her way, she met a Jewish man who had also lost his entire family during the war. They soon married and finally made it to Palestine, where they were welcomed by Sabina's uncle Zvi Vlodavsky (**Hersh Raskin**), who lived in Kfar Saba.

Sabina died in the late 1990s. Her descendants live in Israel.

Zvi (Grisha) Vlodavsky (**Hersh Raskin**) graduated from the Krakow Academy of Fine Arts, became a sculptor, and by 1925 had reached Palestine. He taught music and drawing in Kfar Saba and grew oranges to support himself and his wife. They had no children. Later, however, his sculptures became known even outside of Israel.[10]

Grisha was a warm, welcoming man, who helped Isaac's son Misha and later Sabina to settle in Israel. He died in 1952.

In 1990, as an activist on behalf of Soviet Jews who wanted to emigrate but were denied exit visas, I was invited to a congress of the Jewish Agency for Israel (Sohnut) in Jerusalem. While there, I went to look for Grisha's house in Kfar Saba since I knew his old address, but in place of a small cozy house surrounded by orange trees I found a two-story apartment building where no one had ever heard of the sculptor.

Discouraged, I hurried back to Jerusalem to attend a meeting with General Ariel Sharon, then Israel's Minister of Housing and Construction. The topic was accommodating new arrivals from the Soviet Union.

Before getting down to business, Sharon asked me about my family and what I was able to see in Israel, so I briefly mentioned my unsuccessful trip to Kfar Saba. Sharon perked up and asked me why I went there.

---

10   See Gabriel Talphir, *100 Artists in Israel* (Tel-Aviv: Gazith, 1971).

Hearing the name of my uncle Grisha, he became very agitated, called his wife on the phone, and started exclaiming excitedly in Hebrew.

It turned out that Grisha had been a close friend of Sharon's parents who had also lived in Kfar Saba and had died only recently. Sharon joked that he wasn't particularly fond of my uncle, because whenever his parents had guests, they made young Ariel dust the sculptures that my uncle gave them, and he was afraid to drop or damage them, not to mention that he found dusting boring.

On later trips to Israel, I found Grisha's sculptures at the children's art school in Kfar Saba. We now have five of them at our home near Chicago.

Zhenia Vlodavsky/Kravchenko (**Sheva Raskin**) had settled in Moscow before I was born. She and her husband Mark, also Jewish, had two daughters.

Mark was very different from all the people discussed here. A small-time Soviet manager, he was typical of a large cohort of communists who were promoted by the authorities. Energetic but poorly educated and uncultivated, he was a loud, brash, and unthinking supporter of the regime. After my father was arrested, Mark banned Zhenia from visiting us. She disobeyed him a couple of times, and then, to make her life easier, I occasionally visited her at work to tell her how my father was doing in the camps.

When father returned home, I was still young and yearning for justice, so I implored him to banish from our house all those who turned their backs on us while he was away, especially family members. But he honestly forgave them, because he understood the animal fear that the regime cultivated in people. He did not judge his relatives.

Zhenia died in the 1950s in her mid-fifties from diabetes and heart failure. Seeing her in a coffin, father burst into tears; it probably reminded him of the death of his mother, Chava.

A few more words about Mitia Vlodavsky (**Motya Raskin**), who later became the writer Dmitry Stonov, and his descendants.

By the age of thirty, Dmitry Stonov was an established writer who had already published *The Raskin Family* and a number of short stories. While on vacation, he met Anna, a biology teacher from Kharkov. They were soon married, and in 1931 I was born.

My father continued to write, and in 1934 he became a member of the Union of Soviet Writers. The rest of his life I have covered earlier.

As the son of a political prisoner, I had to face a few difficulties of my own. For the five years that I was a student in the Biology Department of the Moscow State University, I had to conceal the fate of my father, staying away from my classmates, avoiding parties and other social occasions, and not being able to invite anyone to my home.

After graduating, I worked in the field of chemical protections for plants, and this caught up with me in 1979 when we decided to emigrate. The authorities denied us exit visas for eleven long years under the pretext that I allegedly had access to classified materials. And so it happened that my family, like many Soviet families, always had to conceal something. For my father, it was his association with the Workers' Opposition; for my mother, it was her non-proletarian origin; for me, my father's imprisonment; and for my son, the fact that we had applied for exit visas and were denied.

But in 1990, with the help of American Jewish agencies supported by US Congress and the US government, we were finally allowed to leave the country. The Union of Councils for Soviet Jews was particularly instrumental in helping us emigrate and then settle in our new life. And thus the descendants of **Motya Raskin** have finally moved to America.

At the root of everything that happened to us was the hardworking, patriarchal yet modern Jewish family—the family of Meyer Vlodavsky. The novel by Dmitry Stonov is a literary monument to this family.

Leonid Stonov
Chicago, Illinois
May 2018

Miron Vlodavsky (Meyer Raskin in the novel), the father of the novel's author Dmitry Stonov (Motya Raskin).

Chava Vlodavskaya (Chava Raskin), the author's mother.

Sonya Vlodavskaya-Rusevich (Sarah/Sophia Raskin-Rusevich) the author's older sister.

Pavel Rusevich, Sonya's husband.

The sculptor Zvi Vlodavsky (Hersh Raskin), the author's brother, in his studio at Kfar Saba, Israel, with his wife.

Sculptures by Zvi Vlodavsky: *Solomon and Shulamith and Samson.*

Zhenia Vlodavskaya (Sheva Raskin), the younger sister of the author.

Future writer Dmitry Stonov (Motya Raskin) at the commercial school in Brest-Litovsk, 1910.

Dmitry Stonov (Motya Raskin) in Poltava, Ukraine.
1917.

Dmitry Stonov with his wife Anna, Moscow,
1930.

Dmitry Stonov with the writer Georgy Gaidovsky. Poltava, 1923.

Dmitry Stonov, then a correspondent for the newspaper *Gudok*, with a group of surveyors. Altai Mountains, 1930.

Lieutenant Dmitry Stonov on the front during World War II (1943).

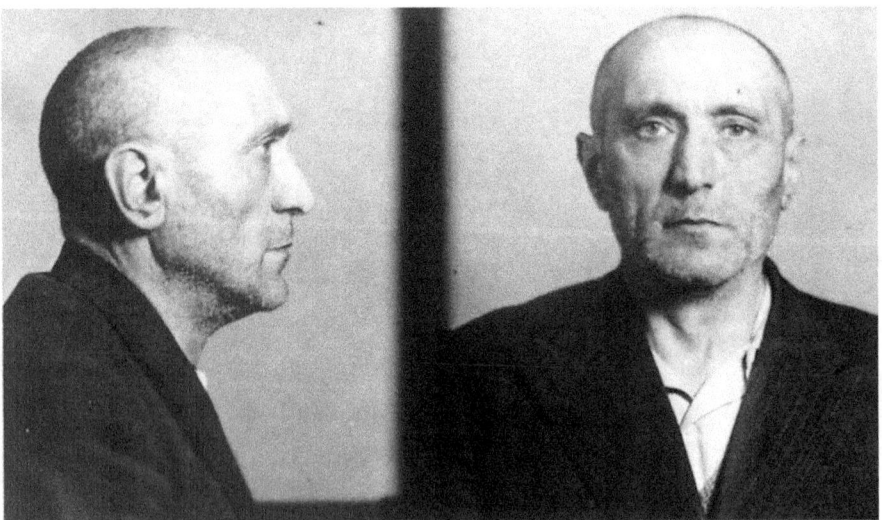

Dmitry Stonov in prison, a week after his arrest. March 13-14, 1949.

Dmitry Stonov with his son Leonid a week before Dmitry's arrest, March 1949.

Dmitry Stonov with his wife Anna, March 6, 1949, a week before his arrest.

Stonov's son Leonid and wife Anna soon after his arrest. Moscow, 1949.

Dmitry Stonov after his release from prison, August 1954, with his wife and son Leonid.

Dmitry Stonov with his grandson Sasha in the winter of 1962, a few months before Dmitry's death.

Dmitry Stonov's (1898-1962) grave at the Vvedenskoye Cemetery in Moscow. The headstone by the sculptor Yuri Chernov.

Map of Western Belarus and Eastern Poland.
The cities whose names are underlined are mentioned in the novel.

lishki
iszki)

Belitsa
(Bielica)

Zheludok
(Zołudek)

Mosty

Koslovshchina
(Kozłowszczyzna)

ovysk (Wołkowysk)

Zelva (Zelwa)

Słonim

xyanka

uzhany
Różana)

Kossovo
(Kossów)

wacewicze) Ivatsevichi

Yaselda

Jasiołda)

anchitsy
rańczyce)

i

Drogichin
(Drohiczyn)

pol

(Niemen)

Molchad

+1060

Dyatlovo
(Zdzięcioł)

Mitskevichi

(Nowa Mysz)
Albertin
(Albertyn)

(Szczara)

Byten

Domonovo

Bobrovitskoe
Ozero

Telekhany
(Telechany)

Ozero Chernoe

Sporovskoe
Ozero

Motol

n

Ivanovo
(Janów)

DNEPROVSKO-BUGSKI KANAL

Lyubcha (Lubcz)

Novogrudok
(Nowogródek)

(Korelicze) Korelichi

Novoelnya
(Nowojelnia)

N. Mysh

Shchara

Lesnaya
(Lésna)

Gorodishche
(Horodyszcze)

Mir

Stolbts
(Stołpce

Goro

Baranovichi (Bara

Lyakhovichi
(Lachówice)

Shchara

Gantsevichi

Vygonovskoe
Ozero

OGINSKI KANAL

Logishin

Parokhonsk

Yaselda

Zhabchitsy
(Żabczyce)

Malkovichi
(Małkowicze)

Tsn

k

Lyusho
(Lusz

Bobrik

Pinsk

Pina

Stak
(Sta

s